The
Lady Loves
Danger

Books by Anabelle Bryant

The Maidens of Mayhem Series

Duchess If You Dare

The Lady Loves Danger

The Midnight Secrets Series

London's Wicked Affair

London's Best Kept Secret

London's Late Night Scandal

London's Most Elusive Earl

The
Lady Loves
Danger

ANABELLE BRYANT

ZEBRA BOOKS
Kensington Publishing Corp.
www.kensingtonbooks.com

For all the other Maidens of Mayhem
who take risks and conquer challenges to better the world.

As always, for David & Nicholas.

CHAPTER I

London, 1817

Sebastian St. Allen eased into the damp corner until his shoulders brushed the soot-dusted bricks of the dilapidated tenement at his back. The night air was still, pungent with the familiar stink of raw sewerage and soiled dreams, as if it too had given up hope. This was Seven Dials, and any man with a shred of common sense wouldn't be found lurking in the streets after dark. An unfortunate soul could lose his life in a matter of minutes and no one would hear his desperate plea for mercy. Still Sebastian remained, lost to the shadows in wait of a thief.

Not any thief, mind you. Not a taker of silks or gin. Nor contraband tobacco. This crime was one of reprehensible depravity. And now, after weeks of following a whisper of information that yielded little more than stains to his fine leather boots, he waited again. The location and sketchy details that led him to this nameless roadway in the bowels of London came through an associate, and while the information had yet to prove its worth, Sebastian wasn't deterred. He'd nowhere in particular to spend his evening and he'd rather exhaust the possibility of interrupting the horrific exchange than second-guess his decision not to.

Pressing a palm to his waistband, he adjusted his pistol as an additional weapon to the blade he carried in each boot. He was an excellent shot and equally lethal with a knife, both skills learned as a means of survival, for while he now resided in a comfortable town house in a better part of London, that hadn't always been his situation.

Hours crawled by and he shifted his stance, his steady focus keen to the squat tenement across the street. His mind dared him to exhume old memories and unpleasant thoughts best left buried in the abyss of the past. Surveillance forced a man to probe his own mind as each minute ticked by, a pitfall of too much solitude and not enough distraction.

Time dragged on until a barely discernible movement snared his attention and brought his focus to a recess of the building across the way. It was nothing more than a slant of gray against black but he sensed the action before he perceived the figure who'd caused it, a slight form in a long cloak with the hood drawn to conceal the face. *A woman.*

With unexpected convenience, the cloud cover dispersed and the waxing moon offered a murky shaft of light. Even with ample distance interrupting the dark thoroughfare, he knew the abilities and limitations of the physical body, gestures of human nature, and above all else, subtle yet graceful distinctions of the female form. Was this woman here to purchase what the thief brought to sell? Not another soul haunted the streets. He muttered a black curse, unable to comprehend the abhorrent evil that drove a person to commit heinous crimes.

The approaching clop of horse hooves from the opposite direction divided his attention. Another beat and he spied the vehicle. Weeks of empty observation and wasted time finally crystalized into possibility. The nondescript carriage slowed at the curb and Sebastian angled his body to gain a better view of what he anticipated to be a swift transaction of contents for payment. The exchange must begin before he interfered. The slightest misstep would spark the thief into flight.

Being on foot, Sebastian couldn't follow the shabby conveyance far, but should someone emerge from the tenement and step forward to receive the goods, he'd be able to perpetrate a rescue, investigate further, and possibly uncover the miscreants involved. He wasn't above pummeling men to gain the information he sought, and he'd question any woman until she supplied the names needed.

The door of the carriage cracked open to reveal a struggle within the interior. With innate stealth, Sebastian moved undetected, at one with the black cast of the eaves above him. He waited, daring only to breathe. To make the slightest sound before the exchange unfolded held the potential to ruin everything. The silence grew louder. He shook off the unwelcome feeling of urgency and slipped his hand beneath his greatcoat to rest atop his pistol, all attention on the carriage door. From the corner of his eye, a blur of motion dissected his concentration for the second time. The cloaked woman stepped forward and he willed her to remain still. She could only mean to receive what was in that carriage and yet he needed to be sure of the circumstances before he acted.

The door widened fully now, its soft rap a lonely echo amid the eerie quiet. The wiry driver stepped down and accepted a writhing bundle, no bigger than a sack of flour. Sebastian's heart seized tight but he forced an exhale to jolt it back into rhythm, the suppressed emotion potent fuel for his anger as fury shot a fiery rush through every muscle and vein.

"Oliver!"

The woman across the way called out and her voice destroyed the silence with resounding alarm. Havoc ensued right after.

With spry reflexes, the miscreant pivoted, tossed the bundle within the carriage and climbed the seat to slap the reins. Sebastian tore down the street in a futile race to catch the conveyance, the agony of what he'd lost almost too much to bear, though rage flamed anew as he turned and started toward the cloaked stranger, motionless and alone on the pavement. Weeks of vigilant observation were ruined by her careless call and now she'd have hell to pay for it.

Delilah Ashbrook stood at the curb immobile, her thundering pulse a threat to coherent reason. Had she just located Oliver and lost him in the same moment? Had she destroyed her only chance at finding him? Fear took hold and paralyzed her reaction for the length of several heartbeats, but she rejected the suggestion of failure. She needed to be strong.

Blinking hard to summon fortitude, she opened her eyes and peered into the night. Her pulse hitched another notch. The broad stranger who'd emerged from nowhere, invisible one minute and in pursuit of the carriage the next, had now turned his attention on her. She couldn't be caught.

Spinning on her heels, she aimed for the darkest alley, heedless of the danger ahead as she fled the danger behind. He gained ground easily, the resounding echo of his boots as they struck the slick stones not unlike the hectic beat of her heart. What did he want with her? Had he watched the carriage in wait of purchasing the child within? What kind of man stole children? Sold them to others to be used for illicit purpose? Her stomach rebelled and she wrapped an arm around her middle, sickened by anyone who'd perpetuate such an unforgivable crime. A cramp gripped her side. She wasn't accustomed to running for very long. *Running at all.* Never mind she wore layers of skirts and a heavy cloak. She dragged in a painful breath. *Cursed corset.* She couldn't get air into her lungs fast enough. Her throat burned but she pushed on.

The alley she'd chosen was narrow, the space between the brick-lined walls barely twice the width of her shoulders. Perhaps the stranger wouldn't fit. He appeared a hulking presence, tall and threatening, as he loomed closer. She reached the end and stalled, taking the next turn at a slower pace, the cramp insistent now. This passage widened and promised multiple escape routes.

She could still hear his approach despite her breathing was loud in her ears. He'd managed to keep her in sight, though she'd done her best to cling to the shadows, pivot between streets and dart around corners.

In a panic, she turned left and aimed at another dim alcove. How long would the stranger pursue her? What did he want? A barking dog sounded an ominous alarm as she passed, and it wasn't until she reached the end that she realized her mistake. Here another threatening form emerged from the darkness. A vagrant whose face was not nearly as discernible as his odor, though she perceived enough to know he meant her no kindness. Gripping the small dagger kept in her pocket, she pulled it out and clasped it with both hands in front of her. The short blade glinted in the moonlight as she retreated with a tentative step, unsure of what he would do but refusing to turn and allow him an advantage. Still, it was all for naught. He snatched the edge of her cloak, reeled her in and belted his arm around her ribs to render her helpless. The stench of his clothing and foul breath caused an involuntary retch.

"It's my lucky night." His left hand covered her breast and squeezed while his right remained locked around her middle. "And now it's your lucky night too."

Terror caused her mind to blank. She still held the dagger but it was useless in her body's position and a scream would be lost to the night. She struggled to think calmly, to react before he violated her further. He jerked backward, reversed their positions and trapped her body against the wall, crushing her to the grease-covered bricks with suffocating pressure as his legs bracketed hers. Desperation tied a knot in her stomach and she dropped the knife lest she impale herself. She was powerless but she wouldn't succumb. She needed to survive for Oliver's sake. She was the only chance he had.

The vagrant shifted his weight and the pressure of his jagged fingernails bit through her sleeve as he yanked her sideways to push up her skirts. She twisted in vain and he scoffed low and ugly against her neck. With horror she realized he'd released her breast to work at the button on his breeches. With immediate rebellion, she fought against the arm that held her captive.

And then, in the next instant, she was free.

The vertiginous force in which she was released left her breathless and disoriented. She steadied herself, one hand flattened on the raw brick biting into her palm before her senses discerned the dull thud of fist meeting flesh.

It was over before she comprehended it completely. The foreboding stranger who'd pursued her through Seven Dials now rescued her instead. The brim of his cap masked his face in darkness, though the moon at his back lent his broad shoulders a burnished glow. She darted her eyes to the crumbled form on the cobbles and backed up farther before she spoke.

"Thank you." The words seemed inadequate. Her pulse still sprinted an erratic pace and her hands trembled.

"I am, if nothing else, an excellent rat catcher." His voice emerged from the shadows, the words spoken matter-of-factly to reveal little as to whether he was friend or enemy. "Are you unharmed?"

"Yes." She breathed deeply as she laced her fingers together in an attempt to calm. "You saved me."

"Momentarily."

His voice was smooth. Refined. And yet when he didn't continue, ill-ease consumed her. The way he waited, fierce and uncompromising, did nothing to reassure she hadn't traded one type of peril for another. She took a moment to straighten her bodice, tug at her skirts and retrieve her fallen dagger.

Still wary, she stood with the knife in hand and he coughed abruptly.

"Are you going to slice an apple?" He moved closer and a shaft of light illuminated his profile. His features looked as hard as his rigid stance. What she could see of his expression remained intense and inscrutable.

"It's protection."

He leaned down and withdrew a long slender blade from his right boot. "This is protection. That is an eating utensil."

She didn't reply, her eyes glued to his knife in wait of what he would do next. Had he saved her from the vagrant's assault so he might perpetrate his own debauchery? But no, he replaced the knife and straightened. He didn't move otherwise and his position held her captive.

"I've waited weeks for that exchange with the carriage, and you ruined it with one careless word." His voice, low and lethal, sparked warning across her skin like a wayward ember.

"I—" She couldn't explain the true reason she was here in Seven Dials, courting her own death while attempting to save Oliver's life. Could it be he wasn't the type of man she initially perceived? She could only distinguish his outline in the intermittent light, but while his dark clothing might cause him to blend seamlessly into the night, there was no denying his presence. He was a man of power. He likely knew influential people. She'd grasp onto any lingering hope if it assisted in Oliver's return.

She pocketed her knife and waited. He'd positioned himself in a way that disallowed her escape and she had little choice but to hear what he had to say.

His gaze coasted over her from the top of her hood to the tips of her boots and it was as if he held her motionless with nothing more than the command of his existence. A tremor that had nothing to do with the chill night air coursed through her.

But he was just a man.

A man who saved her from an abhorrent attacker.

"I owe you my thanks, Mr. . . ." She hesitated, unsure how to proceed.

"St. Allen."

"Yes." She breathed deeply. "Thank you, Mr. St.—"

"Just St. Allen."

"All right." She took a small step closer.

"And you owe me more than gratitude." He delivered this information with some semblance of a grin as his teeth flashed white in the darkness. "I saved you so I can interrogate you."

"Interrogate me?" Her voice rushed out in objection.

"Exactly." He waved his hand as if the gesture explained everything he hadn't.

CHAPTER 2

Sebastian drew a slow breath and watched the woman shift her stance and lift her chin. She was slender of frame, fine-boned and cultured, the innate qualities unable to be masked by the addition of a wool cloak. No doubt a genteel lady or companion to one in elevated social circles. Nevertheless, the woman had experienced two traumatizing situations in the span of an hour and hadn't wept, fainted, or simpered with hysteria. She was stronger than he first believed.

"I'd rather not continue our discussion here."

"You expect me to accompany you somewhere else?" she shot back, her disbelief evident.

He slanted his head in a nod toward the unconscious attacker. "If you have any expectations of leaving at all."

She couldn't argue with that and he turned to go, confident she'd fall in step behind him and accept his protection. Perhaps if he didn't stare at her and instead offered a path out of Seven Dials, she'd be more inclined to answer his questions. Until he understood the depth of her involvement, he couldn't negotiate the mixture of anger and protectiveness at war within him. "Were you here tonight to collect the child?"

"Yes." Her clipped answer sounded reluctant, though he noted she followed a stride behind. Whether fear or preservation motivated her, she'd made the right decision.

"Why did you call out? Surely that couldn't have been the prearranged plan."

"I wanted him to hear my voice."

"So you buy and sell children for profit?" He caught a curse on his tongue. He didn't regret saving her, but he had no use for heartless people who sacrificed innocents for their personal gain.

"No!"

She'd stopped, the sound of his footsteps all at once solitary, but he kept walking and she started after him again. They'd exited into a larger roadway and he indicated an alley to the right.

"The child in the carriage is—"

She seemed hesitant to continue. Perhaps she wondered if he'd pursue her accomplices and spoil the arrangement.

"Yes?" he prodded, shortening his stride so he now walked beside her.

"My responsibility. I'm trying to find him." Her voice went soft as she finished and she may have blinked away tears. She turned her face too quickly for him to be sure, the night too dark.

"How did you know the sale would take place this evening?"

"How did you?"

So, she wasn't so grateful she'd cooperate easily. His opinion of her intelligence increased. "I could help if you convince me you're not one of the criminals."

"If I were, I wouldn't be here with you. I'd be with them." Frustration laced her words.

"Possibly, but there's no reason why you couldn't join them later when you've drawn me away. The carriage might have already returned and sold the child while you ran through alleys and led me on a chase."

This possibility seemed to change her countenance completely. Her eyes flickered with something akin to alarm and he experienced a pang of guilt for purposely scaring her.

"Do you have information? Can you help me?"

Her questions were emotion filled and, Sebastian judged, genuine. She was not connected with the criminals and had taken a great risk to venture out tonight. "If I choose to believe you, we might assist one another. That is, if you truly wish to find the child."

"Yes." Her answer was fast and breathless this time.

Nothing more was said and he quickened his pace, aware she'd need to hurry if she wanted to keep up with him.

Eventually they exited the worst area, though no woman, no matter her cause or social standing, belonged out alone after dark. He strode toward where his carriage waited, the driver alert on the seat.

He turned and she nearly collided with him in the darkness, her attention not altogether focused. He caught the scent of lemons, fresh, clean, and in outright contrast to the filth-lined streets surrounding them. She seemed calmer now, more assured.

"I'll take you to your home or wherever you'd like to go in exchange for a few answers." He opened the carriage door and indicated she should climb inside.

A flicker of hesitation appeared in her eyes, then disappeared just as quickly as she seemingly rationalized the risk. He climbed in after her. When she didn't offer an address, he knocked on the ceiling and his driver slapped the reins with no specific instructions other than to begin. They rolled forward in silence, the tension palpable, and while Sebastian didn't seek to compound her distress, he was anxious to gain information.

He reached into his breast pocket, withdrew a piece of flint and steel, and struck it to flame so he could light the lantern. The sallow glow brought with it a spectacular awareness.

She was young, her skin pale and large eyes luminous. He'd misjudged her in more ways than one, though he didn't discount she'd skulked around Seven Dials in search of children for sale. He examined her face for clues of why that might be, and found she gazed at him with equaled curiosity. She reached up and lowered her hood to reveal a long braid as golden as starlight against her black woolen cloak.

"Why don't you tell me what you know? Why you were in Seven Dials and how you came to be at that particular corner?"

"If only it were that easy." She measured each word carefully. "Besides, I don't know you or your motives. Telling all creates the danger of scaring the criminals into hiding, and then I'll never find who I'm looking for."

"Where should I direct my driver to let you out?" Sebastian liked to change subjects frequently when questioning someone. He found it kept others off balance, and that condition led to unintended confessions and careless admissions.

"The corner of Berwick Street will do. I'll walk from there."

So, she belonged to a finer neighborhood.

The patter of raindrops on the carriage roof mocked her intended stroll home, but he didn't press further. "In all likelihood, our interaction this evening has already convinced those pursuing profit to congregate elsewhere. Another reason why your hasty call ruined a plan that was weeks in the waiting."

She caught her bottom lip between her teeth and her brow lowered in worry. A pang of conscience reminded him to go easy, but he ignored the advice.

"Why would you help me?"

"To seek justice."

"You're a runner, then?" A note of hope laced her question.

"No." At least not literally. On any given day he ran from his past. "The sale of innocent children is an abhorrent crime. I can't allow it."

"I understand."

She couldn't possibly.

He glanced out the window and rapped on the roof. The carriage rolled to a stop at the corner of Berwick Street. The rain had become a penetrating drizzle. Reaching into his coat pocket he produced a card.

"Think about my offer."

The air practically vibrated between them, but after a brief uncertain pause, she took the card without touching his hand. He didn't say more, and when the driver opened the door and she stepped out, he breathed in the scent of lemons left in her wake.

Delilah hurried away from the carriage, barely able to uphold the pretense of strength and control. She still reeled from the shock of seeing a child, possibly Oliver, writhing inside a cloth bag, and then the impact of her error, the loss of opportunity and harrowing experience afterward. What would have occurred if Mr. St. Allen hadn't rescued her in that alley? She didn't dare imagine it in detail. The risk of riding in his carriage alone seemed minimal compared with what she'd already endured.

The rain had soaked through her hood by the time she reached home. She climbed the three steps to the door and entered with her key, mindful to be as quiet as possible. Waking someone would produce inquiries and she had no ready answers.

Abovestairs she prepared for bed as her mind carefully reviewed the events from the evening. She hadn't asked enough questions and knew little more than Mr. St. Allen's name. He was a large, intimidating man with a rich voice that had evoked gooseflesh each time he'd spoken. Too, it seemed, he had some sense of chivalry and a definitive moral compass. He spoke of justice for the innocent and the need to end the horrific sale of children. He might have forced her to any unfortunate circumstance if he'd lacked character, but instead had offered her a safe ride home. She'd noticed an odd charge of awareness accompanied his presence, but exactly how to interpret it, she had no idea. He was a paradox of qualities, for certain.

She settled on the edge of the mattress and at last let emotion envelop her. Regret came swift and sharp, always at the ready to upset her resolve. She'd been so close tonight, only to allow fear and desperation to interfere and ruin her chance at finding Oliver. Pain too fierce to battle sliced through her. She exhaled thoroughly. She didn't possess the fortitude to relive her mistake now.

Padding to the wardrobe, she removed Mr. St. Allen's card from her pocket and moved to the bedside lantern. Much like their interaction, the card was not what she expected. No title or residence was printed on the vellum. Instead, the name of a bookstore stared back at her in bold block letters. She'd already decided she'd visit in the morning. Perhaps Mr. St. Allen's help wouldn't come at too high a price.

Sleep didn't find her easily, but at some point she must have dozed off. She rose and readied for the day with one goal only. She hurried downstairs without eating, walked out, and briskly strode to the corner to hire a hackney.

The Last Page Bookstore was a distinguished two-story building in handsome sand-lime brick on Gilbert Street not far from Bloomsbury Square. Delilah viewed the business from across the thoroughfare and debated what she would say once she went inside. A bookstore was the last place she'd have situated Mr. St. Allen. Something about his gruff demeanor and brawny build suggested images of a smithy or longshoreman, but she dismissed these thoughts as fanciful, most especially when she considered the polished timbre of his voice.

With a huff of impatience, she stopped prevaricating and crossed the street, holding the steady gaze of a dark-haired woman who waited near the curb. She was young, neatly dressed, and unlike others around her in that her bearing seemed intimidating. The interaction was odd, but Delilah dismissed her misgivings. Londoners and their city seemed a world apart from her life in Birmingham. She looked away and aimed for the bookstore.

The door jangled with a cheerful bell once she entered, and the enticing scent of ink and leather assailed her senses. Her heart twisted with a vivid memory of her father's extensive library, when all she need do was decide which book to read next. One of their last conversations rose to mind. She could recall every word, his every gesture. She smiled softly before she pushed the remembrance away. That part of her life was over now.

"May I help you, my lady?" A portly man approached and his amiable grin immediately soothed her apprehension.

"I hope so." She offered a smile in return. "I'd like to speak to Mr. St. Allen."

She glanced about the store in hope he would emerge from a corner as if he chose when to become visible to the world, much as he had last evening, but she only saw banks of shelves filled to overflowing with leather-bound volumes.

"Is St. Allen expecting you?"

She noted the absence of the formal title of address and reminded herself St. Allen had corrected her of the same.

"Yes." At least she believed so. He'd offered her his card. Belatedly she realized she needed to hand it forward.

The clerk accepted the card and examined it a moment before he motioned for her to follow. "Come this way, please."

He wound his way through a maze of overburdened bookcases and narrow aisles that were quick to remind Delilah of her urgent escape through Seven Dials. He came to a stop at a single cherry-wood door. A golden oval colophon hung over the top of the frame but no other sign or markings identified it as special.

"St. Allen will see you on the lower level." The man nodded and walked away, preoccupied by the jangle of the entrance bell on the other side of the store.

Delilah stared at the brass latch and then glanced over her shoulder, the circumstances more than a little unusual—and yet she'd decided to seek St. Allen's help in finding Oliver and therefore couldn't waste another moment. After all, the child's disappearance was her fault in the first place. She should have asked the clerk to announce her arrival. Perhaps St. Allen would have come abovestairs instead.

Placing her gloved palm atop the latch, she opened the door and stared down a single flight of stairs, adequately lit by wall sconces at well-measured intervals. She suffocated her misplaced hesitation and descended. The treads ended in a yawning hallway, a bit dank but dry. It was quiet aside from the creak of footsteps above, and she noticed the corridor widened at the end and possibly turned a corner. Otherwise there wasn't a door or office to indicate anyone occupied the space. This in particular struck her as strange.

Hammering down any resistant trepidation, she walked on, her bootheels clacking a hollow echo against the floor. She'd accomplished half the distance when she heard a sound and spun, her hand flying to her bodice, a gasp on her lips. "Oh, Mr. St. Allen."

She met his direct gaze. He stood a few strides behind her. But how?

"Have I startled you?" A note of apology rang in his voice.

Her pulse raced but she refused to acknowledge it. She hadn't seen a door or room and he most certainly hadn't descended the same stairs as she. However, logic demanded that he hadn't materialized out of thin air.

"How did you come to walk behind me?" She matched his eyes, noting the difference in meeting him in ample light compared to the shadowy interior of his carriage last evening. He was just as tall and commanding as she remembered, but to see his face now caught her as unaware as had hearing his voice moments before.

He possessed striking features, a strong jaw accentuated by the slightest shadow of dark whiskers, a well-sculpted nose too, but by far it was his pale blue eyes that held her mesmerized. They seemed to see inside her as much as the world around them.

"There's a door beneath the stairs." A slight grin edged his mouth. "You likely didn't look backward after you accomplished the flight."

Indeed, she hadn't. Her heartbeat evened out and she relaxed by degree. He closed the distance between them.

"Would you like to discuss what happened last evening?"

The man certainly didn't waste time on idle conversation, but then she wasn't there for that purpose. "Yes. If you can spare a few minutes."

"Let's walk this way and you can tell me what changed your mind and why you've come."

He began down the hall and she moved beside him, not knowing how much to reveal and at the same time desperate for any clue to assist in her search for Oliver. Could she trust this man? Should she tell him everything, or perhaps mete out information in pieces to gauge his reaction? Deciding on the latter, she made the turn he initiated when they reached the end of the corridor.

"My name is Delilah Ashbrook." There really was no reason for her to reveal her societal status. At least not at this time. "And I owe you my humble gratitude."

"You've already thanked me twice. I only did what any decent person would when faced with the predicament."

"Well, that's just it, Mr. St. Allen." She shook her head vigorously. "There were no decent men to be found."

She paused to see what he would say, but he only nodded and they continued walking. "I ventured to that area of Seven Dials in hope I would intercept the sale of a stolen child. I've been searching for a young boy. His name is Oliver. I had reason to believe, and still do, that the child in that canvas sack may have been him." She struggled to keep her emotions in control and steeled herself with a deep breath.

Mr. St. Allen stopped and surprised her when he touched her shoulder gently. She realized he was offering her time to collect herself, but in truth she'd never be emotionally resolved until she held Oliver in her arms again. Regardless, she needed to force emotion aside.

"This child means very much to you."

She breathed deeply and noticed the spicy scent of Mr. St. Allen's cologne water. It was a welcome balm to the acute ache in her heart and brought to mind the flowers in her modest knot garden, the fragrance of cloves and germander, with a note of soothing neroli. Interesting choices for a man so virile and intimidating, and yet unmistakably well suited. The thoughts helped calm her emotions.

"Miss Ashbrook?"

"I apologize, Mr. St. Allen—"

"Just St. Allen."

She inhaled again and was rewarded with the calming scent. "I don't want you to think that I've come to waste your time. It's just not easy for me to recount the situation."

"I understand." He didn't say more for a minute and indicated they turn left and continue walking.

Delilah looked down the hallway ahead. How was it that they still traversed the corridor beneath the bookstore? Her brows drew together and she attempted to make sense of things.

"Would you like to tell me more now?"

She realigned her purpose for being there. "I'm desperate to find Oliver. It was my fault he was taken." Distress threatened to clog her throat and she swallowed it away, forcing out the difficult admission. "Every day that passes lessens my chance of recovering him, and yet last night I was so relieved to finally have found the despicable persons, I reacted without thought and frightened them away. I don't know what to do. I hoped you would."

They stood before a staircase now, identical to the set she'd taken down from the bookstore, except how could that be? Had they walked in a circle? No. She knew that with certainty. In the first hall, there was a crack in the plaster near the base of the left wall as long as her pinky finger. She had an excellent memory and noted the slightest details of her surround. She was confident they no longer stood where they'd once started.

"Why don't you come upstairs and we'll discuss this further?" St. Allen took the first few treads and glanced back over his shoulder.

Delilah followed. Despite her impetuous choices of late, she'd risk anything to recover Oliver unharmed.

CHAPTER 3

Sebastian might have questioned Miss Ashbrook in the hall or within one of the empty rooms he used as an office downstairs, but some misplaced sense of protectiveness or other unexplainable curiosity made him escort her to his home instead. It wasn't every evening he stumbled upon a lovely young miss who single-handedly attempted to thwart a ring of child traders. If anything, he admired her fearless initiative, even if it had been a tad overzealous.

The underground tunnel system used by himself and his associates proved a convenient way to leave one part of the city and appear in another without being detected. He hadn't revealed much to Miss Ashbrook and he was certain she didn't understand the labyrinth of corridors as he maneuvered her through, even though it was by agreement with his associates that no person be knowingly taken within the grid at the risk of exposure and ruin.

Except he hadn't stopped thinking about Miss Ashbrook since the moment she left his carriage, especially the peril she'd placed herself in by entering Seven Dials and almost not leaving. Something about her captured his interest and not just for the information she might possess. He was relieved when she'd shown at the bookstore this morning. Her pursuit of the criminals wasn't the ordinary clue that inspired him to work harder toward solving a problem. She intrigued him despite he didn't know her well.

Now he noted his memory hadn't served him as accurately as was habit. She possessed an uncommon beauty that went unnoticed in the chaos of last night, her skin flawless and fair, her hazel eyes crystalline. With her seated before his desk in his study, he matched her perspicuous gaze and waited for her to continue her story.

"I realized after the carriage ride home I didn't ask you nearly enough questions."

"You were recovering from two appalling incidents in a relatively short period of time."

"True." She nodded and he watched as sunlight from the egress windows on the left wall shimmered down the length of her hair and back up again. Did her tresses smell like lemons too? Even coiled, the golden strands reached midway to her bodice. How long must it be when not artfully arranged? He rubbed his fingertips together to quell a beat of restlessness.

"How did you discover the meeting place for the exchange? Do you know where they'll be again?"

It wasn't like him to be distracted easily and the questions she peppered at him restored his attention. He didn't share often when it came to information; personal, business, or otherwise. At least not until one earned his trust and few people had accomplished that.

"I've a special interest in anyone attempting to sell or purchase a child with an intent to put an end to the miscreants who perpetrate these crimes," he replied. "It's a tragedy orphanages and charitable organizations are overburdened to the point where they can no longer assist in finding abandoned urchins a kind home; but no one, not child or adult, deserves the future that awaits at the hands of a criminal."

He'd developed a skill for avoiding questions he'd rather not answer. He'd begin with a fact that partially supplied information and then continue with a generalization composed of common knowledge. It was easy to be vague and deflect attention once he'd honed the craft. He didn't lie. Lies complicated rather than simplified things and he had no desire to lie to Miss Ashbrook. Nevertheless, omitting information fell within the boundaries of fair play. It appeared she carried a significant burden, one he had yet to decipher. It was his turn to uncover answers.

"How did you know of the address in Seven Dials?"

She swallowed and darted her eyes away before she answered his question. "I frequented several establishments along the Thames. Disreputable taverns and pubs better left to the scourge of society." She said this with no judgment, just a retelling of fact. "I inquired where a woman might rid herself of a child when found in the family way. Any information I gathered would shed light on where children are bought and sold." Her voice trailed off as if speaking the words aloud abhorred her as much as the act itself. "I had no other choice. I should never have taken my eyes from Oliver, not even for one moment." She'd spoken softly, but he knew, able to read her lips from across the desk.

"Have you no husband to assist in your efforts?" He filed that question under information gathering, though he had no idea where it came from. Regardless, it wouldn't hurt to have the knowledge. Collecting facts and details was an essential part of his work. Besides, Miss Ashbrook hadn't identified herself as a genteel lady, but every action, from her disposition to her diction, told him things weren't as they seemed.

"No." She didn't elaborate and instead removed her gloves and pulled a small cloth pouch from her pocket. "This is a miniature of Oliver. It was completed earlier this year for his fifth birthday." She paused, another item in her palm catching his eye. After a moment he realized it was a lock of hair tied with a blue ribbon. "I have failed him in every way."

"You're alone then?" He didn't mean to appear rude by inquiring of her relationship status, but the lady was proving a riddle and if they were to help each other, he needed to know more.

"No." She frowned, still looking at the keepsake in her hand, her answer distracted.

"Are you his governess?" There was no way Miss Ashbrook

could be the child's mother. It was unfathomable, not just by her lack of husband or young age, but more so that her constrained emotion and successful struggle bespoke of a different type of relationship. A loving mother in this situation would be overcome with worry, unconsolably distraught and most likely unable to pursue results. Of course, his theory wasn't an absolute, but he believed it true and his gut had a way of being right about things.

"No, I'm not." She inhaled deeply and her face cleared of emotion. "Can you help me?"

"Our concerns mirror each other and I'm impressed by your ingenuity in gaining information, but by your own admission, you've put yourself in harm's way at least three times. Asking questions at a tavern is almost as dangerous as entering Seven Dials and confronting the malevolent darkness that lurks in that part of the city. Your decisions are reckless and unwise." He leaned forward on the desktop, a thread of protectiveness making his voice low and firm. He didn't like the idea of her running around the worst areas of London on a one-woman mission to find a single child, and while he didn't mean to chide her or use a disapproving tone, he meant to discourage any future dangerous endeavors on her part.

"I have no choice. Even if you decline assisting me, I'll continue to seek out the horrible men who've stolen Oliver. I'm determined to find him." She stood up and paced away from his desk as if the distance would solidify her ultimatum.

Sebastian also rose and came around his desk, unsure if she would make for the door. He didn't want to upset her, but he also knew people who sold children were ruthless and would think nothing of eliminating any threat to their business; even a beautiful young woman with uncommon hazel eyes.

"When you tell me the name of the tavern where you learned of the exchange, I'll seek out the same despicable reprobate who supplied you with information the first time and extract everything he knows." It was good practice to assert compliance. At times it lured the resistant participant to capitulate.

Her brows rose at his use of the word *extract*, but she didn't comment, so he pushed a little harder. "As you well know, Oliver's time is running out even as we stand here and discuss the problem."

"I'll tell you but only if you agree I may accompany you." Her voice firmed from confidence or rebellion. He didn't know which.

"I can't allow that." He closed the distance between them and met her gaze to ensure she understood the decision was nonnegotiable.

Her expression grew intense, the pale green of her irises seemingly changed to emerald with her anger.

"I hoped telling you of my problem would aid my efforts, not exclude me from righting this wrong."

"I have no intention of doing that. However, you need to be apart from this. Your emotions interfered last night, and if that happens again it would put not just you in danger, but the child you mean to save." He softened his tone in an effort to convince her to see reason. "I have friends who are skilled in this type of work."

"Friends?"

"Associates. People who are able to ferret out distasteful information and handle specific, unique problems as they arise."

"I don't understand. I don't understand any of this." She rotated in a slow circle and assessed the room around her. "Am I still in the bookstore?"

"No." He wouldn't lie to her. "You're in my home, my study actually."

"Your study?" She looked at him as though she knew he distorted the truth. "If I draw the curtains wide, I won't see Gilbert Street, will I?"

She didn't make a move to prove her theory. The lady was far too clever for her own good.

"If you wish to rescue Oliver as soon as possible, I need you to tell me everything you know."

"I'm no watering pot or wilting lily. I insist on being part of this plan. Danger to my well-being shouldn't play a role in decision-making. Last night I needed your help, and that caused me to climb into your carriage. It was a conscious and purposeful risk."

"That and a fair amount of shock," he added, annoyed she'd disregard her safety so readily. "As I see it, you had little other choice. Seven Dials is no place for a woman. What would you have done if I wasn't there? Did you plan on confronting the men in that carriage, with your paring knife?"

Her eyes widened and she didn't answer.

"Had I not followed you into that dark corner . . ." He left that sentence unfinished.

After another beat, her posture eased. She faced him, her chin high and resolute.

"It's true, so far, London has been unkind. I once thought coming to this city offered a chance to live a dream, but circumstances have changed drastically."

"Indeed, this is no dream." He moved closer, acutely aware of all the unknowing clues she'd offered him. She wasn't from this area and viewed London as an idealistic solution to some preconceived illusion. She was the perfect prey for the thugs and criminals who crawled the streets after dark. "What almost occurred last night was a nightmare. What happens to the children who disappear off the streets of London is another horrific reality."

"Yes, I know." She shuddered and rubbed her palms up and down her upper arms, though the room was warm and comfortable.

"Are you ready to tell me what I need to know, Miss Ashbrook? It's the only way I'll be able to assist you."

Delilah searched St. Allen's eyes for a sense of trust and sincerity and found it, even though the day's unlikely events confused her more than she'd ever admit. Time blurred since Oliver was stolen. Emotional distress interfered with clear thinking. She required help, and every precious minute mattered.

She needed to confess the whole of it. *Or at the least, most of it.*

It was the only way to secure his assistance, and considering she held all the blame, she'd take any chance necessary to recover Oliver safely.

Nodding her agreement, she reclaimed her chair. Then he surprised her and sat in the chair at her side instead of returning behind the desk.

"The tavern I visited, well, it was reprehensible." She stalled in her answer, uncomfortable with uttering the explanation.

"The Three-Legged Pirate?"

She shook her head.

"The Drunken Doxy, Salty Pearl, Old Cock's—"

"Mr. St. Allen." She cleared her throat and flared her eyes to discourage any more suggestions on his part as heat stole up her cheeks. "It wasn't any of *those* establishments." She hurried on lest he continue. "I visited the Devil's Bedroom."

His lips twitched and she wondered if he'd purposely sought to lighten the mood and now suffocated a grin at her expense. "I can see why that name might be distressing to voice aloud."

Delilah went on, anxious to fill the uncomfortable silence.

"Oliver is the son of my lady's maid, Beth. He was snatched from the streets while under my care." She blinked rapidly and continued the retelling, stark and sorrowful in the room's patient quiet. "It was last Thursday, half eleven in the morning. I took him shopping for his mother's birthday. Beth is more like a sister to me than a servant. She's my dearest friend, but she never wished to come to London. I'm at fault for that decision too."

St. Allen leaned back and crossed his ankles, though he never stopped watching her face and his silent observation caused her heart to thrum louder in her chest. Already it was as if his eyes looked into her soul. What would he think when he heard everything she had to tell?

"Since the death of my father two years ago, I've lived an uncomplicated life in Birmingham. It was just the two of us. My mother passed when I was a young child. Father's death was unexpected and it left me quite alone aside from the modest staff. His sister, my Aunt Helen, had visited Birmingham and her fervent wish was that I relocate and come to live with her here in London. At first, I wasn't ready to leave my childhood home and the many lovely memories, but upon my aunt's insistence I finally agreed.

"I grew excited by the idea of embracing a new experience, but Beth feared the city and a more complicated lifestyle. She too had little family aside from her son and we all resided comfortably together before circumstances brought us here. In truth, Beth had little choice in the decision. Finding another household that would hire her and also support her son would prove difficult. I became as persistent with her as my aunt's efforts to persuade me. I wanted Beth to be happy with the move, and selfishly worked at convincing her to agree. It was due to Oliver's hopeful enthusiasm and desire to see the many sights of London that Beth reluctantly decided, but I know she was frightened. Yet despite her own misgivings, because of our friendship and bond, she put her trust in me. And now I've failed her in every way."

By the time she finished, tears stung her eyes. She turned away from St. Allen to focus on the navy-blue drapery as she composed herself. She didn't wish to appear weak or foolish.

"I'm sorry to hear all that has come to pass, but you mustn't blame yourself for the evil deeds of those involved in stealing children. It's a prolific and heinous problem. Street urchins have no advocates. No one fights for their survival or mourns their loss, though hundreds of nameless orphans roam London's streets, some runaways, others are bastards discarded by peers and quickly forgotten. Aside from the occasional charitable donation, most of upper society turns a blind eye to the plight. I'm sure you meant well by the choices you made."

The richness of his voice expressed more than compassion. It almost sounded as if he understood her despair on a deeper level, but she couldn't sort her own emotions enough to readily label what qualities he'd revealed. She composed herself and turned back to face him as he continued speaking.

"There are places where these deviant criminals keep the children they've stolen. It's short-term at best. Most often they respond to supply and demand. When they are approached with a proposition, they snatch a child from the streets that fulfills the customer's request. Small boys are sold as chimney sweeps and young girls to a worse fate, in many instances prostitution on foreign soil."

Delilah shuddered, the abhorrent practice too ugly to envision. She twisted in her seat and searched his face in hope of replacing the immediate image with a more preferable one. He stared at her, that same intensity in his gaze. Why would he help her? Why did he also wish to rid the streets of criminals and vermin? He was a tall, handsome man who would easily grace any ballroom and cause ladies to swoon.

He reached into his coat and retrieved a linen handkerchief. She took it and held it in her hands for lack of something to do.

"Oliver may have been in the carriage last night, or it was another unfortunate child in that sack. An innocent victim. Either way, I'm heartened that you've told me the truth."

His voice lowered to an entrancing timbre that resonated over her skin. She was reassured she'd made the right decision.

"There's more I should tell you, I suppose." She realized belatedly she'd mutilated his handkerchief into a rumpled mess and now attempted to smooth it on her skirts, distracted by the task for a moment.

"Go on."

"At first I thought to employ a runner. He arrived at my aunt's address and listened to my story, but once he learned I spoke on my servant's behalf and not a peer or relation, he dismissed concern with a callous explanation that the city is dangerous and lost children difficult to locate. He suggested Oliver ran away on purpose. I could tell he didn't care enough to search for him."

"Bow Street is undermanned and overtaxed, though that hardly assuages your worry or exonerates their dismissal."

"My aunt called the physician who treated Beth with laudanum. Telling her what had occurred during my outing with Oliver was the hardest thing I've ever faced in my life. Worse than my father's death. But now Beth just lays abed. It's as if I've broken her heart and with that, her will to live." She leaned forward, imploring him to listen. "My aunt doesn't know what I'm doing, of course. She'd never approve and likewise is too entrenched in society's censure to understand completely. But Beth is the sister I never had. Her son is like my own family. That's why I must continue my search. I need to right this wrong." She paused, steely resolve hardening her tone. "I need your help, but I won't have you exclude me in the process."

CHAPTER 4

Sebastian met Miss Ashbrook's gaze. When she'd turned her wide, hopeful eyes in his direction something in his chest squeezed tight. He had no time to examine it, but knew it dangerous indeed. Emotion had no place in his decision, and more often than not, disappointment was the outcome.

"I will do everything in my power to find Oliver, Miss Ashbrook." He kept his voice solemn.

"Delilah. You should call me Delilah." She attempted another smile, somewhat wobbly and all the more charming for it. "I don't see why we should stand on formality when we'll be keeping company and working together."

"About that," he began, but her face immediately reflected the same earlier defiance, and he wondered if there wasn't a better way to approach the problem. "Your involvement requires I take additional precautions. As I've already stated, my associates and I can use the information you've supplied and—"

"No." She shook her head and he again caught the scent of lemons. "My aunt is highly respected in London society. She wouldn't be pleased if she knew I'd taken matters into my own hands. Aside from the obvious impropriety—"

"And implicit danger," he interrupted, suspecting where her little speech led.

"She reviles scandal. The whole reason she insisted I come to London grew from her concern people would talk about my rustication in Birmingham and her lack of familial responsibility. She'd previously mentioned me to her many acquaintances and shared the assumption that upon my father's passing I would journey to London. She fancied she'd find me a suitable husband. Clearly, she never expected my resistance or reluctance."

He began to understand the slight woman in front of him had an iron will to match her inner strength. Perhaps he'd misjudged her in much the same way as her aunt, by appearance and lovely hazel eyes, hair the color of sunshine.

"Nevertheless, these are the facts and circumstances which led me to Seven Dials and now to you."

She placed her hand on his forearm and his first thought was to move away. Not because he disliked her touch, but oddly because he immediately wished to draw her into his arms. There was nothing scandalous about her gesture and yet it evoked all kinds of improper thoughts. Thoughts thoroughly misplaced considering the subject they discussed; still, his brain had no trouble at all supplying them. It could only be sympathy for her situation that caused the reaction. An inappropriate and unexpected vein of protectiveness too. He laid his palm atop hers, meaning to remove the contact, but then left his hand there instead. *For reassurance only.* What he had to say wouldn't be received easily.

"If your aunt already disapproves and fears societal censure, why would you insist on tempting that very same outcome? Your explanation sounds contradictory. This type of work requires late hours in dangerous settings with disreputable people. The worst of humankind, actually. Your aunt wants what's best for you and I'm of the same thinking."

"What's best for me is to find Oliver and return him to Beth. I'm responsible for his disappearance." She slipped her hand from beneath his and laced her fingers in her lap. "I'll never forgive myself until I exhaust every resource. Say you'll help me, St. Allen."

He exhaled long and thoroughly as he voiced words he'd no doubt come to regret. "It goes against my better judgment, but tonight only, for the purposes of identifying the person you spoke to previously, I will make an exception and agree. I'll send a hackney to the corner of Berwick Street. From there, we'll meet and proceed to the tavern. You're not to engage or interfere. My associates will be blended into the crowd. Do you understand the arrangement?"

"Yes." She popped to her feet, something akin to relief on her face. "Thank you. That will do." She offered his wrinkled handkerchief forward.

"You may keep it."

She pocketed the linen and then thrust out her bare hand as if to shake on their agreement. "Do I have your word?"

He noticed her slender fingers, her skin pale and soft, no doubt. He stood and clasped her hand within his. They remained that way a moment too long, his eyes matched to hers as an unsettling calm swept through him. Perhaps she experienced it too. A pink blush stole over her cheeks.

"I really should go." She backed away a step and walked toward the door. "My aunt will wonder as to my early errand, and with Beth unable to assist, she won't think well of me being out without a maid or footman."

"Proving my point yet again, Delilah." He paused, considering their familiarity no matter the uncommon circumstances that brought them together.

"I'll meet the hack on Berwick Street. There's a lovely lamppost on the corner. The lamplighter always arrives by half eight."

She had no reason to worry over her safety. He'd have someone keeping eyes on the corner long before she arrived this evening.

"I'll see you then. Don't be late." He gestured toward the door. "We should go downstairs and return to the bookstore."

They walked through the corridors in amiable silence for a stretch until he paused at the foot of the stairs leading to the Last Page Bookstore.

"This is clever." She nodded and began the flight. "How smart to have your home attached to your place of business."

He didn't correct her misconception, gladdened she hadn't thought too closely on the underground corridors. A sense of compunction crept to mind. Why was he actually allowing her to participate in his plan? Had he encouraged it simply because he'd like her to feel better? To alleviate her guilt? Or was there another reason? The warm pressure of her touch when she'd laid her slender hand on his arm lingered.

She reached the top of the stairs and only paused for a quick glance over her shoulder before she opened the door and crossed the threshold.

He wondered if she understood more than she revealed, or maybe if the situation causing her turmoil didn't allow her to sort everything to exactitude. Either way, he waited for the familiar click of the latch and then turned and aimed down a different path, one which he'd walked more times than he could tally. He had an appointment this evening, in a tavern where he hoped to discover information leading to the recovery of little Oliver, or another innocent child taken from the streets. He'd need the assistance of a few associates and he knew exactly where to find them.

Delilah hurried up the limestone steps to Aunt Helen's stylish town house and let herself in with the key, only to find her aunt paused in the foyer, her stout figure at mid-pace as she bustled back and forth.

"There you are." Aunt Helen rushed forward and gathered Delilah into her arms for a tight embrace. "I was worried about you."

"About me?" Delilah returned the hug and then withdrew to assess her aunt's concerned expression. "I left you a note stating I'd be out this morning. Whatsoever has you upset?"

"I don't like the idea of you moving about the city without me or at least without the company of a maid or footman. It isn't proper and considering the events of late . . ." Helen *tsk*ed her tongue in a sound Delilah knew well.

Removing her wrap, Delilah followed her aunt into the drawing room, though she was anxious to check on Beth. She understood why her maid was beside herself with grief and worry. While the doctor-prescribed laudanum numbed the truth of the situation, Delilah wished to explain how she'd enlisted the help of a man who seemed to command the world around him.

Delilah had contemplated St. Allen the entire ride home, replaying their conversation verbatim, able to think more clearly after separating from his company. When she sat beside him in his study, she'd become so acutely aware of his nearness she'd almost relented and agreed to allow him to visit the tavern alone. Luckily, her desire to right the wrong she'd perpetrated overrode distraction. She had to witness every interaction so she could be sure there was no stone left unturned.

That's not to say she didn't want to lean into St. Allen's strength and draw courage from him the same way one quenched thirst with a long drink of water. When she'd touched his arm it was solid muscle beneath her fingertips. She knew immediately he would keep her safe. This entire situation had shaken her to the core, and the lonely sense of vulnerability she experienced often kept her awake at night.

St. Allen radiated strength and reliance. He spoke of the plight of street orphans with knowledge and compassion. What of all the other children besides Oliver? Another pang of sorrow sliced through her heart. St. Allen was a good man to want to right the wrongs of those less fortunate.

She slid her fingers into her skirt pocket and touched his handkerchief tucked inside. She'd wrapped it around the pouch holding the miniature of Oliver and lock of his hair.

"Shall I ring for tea?"

Aunt Helen's cheerful bid penetrated her thoughts and drew Delilah to the present. Apparently, her aunt's amiable demeanor was restored. Delilah would need to be more careful of evoking Aunt Helen's concern. She didn't want to become another burden; even more now that Oliver's disappearance distressed the household. The overwhelming feeling of helplessness made her wish she could scour the streets in search, despite she knew the foolishness and futility of that idea. The only way to find Oliver was to confront the men who'd taken him in the first place.

"Yes, tea is always a good idea." She settled on one of the overstuffed chairs before the hearth. "Have you looked in on Beth?"

"She's in a terrible state. My heart breaks for her." Aunt Helen took a chair after she rang for Mrs. Dunn, the housekeeper. "I've written a few letters to people of influence who may lend help in this situation, but I don't hold much hope for a prompt reply. I never considered the desperate plight of street children and how it impacted so many lives. In the worse lesson possible, I've learned London is not as idyllic as I've always believed."

"I'm truly sorry to bring this trouble to your door." Delilah fairly whispered the words. Her aunt had offered her a home, companionship, and a rightful place in society so she might find a suitable husband and secure future. In return, Delilah caused tragedy, sorrow, and a shocking revelation that permanently marred her aunt's perception. Still, the stark reality was one every Londoner should strive to improve.

"Dear, please don't apologize. What happened on Jermyn Street is not to be relived now in our home. We've notified the authorities. I can't imagine what else can be done. It's a tragic accident and well . . ." Aunt Helen picked at a thread on her skirt, apparently unsure how to complete her sentence.

"Yes." Delilah sought to relieve her aunt's discontent. "I know."

She also knew the crushing weight of guilt. She alone was responsible for Oliver's disappearance. He was stolen while in her care. If she allowed the anguish of her regret to take control, Delilah believed she too would need a healthy dose of laudanum. But intelligence warred against that surrender. St. Allen's help was timely because she'd do anything and everything to rescue Oliver. Having St. Allen by her side offered hope, however slim the realistic possibility. She needed to tell Beth of this development.

Assuring her aunt she'd return for tea shortly, Delilah went upstairs to the servants' rooms. She found Beth seated near the single window, her focus on the street below. Delilah knocked on the doorframe lightly in an effort not to startle her friend.

"May I come in?"

Beth didn't move at first but then she turned, and her forlorn expression solidified Delilah's determination.

"I keep waiting to see Oliver run up the lawn or be returned by a Bow Street official . . . somehow come back to me."

Delilah settled on the seat beside her maid. "Of course. I want that too." She placed her hand atop Beth's in the same way St. Allen had offered her reassurance. "I know someone who may be able to help us."

Despite the lingering lethargy of the physician's prescription, Beth's eyes immediately brightened. "Please tell me."

"I met a man who is also interested in stolen children."

"A criminal?" Beth looked aghast.

"No. Nothing like that." Delilah shook her head in the negative. "He fights against horrific crime. He wants to help us find Oliver."

"How will he help? What will he do? How can one man fight against these horrible thieves?"

Careful not to instill misplaced expectation, but likewise praying the arrangements this evening would lead to Oliver's recovery, Delilah continued. "I'm meeting him later. We hope to gain information that will lead us to the men who took Oliver and likely many more children from the streets."

"Dare I wish it true, but it sounds too dangerous a risk."

"St. Allen will protect me."

"St. Allen?"

"That's his name, though he hardly looks the saint." Delilah was quick to conjure an image of how he'd appeared in Seven Dials. Tall, unyielding, and lethal; the shadow of whiskers along his jaw, his thick hair and piercing liquid eyes that held her in sharp scrutiny as they took her measure. He'd materialized from thin air and vanished into the night the same way. When he'd climbed into his carriage and filled the seat across from her, the interior had shrunken by the broad width of his shoulders, the space between crowded by his long muscular legs. She blinked to clear her mind. "I can't make a promise we'll have more information tonight, but I will promise I'll never stop looking for Oliver."

Beth's eyes filled with tears and she turned toward the window again. "I know, my lady. I know you will."

CHAPTER 5

Sebastian was relieved to see two of his associates at billiards when he entered their meeting place. Malcolm Vane slanted a glance in greeting while Tristan Darlington hardly spared him notice, his focus on the shot before him. The clack of the ball and subsequent thud as it butted against the felt-covered table and missed the netted pocket evoked a black oath.

"St. Allen."

"Vane."

"Darlington has volunteered to lose to me again if you'd like to get in on our wager."

"The only thing I'm losing is my temper as I listen to your tripe. No matter how you bait me, you'll not win against my skill today," Darlington objected quickly.

"That's not skill, that's luck."

"Only the good get lucky, Vane."

"Luck and skill combined, no doubt," Sebastian interjected. The two were known to bicker like brothers, though one was a respected peer and the other a product of the streets. Their distinct abilities set them apart and at the same time brought them together.

"Always the slick negotiator, aren't you?" Darlington commented.

Sebastian approached and watched several shots in succession until Malcolm sunk the last ball and both men replaced their cues, the earlier prediction now a reality.

"Speaking of luck, did you have any with your surveillance?"

Sebastian pondered a justified response. "Yes and no."

"A bit of both?"

"I didn't confront those involved as planned, but I saved a woman in trouble who in turn seeks the same justice." Sebastian eyed the brandy on the sideboard, undecided whether he cared for a drink. "Her attacker deserved my knife buried in his gut, but the lady experienced enough shock for the evening. She didn't need another nightmare to add to the one she's already living." That was it, wasn't it? The reason he'd allowed her to convince him. He felt sorry for her.

"A woman in Seven Dials at night," Vane considered aloud. "She owes you a debt."

"I don't see it that way."

"To venture into the vilest part of the slums alone is asking for the worst possible outcome," Darlington replied offhandedly.

"Agreed." Sebastian didn't feel compelled to add more to the story. Delilah seemed reluctant with every word she'd uttered and he'd share her story judiciously.

"It conjures images of a female avenger in search of innocent children."

"More an angel." This comment earned him a curious glance and prompted Sebastian to continue or else invite their relentless jibes. "We're pursuing one of her leads this evening."

"We are?" Malcolm motioned in the space between himself and Tristan.

"Or you and the avenging angel?" Tristan asked.

"All of us, actually." Sebastian didn't hesitate at pulling his associates into the fray. It was the primary reason they'd accepted their positions as intelligence agents in service to the Crown. Their purpose was to covertly solve crimes in London and they were damned good at it. Sebastian had saved their arses before and risked his own at their request too many times to count. He supplied a brief explanation of what he knew and planned going forward.

In a familiar routine, Tristan went to the sideboard and poured three glasses of brandy as they fell into conversation with ease. Then he reclaimed his chair, set his drink down on the side table with his assured arrogance neatly in place. "Since when do we include outsiders in our matters?"

"It was the only way she'd agree to supply the information I needed," Sebastian answered.

"Shrewd terms."

"Determined, more likely." A ready image of Delilah Ashbrook formed in his mind. She was brave, he'd give her that. And beautiful, though he shouldn't notice. That quality had nothing to do with what they hoped to accomplish this evening.

"It will be difficult to find the boy." Malcolm exhaled and leaned back in his chair. "He was likely taken to be sold."

"I thought the same thing."

"Abductors of children ordinarily prey on the overlooked, the lost and hungry, not children of the aristocracy. Peers will employ every avenue at their disposal and cause a ruckus," Tristan added.

"I suppose we'll know soon enough if a ransom demand follows." Sebastian said the words and strove for an even tone as a somber silence enveloped the room. After years of pursuit and rescue, Sebastian knew the plight of street urchins all too well, not discounting personal experience. But he wouldn't reopen old wounds even though the past was always anxious to rush in. Instead, he would find Oliver.

"So where are we going this evening?" Tristan moved to the sideboard and replaced his empty glass.

"The Devil's Bedroom."

"A convenient location if nothing else." Malcolm also stood.

The Government had a corridor entrance two blocks over from the tavern in question. The King's Elbow was a small pub which catered to the honest and hardworking people of the area instead of the miscreants and thieves who lurked near the docks. The various locations atop the corridors kept the agents hidden in plain sight and allowed for easy relocation without visibility.

"I'll meet you there at nine."

"Where am I going at nine?" A female voice chimed in but none of the men turned in reaction. Eva Fields was another of the Crown's agents and her comings and goings at the offices were a natural occurrence as much as their own. No one knew anything about her except what she'd decided to share, and that was little. But her ability to make mishaps nonexistent, generate a powerful thread of gossip whispered in the right ear to influence those in power, and fix a potential scandal with seamless eloquence, qualified her as an important member of the group. Like the others, she meted out consequence, punishment, and justice with precision.

Sebastian reiterated their earlier conversation without embellishment. At times he suspected Eva held an unspoken affinity for him, and that concern caused tension. He immediately squelched any thoughts of romance she might entertain, whenever they were alone together, but he wasn't altogether certain she realized his intent, even though he'd spoken plainly. Mixing business with pleasure was a definite misstep and he had no desire to turn their professional relationship into a personal one.

"Jermyn Street is a popular place for danger and misdeeds these past two days." Eva picked up Sebastian's brandy and finished what was left in the glass. "That's the same location where the Duchess of Grandon was accosted earlier this week."

"Accosted?"

"Perhaps that's too strong a word. She's quite fine, although the assailants made off with a possession more treasured than all her priceless jewelry."

"And that would be?"

"Cygnet, her pure white Pomeranian."

"A dog?"

"Someone attacked the duchess to get her dog?"

"As strange as it sounds, it could only have been prearranged.

The duchess was near Jermyn Street to take tea with a friend, as she does every first Thursday of the month. Once outside her carriage and accompanied by two footmen, she stopped on the walkway to allow a young boy to meet Cygnet. The dowager adores children almost as much as her pet. Cygnet is like her child, actually. Unfortunately, doing this was the distraction the thieves needed. They jostled her intentionally and snatched the pup while the footmen recovered the duchess. It wasn't until Her Grace was righted and protected by her footmen that she shrieked with horror because Cygnet was gone."

"Perhaps the pup was happy to be free of his leash and simply ran down the street and escaped by his own will." Darlington suggested.

"No." Eva shook her head, her expression chagrined. "Cygnet's leash was cut. Sliced clean through. No one heard a bark or saw a thing, all eyes focused on the falling duchess and the bevy of footmen anxious to prevent her injury."

"It's just a dog." Vane shook his head in a show of how ridiculous he thought the conversation.

"Not to the duchess. Cygnet is the child she's never had. She dotes on him like a little prince from his polished nails to his priceless collar fashioned from a collection of heirloom diamonds."

"Now we're getting somewhere," Tristan interjected. "Priceless diamonds add a whole new perspective to things."

"When did this occur exactly?" Sebastian had followed the discussion carefully, his mind at work.

"I haven't all the details but I know it was sometime Thursday, as the duchess approached the teahouse."

Sebastian needed to question Miss Ashbrook, *Delilah*, more thoroughly. It couldn't just be coincidence, could it? Jermyn Street was a main thoroughfare in the shopping district, not some dark alley in the middle of Seven Dials. Crime wasn't even a consideration during the daylight hours. Something was afoot and he was determined to discover what it was.

*   *   *

Once darkness fell it was easy for Delilah to slip out of the house undetected. Aunt Helen retired early, and with a few chosen words to the household staff, Delilah ensured no one would look in on her for the rest of the night. Now, she hurried to the corner of Berwick Street, her cloak wrapped tightly, her pulse as anxious as her steps. St. Allen had assured a carriage would arrive and bring her to their assignation. She'd barely stepped to the curb when it materialized out of the lazy fog and rolled to a stop before her. The lamppost lent a soft glow to the otherwise vacant area, and when the door swung open she took the steps and settled on the seat, surprised to see St. Allen on the opposite bench.

"Oh." She drew a deep breath, again reminded of his intense masculinity, his presence inside the interior somewhat unsettling. He didn't intimidate her despite he had the look of a coiled snake, his watchful eyes in wait of the perfect moment to strike, his body all potent strength and lean, carved muscle.

He might not be suited to a bookstore necessarily, and his presence in Seven Dials last night still remained unexplained, but nevertheless he'd saved her from inconceivable danger and now worked with her to find Oliver.

The carriage jerked forward and she caught the edge of the cushion to keep from swaying across the divide. "I didn't expect you to be here."

Did the words sound pleased or disturbed? He quirked an amused smile in her direction.

"I thought it wise for us to discuss the plan before we entered the tavern." His dark brows raised as if even a simpleton would see the necessity. "My riding with you makes it all the more convenient to explain what will happen this evening."

Delilah listened, not wishing to appear foolish. Her solitary thought had been to find Oliver and return him to his mother, but she was learning quickly how impulsivity and poor planning would ruin any chance they had at that outcome. The information

St. Allen could provide about this unfamiliar city proved invaluable. She ran her eyes over him, his disheveled appearance yet another portrait of an intriguing man.

"Your clothing . . ." She noted his loose trousers and lack of a waistcoat or jacket. His white shirt was wrinkled, the sleeves rolled to reveal a dusting of dark hair on muscular forearms. He wore no cravat, the slender vee of skin at his neck dimly visible in the soft glow of the carriage's lantern.

"We're going to a tavern, not a ballroom." Again, one side of his mouth hitched upward. "But you can't be seen, so you should keep your face shadowed by your hood whenever possible."

She nodded for him to continue.

"Once we're inside, I'll need you to practice the utmost discretion and indicate the man you spoke to last time."

"What should I do? How will you know?"

"A brief description of his clothing and location whispered in a low tone should suffice. My associates will already be scattered about the tavern at the ready to act if needed. You'll take a corner table with another one of my associates, and after I've made contact, he'll see you home safely."

"Where will you go?"

"Wherever the information leads me."

"Let's hope it leads you to where Oliver is hidden." *Because I'll be following right behind you.*

He paused and she watched as his jaw tightened. From the way he avoided her eyes, she wondered what secrets he kept. Regardless, whatever he meant to say next wouldn't come easily.

"Do not be appalled when I pose as someone looking to purchase a child."

"No." She pushed her hood backward so she could meet his eyes clearly. "I know this must be done to accomplish our plan."

"If there's any kind of disturbance, my associate has been instructed to take you out immediately."

He reached across the interior and grasped the sides of her

hood with both hands to replace it and conceal her identity. One hand dropped away but the other lingered and her breath caught, unsure what he would do next.

"There are no guarantees, Delilah." He stroked a line down her cheek with his fingertip as if tracing the track of future tears. "Be strong."

He thought her weak? She'd allow him the misconception, and while she wouldn't take advantage of his kindness, no doubt she'd gain more if he believed he served as her protector.

The carriage jerked to a stop and he cupped her jaw to steady her from the unexpected jolt.

"We've arrived."

She drew a deep breath as he pulled his hand away, his touch imprinted on her skin, her heart in a frantic beat.

Never allow emotions to control a decision. Never allow someone to discern your emotions. Never—

They'd reached the tavern door midway through Sebastian's recitation of personal rules. He'd made a costly mistake. Delilah was a distraction. Well, mostly her moonlight-golden hair and citrusy scent. Worse than a distraction, she was his responsibility, which included her implicit trust and the overwhelming hope alive in every glance from her lovely hazel eyes. If a ruckus broke out at the tavern or he pressed too hard on the man she indicated, he'd be more worried over her safety than acquiring the information needed. He'd broken an important rule, but it was too late for regret. He blew out a rough exhale to refocus on the task at hand.

Once inside, he ushered Delilah to a table near the corner and waited for her to scan the interior. It was still early and the crowd was lean. This type of tavern drew a mix of rough element, curiosity seekers, and simple hardworking people who wished for a cheap ale after a long day. Nightly disturbances were part of the tavern's spectacle. A few couples enjoyed a meal at the far tables and a handful of men congregated around the bar, their boisterous conversation forcing attention from those around them. He noted

Eva near a ladybird at the opposite corner. Once Vane slipped into the seat next to Delilah with practiced ease, Sebastian claimed the third chair.

"I don't see him. He's not here." Delilah spoke the words in a soft whisper though her distress was evident.

"Let's give it some time." Sebastian eyed Vane across the table. "I'll make my way to the bar and drop a few intentional inquiries. It will be easy to decipher if anyone can help with my problem." He lent a quick glance to Delilah and stood, not waiting for confirmation from his friend. He turned, alerted to the voices near the bar as they escalated into what could only be an argument between two men who should have stopped drinking an hour earlier.

Sebastian stalled, waiting to see if the men would resort to brawling, but the disagreement escalated too fast. Instead of common fisticuffs, an empty bottle flew across the room and shattered on the wall above the table where Delilah sat. She gasped loudly. If she hadn't been wearing her hood, a shower of glass would have rained down upon her.

"Remove the lady." Sebastian aimed his order at Vane, though he kept a close watch on the instigators. One of the men cursed loudly while the other brandished a broken bottle in retaliation. With haste the area cleared of patrons, but some onlookers encouraged the men to fight, interested in a show of savagery. Others abandoned their tables and made for the front of the tavern, intent on leaving. All around them commotion swelled. Still, he heard Delilah over the rising din.

"I'm not leaving. I haven't had time to look at everyone."

He hadn't expected her to object and shook his head in the negative. "Never mind about that."

The likelihood of anything constructive happening now was slim, the entire tavern transformed from public gathering place to disorderly chaos in a matter of minutes. Ironically, it was how the establishment perpetuated its ridiculous name.

Reaching for her hand, Sebastian helped Delilah to her feet. Her hood fell back and a long braid tumbled over her shoulder.

Across the room, the fight had begun in earnest. People near the bar yelled insults and jibes, more interested in the spectacle than in resolving the issue. Even the barkeeper stopped filling tankards to watch with rapt attention. Conversely on both sides, groups of people pushed anxiously forward in an attempt to clear from danger and leave.

Brawls had a way of becoming contagious, and while the crowd seemed satisfied with the display offered at the moment, there was no telling when the situation could change. He needed to move Delilah toward the exit and out into the waiting carriage. He had a few other ideas where a deal could be made to buy a child, despite the very thought disgusted him. Hopefully she would be content with altering their plans.

Across the floor, the front door opened and several newcomers entered, at least half a dozen, their voices jovial. Sebastian could only see the faces of the first three and he shifted his position at the same time Delilah managed to squeeze through the crowd and join him at his side. She was supposed to remain with Vane, and yet she stood beside him now. Near the entrance a tall, thin man in a black cap broke away from the group and scanned the room, his attention settling on Delilah a moment too long. Sebastian blocked her with his body and took a step in the opposite direction, urging her farther into the tavern.

"Pull up your hood and stay with me."

He stared into her eyes and without waiting for an answer, clasped her hand and tugged her deeper into the press. He had to get her out of the tavern and away from the carriage driver from the past evening. The driver had looked at Delilah with a note of recognition and with that, no question remained they needed to disappear as quickly as possible.

Shoving through the crowd of gawkers, Sebastian spared a quick glance behind him and noted the driver pursued them now, his gangly height easily observed over the other patrons who pushed and squabbled to find a better vantage point to observe the brawl at the bar. Thankfully, the swell of customers interested in leaving impeded the driver's advance, but not so many people that it would prevent his progress for long. At one point, a woman in a long cape brushed against Delilah and caused her to gasp. Sebastian tightened his hold on her hand and worked harder to maneuver through the crowd. When he reached the rear of the room, he pushed through the swinging panel used to access the kitchen and half guided, half hauled Delilah along with him. He didn't stop until he exited the back door and hurried her around the side.

Unfortunately, the area offered them little opportunity. Several men congregated at the corner of the building where one of them relieved himself on the tavern wall. There wasn't a clear path to safety although a few hackneys waited several strides away. The hacks could be useful as an adequate place to hide.

Within the next moment, the back door swung open and the same wiry driver exited, his footsteps hollow on the slates as he moved hurriedly in their direction. Decision made, Sebastian pulled Delilah hard and tight against his body as he melted into the shadows between two waiting cabs.

CHAPTER 6

Mistakes. Tonight, he was making one after another. Holding Delilah against him and waiting in the dark proved a harder task than he'd anticipated. *Harder.* Absolutely. She remained motionless and yet his body hummed on high alert, attune to every exhale, her fresh lemony scent, the press of her warm soft breasts against his chest and their shared heat as they cocooned between the hackneys.

The threat of discovery had passed, but he waited still. He should release her, though he told himself an extra few minutes of safety in hiding would guarantee no one met with harm. To attack the driver would set off a chain reaction, no doubt stirring everyone in the Devil's Bedroom into a massive brawl. While he was confident in his ability to protect Delilah, he had no desire to waste time cleaning up the overflow of such an event.

After another few minutes, only the sound of normal business emanated from inside the tavern and he guided Delilah silently around the rear wheels of the hack and down the line until he reached his own carriage. Without a word he opened the door and motioned for her to enter. Then he took the opposite seat and rapped on the ceiling.

Though he said nothing, her eyes gazed at him intently, glistening in the light of the interior lantern. Without thinking he leaned closer. He'd labeled her eyes hazel, but he couldn't be more wrong. Up close each iris held a universe of beauty, soft mossy green with tiny constellations of shimmery gold flecks. Yet his moment of adoration was short-lived.

Without warning her expression collapsed and she drew a shuddered gasp, the impact of the evening finally taking hold.

"I—" She struggled to catch her breath, whether the race through the tavern, necessity of hiding, or now the intensity of their escape, she seemed beside herself with emotion.

"Don't talk," he suggested. "Just try to relax while we get away from here."

"But what of Oliver?" She shook her head vigorously, the cloak wrapped around her shoulders awkwardly, the hood twisted off to one side.

"No one would be willing to talk to us at the tavern with that melee going on." He watched her carefully. Was it upset or anger in her reaction? He had little practice with women and tender emotions. "We'll try again, or at least, I will."

Her eyes flared and she squeezed her hands together in her lap, the knuckles blanched white. The last few nights had been unthinkably unkind. He sensed whatever reserve of strength she'd salvaged was nearly bled out.

Leaning forward, he braced his forearms on his knees and sought to reassure her. "I had to remove you from the tavern. Aside from the brewing trouble started by the two fools at the bar, the wiry driver from last evening spotted you in the crowd."

"I saw him. I can picture him in my mind's eye and describe him to the tiniest detail." Her voice fairly vibrated.

"What's wrong?"

"I'm angry. I'm frustrated and discouraged."

"Nothing good would have come from that confrontation. From this point on I think—"

"I'm never going to find Oliver." Her rapid breathing turned whisper thin. "I lost him. Right in front of me, I lost him and now he may be hurt, harmed. Worse, he may be—"

A wretched sob interrupted and Sebastian sensed she bordered on hysteria. He grasped her hands within his. They were ice-cold despite the overly warm temperature of the interior. "Miss Ashbrook?"

"I never should have allowed him out of my sight. He just dashed off. He didn't listen. I called after him. Several times. But it all happened so fast." Anguish distorted her words.

"Miss Ashbrook? Delilah?" He rubbed the backs of her hands vigorously within his own and when she showed no answer other than a broken sob, he hauled her atop the bench beside him, her skirts and cloak draped across his legs where they overlapped. Bloody hell, she'd been through so much in the last three nights, but he couldn't have her falling apart. He needed to regain her attention and a slap wouldn't do. This situation wasn't like any other and warranted a careful approach. She was strong and brave, but clearly at the moment she was overrun with emotion.

He released her hands and cradled her face, forcing her chin upward so she couldn't avoid his eyes. He noticed the shadows of fatigue under her eyes and creases of worry at her temple. "Delilah. Take a deep breath. Try to calm yourself and listen to me. We'll find Oliver."

Another rule broken. An empty promise. He had no idea how any of this would end. The boy could be sold into oblivion, a victim of depravity—or worse, no longer on their side of the earth.

A wispy sigh shivered through her and her chin trembled in his hands. Dammit to hell, he was no good at consolation. A haunted look shadowed her eyes now and he searched his mind for something to say that would ease her distress. He needed a distraction. Something to shock her out of her dismay.

She appeared so vulnerable. So full of despair. His heart tightened and he swallowed hesitation as he made yet another mistake in a long list.

Delilah stared into Sebastian's eyes, caught by the intensity of his expression. Could it be tenderness? How ridiculous. That made not a whit of sense. Scattered thoughts crowded in, emotion inundated her heart, her pulse frantic and stomach in knots. However, the longer she matched his heated gaze, the calmer she became. His nearness and unyielding strength comforted and at the same time distracted, all in a good way. When he clasped her face within his bare palms, so warm and strong, her breathing evened, her heartbeat steadied.

Regardless, she never expected what happened next.

He slanted his face down to hers and his slight hesitation caused a lock of hair to fall forward on his brow. When his mouth met hers, it was a gentle brush of his lips surely meant to soothe her, but somewhere between his intent and execution, circumstances changed. Another beat of her heart and he captured her lips in a kiss that sent the world spinning on its axis, faster than her rapid pulse, more frenetic than their race through the tavern yard. She didn't think. She wanted comfort. To feel safe and cherished. Just for a moment. And so, she gave herself over to his kiss and returned his attention with uninhibited honesty.

The press of his lips caused a tingling sensation like sparks dancing along her nerves to spiral in a steep whirlwind low into her belly. She relaxed into him and he growled a deep noise of appreciation that somehow vibrated through her no matter only their mouths touched, his fingers wrapped loosely near the neck of her cloak.

She'd never kissed a man before, not in a romantic manner, and yet she must be doing something right. He seemed to enjoy the kiss as much as she. She wished she could silence her brain completely. Force her mind to stop analyzing their embrace. St. Allen was handsome and compelling. He commanded the world around him. Yet for all the ruthlessness in his outward appearance, she sensed a deep tenderness within him. The contradictory qualities intrigued her. She could easily succumb to his charms, but that wouldn't be in her best interest. If he'd aimed for distraction, he'd achieved it and she'd be wise to leave it at that.

The carriage hit a rut with a hard jolt and the reverberation shook them apart. For a moment, neither of them spoke. Then she withdrew and huffed a breath in hope a little oxygen would clear her mind. St. Allen reclined against the squabs, though his eyes watched her every move.

"Why did you . . ." She stalled midsentence and pressed her fingertips to her mouth. They tingled still. But kissing—kissing should be the last thing on her mind, even though there was no ignoring the undeniable spark that danced between them when their lips touched.

"You were upset from the scene in the tavern. I hoped to calm you."

Hardly. Her heart thundered and her pulse thrummed. Electricity sang in her veins so vibrantly, she no longer felt tethered to the earth. "Do you always kiss people to settle their nerves?"

"No." His eyes twinkled with what could only be amusement at her inquisitiveness, and his voice lowered to an enticing timbre. "But you were *very* upset."

The husky tone of his words skittered over her and when she didn't reply he continued. "I'll take you straight to Berwick Street. You've had enough excitement for one night."

No, she couldn't return home. The hopelessness and helplessness of that choice was enough to break her heart yet again. She needed to find out what they would do next and how they would search for Oliver.

"Could we ride around a little? Right now, I'm too distraught to sleep."

"Of course." He knocked hard on the ceiling to be heard over the traces, and when the driver opened the panel, St. Allen instructed him to keep moving with no particular destination. "I need you to tell me everything about the day Oliver disappeared. Every single detail. Don't omit a thing or dismiss it as minor or coincidental. Can you do that?"

"Yes." She nodded as she adjusted her hood and opened her cloak. Anything that would aid in the safe return of Oliver was imperative to remember. Relying on St. Allen rankled, but women were limited in London society and she had no other recourse than to enlist his help.

She exhaled thoroughly and began. "We were on our way to Hanson's Millinery on Jermyn Street. I wanted to purchase a new bonnet for Beth's birthday gift, with a matching velvet ribbon as a present from Oliver. He insisted on accompanying me and I saw no harm in it. He was very excited about seeing the city. We took a footman with us and used my aunt's carriage." Delilah shook her head and paused to collect her thoughts. Blinking hard, she took a deep breath, summoning her remembrance of the scene in intricate detail. She'd made a poor decision, or at least her good intentions had gone terribly astray. She flicked her eyes across the interior, but St. Allen only watched her silently, his pale eyes bright with a mixture of encouragement and empathy.

"The shops were busier than I anticipated. I don't know what I expected actually. I believe now, my view of London life was skewed. But regardless, our driver managed to maneuver brilliantly and align the coach with the storefront where we were quick to alight. I had hardly smoothed my skirts when an elaborate equipage turned the corner and captured everyone's interest, most especially Oliver's. His eyes grew wide with fascination and he pointed toward the street with excitement. Four dappled grays pulled a grand barouche, their manes braided with colorful ribbons, the ends dancing wildly in the wind. I was pleased the outing brought this unanticipated spectacle. Even the liverymen were dressed in their finest, a dashing blue and scarlet pattern with shiny brass buttons that glittered in the sunlight. The carriage could only hold someone very important and I allowed Oliver to watch. In truth, I was equally transfixed by the display. I only wish the crest had been visible upon the door." She couldn't disguise her reproach at her poor judgment. She should never have taken her eyes from Oliver. Not for one moment. Still considering her obvious and detrimental mistakes, she paused. St. Allen had leaned in while she'd spoken, his eyes never leaving hers.

"There's no need to embellish the story." St. Allen spoke quietly. "I imagine you've relived it many times, but only the facts will serve best in locating Oliver."

"I *am* relaying facts." Delilah stifled a spike of irritation. "I've always had the uncanny ability to remember things in frightful detail. My father would tease me that I could recall a conversation from a decade ago and recite every word correctly."

She might have been wrong, but if St. Allen's expression was any indication, she'd raised her esteem in his regard.

"How clever." He offered her half a smile. "For some that would be a very useful tool."

He didn't say more and so she continued.

"I reached for Oliver's hand and nearly had it in my grasp when his little fingers swept across my palm. A small crowd had formed quickly and he wished to see too. Being so small he simply slipped through the legs of those who filled the curb. I followed right after him, but it wasn't as easy for me to make my way, and any gentleman's greatcoat or lady's skirts hid Oliver from view. Then, a woman's cry rang out. A dog barked sharply, twice in a row. It was as if time slowed at that point." She relayed the memories even though they sliced like thorns into her heart. "The crowd shifted and swayed and I continued to fight for a view to the scene unfolding on the pavement. The footman and driver from the fancy coach jumped down from the boot. It seemed as if suddenly everyone was in motion and I frantically searched for the sight of one little boy among a gathering of dozens. When I at last managed to gain a clear viewpoint, an elderly woman stood at the center of the upset. She was in tears, though her panicked shrieks echoed my own as I searched the crowd for Oliver. I called his name out over the noise, but between the lady's exclamations, the onlookers, and busyness of the street, I knew he likely couldn't hear me. The distraught lady was hurried back to her carriage, and those who'd gathered began to disperse. I didn't discern more than a blur of color. I was frantic and at the same time confused and horrified by the truth. Oliver was nowhere to be seen."

Their carriage rolled to a stop but she hardly noticed. She knit her fingers in her lap, only to separate them again, her emotions frayed from the bleak retelling.

"You mustn't blame yourself."

St. Allen's deep voice and kind words were likely meant to reassure her, but she had no one else to blame. She'd lost Oliver and it was up to her to find him.

"Now you understand why I must be part of the search." She drew a deep, cleansing breath. "It's my fault Oliver is lost. Stolen. Had he watched the scene and not been taken he would have been there waiting for me as soon as the crowd dispersed. I searched the nearby streets and questioned people in the shops. I called after him for over an hour. No one had noticed a young boy. At least no one I'd spoken to."

"I believe the woman in the elaborate equipage at the center of the scene was the Duchess of Grandon."

He spoke so matter-of-factly Delilah wondered if he understood the depth of her desperation, but when she looked to him in the dusky lantern light, she again saw understanding in his eyes. "How would you know that?"

"A number of ways, actually. Livery colors are individual and identifiable, as was your description of the livestock."

"You've memorized uniforms and horseflesh?"

"It's useful information."

"I imagine so." It was her turn to be impressed with his knowledge and skill.

"And too, an associate mentioned the Duchess of Grandon was accosted last Thursday on Jermyn Street as she neared the teahouse where she regularly takes refreshment."

This addition to the conversation prompted her to breathe a little easier, and when she met his eyes, the reassurance she saw there pushed away the lingering remnants of regret, at least for the time being.

"Now I understand why you took the trouble with the livery."

For a long moment, neither of them spoke.

"I'll devote my attention to the duchess to assist in our search for Oliver," he said at last.

"You will?" His statement brought about her immediate focus. "Don't you mean *we* will?"

"This provides us with a strong avenue forward."

His high-handedness in assuming he had all control erased any kinship they'd formed. Her temper simmered as he continued.

"I'll look into the matter from now on. You shouldn't place yourself in harm's way."

She had no intention of relinquishing her participation.

"I don't know the Duchess of Grandon, but perhaps my aunt does," Delilah answered. "Any social events and introductions have been few since I've arrived. Everything in the household has stalled now that this situation has transpired."

"I'll contact my associate and learn what she knows of the incident as well."

"Yes. All information is good."

He didn't say more and Delilah wondered who his female associate might be. The man was a mystery as much as Oliver's disappearance, except St. Allen was here in front of her. She'd seen a few women at the tavern tonight, but there was no way to know if they worked with St. Allen or were local patrons out for something to eat and drink. And then there was the woman who purposely bumped into Delilah as she and Sebastian struggled through the crowd toward the rear exit. Delilah recognized her as the same woman who'd held her attention outside the Last Page Bookstore.

Except tonight the woman had pressed something into Delilah's hand and Delilah had pocketed it immediately, not wanting to lose the paper. She would look at it when she was home in her bedchamber. It could be nothing at all; although, the circumstances were strange indeed.

Tension invaded the interior of the carriage. She glanced to St. Allen in an attempt to read his thoughts but came away with little more than an assessment of his full mouth and the heated remembrance of how he'd held her against his chest and kissed her distress away. She needed to leave before she said something she might regret. There was no room in her thoughts for foolish emotion.

"Thank you for all your help tonight." She gathered her skirts and prepared to leave.

"I will send you a message if I discover anything useful."

"But how will you know where—"

He knocked on the roof and the driver jumped down to open the door and extend the steps. The lamplit corner of Berwick Street stood in wait, the night air heavy with humidity.

"I'll send you a message."

He didn't say more and Delilah left the carriage and hurried toward home. She glanced back and saw St. Allen on the pavement, watching her all the way to her aunt's front steps. She was new at subterfuge, but what harm could come from allowing him to know her address? He needed to send her word if he found Oliver. After all, that was the purpose of their association. Nothing more.

CHAPTER 7

Dawn arrived with its unusual brightness and inspired a similar burgeoning confidence in Delilah. Sebastian meant to keep her safe at home, tucked away until he discovered information concerning Oliver's disappearance, and she appreciated his well-intended gesture, but she couldn't do what he asked. She couldn't remain idle. Not while Oliver was lost to all of them. Not while other children were in danger.

With Beth overcome by the circumstances, Delilah had no need to make excuses to her aunt for the lack of a maid to accompany her, but instead promised to be most careful and keep the carriage and footman nearby at all times. She instructed the driver to take her to Cavendish Square and set out as soon as she'd finished breakfast, placating her aunt with a version of the truth. Delilah *was* completing an errand this morning. It just so happened to be visiting the address on the mysterious scrap of paper slipped to her the night before. It might prove nothing more than a foolish mistake, but she couldn't be sure, and if she'd learned anything within her brief association with St. Allen, it was that no clue should be left unpursued.

When she arrived at the Mortimer Street location, the carriage aligned with the curb and Delilah wasted no time climbing out to the pavement. She surveyed the modest limestone building labeled Wycombe and Company with its nondescript grid windows and quiet façade. Next door was a haberdashery that reminded her too much of the task which had led to Oliver's abduction. This realization solidified her resolve and she climbed the three stairs and dropped the brass knocker.

The door opened immediately and a petite woman with russet hair greeted her.

"I wondered when you would finally visit us. Please come in."

Delilah's eyebrows climbed with interest at the expectant greeting and she followed the woman inside for no other reason than to understand the circumstances better. The building's interior was well maintained and cheerful, albeit spared of ornamental decorations. She continued through the hall and up to the second floor, where things changed dramatically. The walls were papered with a floral design, soft welcoming furniture was arranged artfully, and two more women, one who poured tea at the large walnut table, looked up with congenial expressions upon their faces.

"Welcome." The tall, slender woman smiled and set down the china pot. "Your timing is excellent."

With little more than a nod, Delilah walked to the table beside the woman who'd greeted her at the door. The situation was most curious and she was anxious to understand further.

"Thank you." She removed her pelisse and took a seat beside the fair-haired woman who hadn't spoken yet. "I'm Lady Ashbrook."

"Oh, yes." The woman from the door nodded. "I'm Lady Julia Wycombe. This is my building. The three of us share this space as an office of sorts."

Delilah looked around the room, her gaze coasting over the furnishings and décor that spoke more to a home interior than any business she imagined. "I don't understand." She pushed her teacup toward the center of the table, unsure what to make of the morning so far. "Why am I here?"

"We're interested in helping you if the circumstances require it," the fair-haired woman beside her answered. "I'm Phoebe, and

Diana poured your tea. Julia has graciously provided this property so we have a common meeting place to work."

"And that work is . . ." Delilah remained terribly confused. Why had these women summoned her? And why was it done with such mystery if they operated a business here in the middle of the city?

"We strive to make London a better place. To right wrongs and correct issues that cause others harm and upset. Females are too often dismissed and overlooked." This came from Diana, who glanced up briefly from adding cream and sugar to her tea. "Julia thought you might be in need of assistance."

"So I *accidently* bumped into you in the Devil's Bedroom and pressed our address into your hand. I was there pursuing another matter, but I noticed St. Allen." Julia smiled, apparently pleased with her approach. "I'm encouraged you've acted on instinct and didn't dismiss the note as a useless scrap."

No doubt everyone noticed St. Allen. There was a compelling quality to the man that commanded one to pay attention to him even though he had a unique talent for remaining invisible when he wished to be. "You were sure I would come?"

"No, not at all. But we hoped you would." Julia took another sip from her cup and the room fell silent.

"I couldn't neglect a single opportunity if it offered some type of clue to solving my problem." Delilah shook her head in the negative, beginning to relax as a seed of an idea took root. Could these ladies help in her search for Oliver? Were they already aware of her distress? Could that be possible? She sincerely doubted Julia Wycombe spent all her evenings at that horrid tavern pressing notes into people's palms. "But how did you know?"

"Know what?" Phoebe asked, her eyes guileless.

"That I am troubled? That I needed help?"

All three women laughed outright, not one of them embarrassed to express their opinions openly, and Delilah smiled despite herself.

"We're familiar with St. Allen's efforts," Julia answered once their laughter ended. "Although I've never known him to involve an outsider, never mind a lady, in his investigation. Men can be rather obstinate in that manner. You must have insisted strongly enough for him to reconsider."

"Yes, I did. Our paths crossed unintentionally in Seven Dials the other evening—"

"Seven Dials?" Diana's eyes widened and Delilah had the notion she'd somehow raised her esteem in the other's opinion.

"Yes. Horrific circumstances brought me there." She wasn't sure yet what the women meant to propose, if anything, so she didn't continue. She busied herself with reclaiming her tea and taking a sip.

"You are either brave or desperate, to put yourself in such a dangerous place." Phoebe softened the latter of her comment with a frown. "Maybe both?"

"I don't know about bravery, and danger is of no consequence as I am truly desperate." She was, and thereby it couldn't hurt to enlighten the ladies further. "I'm searching for my maid's young son, Oliver, who was stolen off the street. He was in my care at the time and we are all heartsick over the incident. The three of us, my aunt, maid, and myself, are a close-knit family of sorts. Bow Street isn't interested in helping us, and with no other resources at hand, I took it upon myself to search for him. I can't bear the agonizing thought he's scared and alone somewhere. He's only a child." Emotion threatened and she blinked hard to force it away. "Are you able to help me? Is that why you wished for me to come here?"

"Yes." Julia settled in the chair beside Delilah. "St. Allen also works toward bettering injustice, although I understand he acts for personal reasons as well. His attention may be divided. But we work to help London. We want to help you."

"Do you know Seb . . . St. Allen well?" Delilah tried to sort the information and make sense of it all. She'd accept anyone's assistance in the search for Oliver.

"Not especially," Diana answered. "He and few of his associates have made our efforts more difficult at times, but other than happenstance, we have no history."

"Does he really work at a bookstore? What kind of personal reasons motivate him?" Delilah suddenly had more questions than she could voice.

Julia Wycombe tapped the side of her teacup with her pointer finger. "I can't speak to any of that." She paused, but only for the length of a breath. "Now that you're here and you understand our intent, we'd like for you to tell us the details of Oliver's disappearance. Together, we will gather information and attempt to recover the child if possible."

"I knew you were clever and intelligent," Julia added. "Not just because you somehow convinced St. Allen to allow you to join him at the tavern, but by not dismissing the slightest chance or opportunity of hope by visiting us here."

"Why were you in the tavern?" Delilah couldn't help but ask. "It's not a very welcoming place."

"No, some parts of this city are a far cry from a ballroom or garden party, although you likely already realized that from your visit to Seven Dials," Diana answered. "But you needn't worry about anything aside from your own troubles."

"Would you allow us to help you, Lady Ashbrook?" Julia replaced her teacup and looked at her directly.

"Of course. I'll tell you everything I know." Delilah glanced at each of the ladies in turn. "Is it just the three of you?"

"Now it is." Phoebe said. "Our dear friend Scarlett left our group last month and married a duke. We are quite pleased for her."

"Oh." Delilah didn't know what to make of that, but then again, when she'd set out this morning she'd had no idea she'd be taking tea with a vigilant trio of females who served as London's guardian angels. It certainly couldn't hurt to have another force working to locate Oliver in London's population. She'd tell them everything she knew and hope for the best.

"Most importantly, we won't exclude you," Phoebe continued. "You'll be included in every effort we make to find Oliver."

"And all the other children?" Delilah couldn't help but add. The thought of children being stolen and abused kept her mind in a constant state of turmoil.

"Sadly, we'll never be able to rid London of all the miscreants and criminals who prowl the street with foul intent, but we make a difference." Diana added, "We do what we can with the abilities we have to assist anyone in need."

"That's very noble. I appreciate your help. I'll do anything to have Oliver returned." Delilah took a deep breath. "Let me tell you what I know."

With careful yet artful finesse, she did just that, although she omitted any exchanges with St. Allen, most especially his kiss. That information had no bearing on the search. She didn't wish for the ladies to think her frivolous, since she had no way to explain her compliance when Sebastian initiated that kiss. At any other time, the gentleman would have earned himself a stinging cheek.

"Are you free this afternoon?"

"In the early hours, yes." Delilah leaned into the conversation, already intrigued. "Later in the day, I'm accompanying my aunt to a social event."

"Or we could leave now," Phoebe suggested. "At times daylight offers an advantage to the information we seek and the ability to view things often left in the dark."

Delilah wondered at Phoebe's cryptic comment. "Yes, I can go now. I'll need to send a message to my aunt that I may be later than expected. I wouldn't wish to cause her to worry. We've all had enough heartache lately."

"We can take care of that for you." Diana rose and went the sideboard before she returned to the table with a small pad and pencil.

"You certainly work quickly." It was all a little overwhelming, but if there was a chance any of this could help locate Oliver, Delilah wouldn't be deterred. "I'm ready."

"Let me tell you what I have in mind." Julia took control of the conversation and the four women began their planning.

Sebastian made his way to the offices in hopes he'd find the one person who already possessed information seemingly connected with Oliver's disappearance. His effort was rewarded. Eva glanced in his direction as he neared the table where she sat, papers strewn across the blotter in front of her.

"Late night straight into morning?" It was an innocuous question. Something to lead into the discussion he meant to have without veering into anything personal. Conversation was often dangerous with Eva. He didn't want his words misconstrued.

"That's the only kind, isn't it?" She looked up and smiled slowly. "Come keep me company." She gestured toward the chair beside her.

"I've too much energy to sit." He moved toward the hearth and back again. "Have you learned anything about Jermyn Street? How is the duchess faring?"

"Well enough as she recovers from the fright. She expects a ransom note or some type of extortion in the near future. Apparently, this isn't the first time someone has made a threatening advance toward her, but being concerned over society's perception, she's kept it all hush-hush and inadvertently placed herself in harm's way."

"Isn't it like the uppers to believe they are above nefarious crime?"

"Only because they perpetrate their conspiracies in fancy Mayfair drawing rooms instead of the dank alleyways of Seven Dials." Eva shook her head as she answered.

The mention of London's worst slums brought his mind immediately to Delilah's situation, not that the lady wandered far from his thoughts. Why was that? He couldn't afford mild curiosity to dull his focus. Yet he was doing just that. Eva was still speaking, unaware his attention had drifted.

"Either way, it's clear it isn't a random sneak or snatch, out to pad his pocket."

"You mentioned that. Have you gained any details about the incident itself? Something you didn't know when we spoke earlier?" He stalled a few strides from where she sat, but then she did exactly what he'd hoped she wouldn't and stood, approaching him as she spoke.

"Gaining access to the duchess is the problem." Eva gave him her full attention and stopped less than a pace away. "She plans to attend a ball this evening and I thought we could go together, slip into the crush via the terrace and flush out information. Otherwise, access to Her Grace is more guarded now than ever before. I'm a little surprised she's carrying on with her social schedule, but I've heard her described as obstinate, so no doubt she refuses to be intimidated by any perpetrator." Eva folded her arms over her chest and the motion lifted her bosom higher.

"Why the charade?" He avoided the ton and preferred it that way. "My usual method of information extraction is always successful."

"Indeed." She laughed softly and dropped her hands to her sides as she moved even closer. "I would also label you uncompromising, even stubborn, but I know you'd argue the point just because you refuse to be pigeonholed. Regrettably, your chosen manner of information reconnaissance won't work in this situation. The duchess is well guarded and no one, not even a tall, handsome man of mystery, will be able to lure her into a private setting."

It was best to ignore Eva's compliment. "The duchess won't know I'm there until I make myself known."

"True, you are gifted when it comes to invisibility, but Her Grace won't be left alone, thereby refusing you the opportunity to suddenly appear from the shadows." Eva arched an eyebrow that was as much invitation as it was challenge. "My idea makes sense. You and I work well together in all situations, wouldn't you agree?"

Eva's explanation was practical, though he didn't like the gleam of innuendo in her eyes. He didn't reply and she continued her efforts to convince him.

"Since your interests seem equally aligned, what do you say? Will you escort me this evening?"

Sebastian cursed mentally. He'd walked right into that one. Refusing would be awkward, if not counterproductive to finding Oliver. And it was only one evening. One ball. Though he wasn't so foolish to believe Eva wouldn't somehow finagle a dance from him or worse, involve him in some dark room surveillance that allowed her an advantage. Had she been cured of her starry-eyed notions where he was concerned? He hoped she'd taken his polite rebuff seriously. Romance and business were a horrible combination, and since he had absolutely no interest in Eva on a personal level, he didn't wish to poke a stick in a wasp's nest to encourage something that would only have a messy ending. Something with the potential to ruin their association with the agency or impede their work. Her contributions to every investigation were important and her work ethic unmatched. It presented a difficult situation to navigate at times.

"All you need do is tell me the time and place." He cleared his throat and met her eyes. "I'll be there."

CHAPTER 8

"We've arrived." Phoebe settled a gloved hand over Delilah's. "Are you ready?"

"Yes." Her answer was tentative at best. The way Phoebe spoke of the Foundling Hospital, as if it was a horrible place, caused Delilah's pulse to race. She'd always believed otherwise, but then again most of what she'd assumed of London had been revealed as false.

The hack arrived in Bloomsbury and Phoebe paid the driver. Delilah viewed the imposing gate and stone edifice at the front of the building before her. It made sense they should inquire within. There was always a slim chance somehow Oliver had been left at the hospital. She wouldn't have thought of the idea on her own. It was smart to rule out the possibility. She wondered idly if St. Allen had the same notion. Perhaps he'd already checked the hospital, making this a fool's errand, but she hadn't spoken to him so she couldn't know.

"We'll go around the back while Diana and Julia call at the entrance. Their hack is pulling to the curb now."

"I don't understand." Delilah hurried to follow Phoebe as she skirted the entranceway to the courtyard. The property was large, and had the hackney left them on the street they'd never be able to proceed without being questioned by a guard or worker. "Aren't visitors welcomed here?"

"Not without an appointment," Phoebe explained in a hushed tone, still on the move. "We don't have time for that. Julia and Diana will create a reason to draw the clerk to the girl's wing while you and I enter the boy's wing. Are you ready?"

Before Delilah could voice even one more question, Phoebe unbuttoned her waistband and dropped her skirt to reveal a pair of black, tight-fitting trousers that made scaling the low-lying brick wall possible. Phoebe then proceeded to the back door and removed a small tool from her pocket. She had already unlocked the gate and motioned Delilah to hurry before the series of actions registered.

"You're wearing trousers."

"We all do at times. The required skirts and underskirts of women's fashion are rarely convenient for our outside interests." Phoebe placed her hands on her hips, her explanation matter-of-fact.

"I daresay you have the right of it. You made everything you just did look simple."

"It wasn't very difficult." Phoebe flashed a brief smile. "Various unusual skills come in handy for the work we do and we all share our knowledge. We'll be happy to have trousers made for you if you'd like."

"Me? Doesn't it feel as though you're walking about in your drawers?" Delilah whispered.

"What it feels like is *freedom*."

Delilah didn't know what to say to that and followed on Phoebe's heels into a small vestibule and then down a long hall. An assortment of sounds echoed in the corridor, some friendly and others not. The prevalent sound of crying created a sorrowful background Delilah had trouble dismissing without consideration. The children here were fed and given a place to sleep, but she doubted any of them were happy. Her heart broke a little with the knowledge. If only there was something she could do.

"Come this way." Phoebe tugged on Delilah's elbow and together they moved toward a long hallway marked with dozens of open doors.

"Is this it?"

"Yes," Phoebe whispered, and waved her forward, but they were immediately stalled when a large shadow crossed their path.

They flattened against the wall and waited.

A tall guard strode past, followed by two stout nurses. They spoke in hushed tones as a single line of boys filed behind them. The children were quiet, their clothes dingy and ill fitted.

The scene before Delilah made looking for Oliver incredibly convenient, although her heart squeezed tighter as she watched child after child with the same sullen expression. There must have been forty boys in all, yet Oliver wasn't one of them. Once the guard and nurse were out of sight, Phoebe touched her arm and reclaimed her attention.

"They're likely off to the bathing chamber." Phoebe moved from the shadows and waved Delilah forward. "It's much easier to wash the boys as a mass group than individually."

"Oh." A world of emotion was contained in that one word. Delilah couldn't imagine the lack of privacy or awkwardness the children experienced, most especially the young girls, if indeed the same practice occurred in their assigned wing. "What will we do now?"

"I had hoped for an easy resolution and we'd discover Oliver here, but there's another place to look. Unfortunately, it's not nearly as pleasant."

Delilah's brows rose in reaction. The orphanage was anything but pleasant. Someday, she'd like to work to improve these conditions. The hardships each child faced seemed utterly unfair.

"This way." Phoebe moved silently down the hall and they were soon free of the building and outside again. As if by planned magic, Julia and Diana met them near the curb.

"As we might have expected, the resolution to this problem will take a bit more investigation." Julia waved the ladies closer and they moved to the roadway. "I've another idea that may prove more fruitful."

"This is a lot to see and understand. I'm saddened by this deeply." Delilah glanced over her shoulder at the orphanage building before following the ladies to the corner where hackneys waited for hire.

"True, and you're brilliant." Phoebe leaned in and nodded enthusiastically. "I think she's a natural, ladies."

"That does sound promising, doesn't it?" Diana added.

"I'm not sure I know what you're talking about," Delilah replied. "But unfortunately, I need to return home. I'm attending an event with my aunt this evening and I refuse to cause her reason to worry about my welfare."

"That's understood." Julia signaled to a driver, holding two fingers up in a gesture of command. "Why don't we continue this tomorrow morning? What time will you be able to meet, Delilah? We like to conduct business at first light before London is even aware we've pursued our goals."

"How clever. I can join you as early as you wish. You need only to include me in your plans."

"Then share my hack and Phoebe and Diana will follow. I know exactly what we need to do next."

Delilah settled on the banquette across from her aunt and wondered for the hundredth time what Mr. St. Allen was involved in this evening. He hadn't contacted her, and while her morning with the ladies at Wycombe and Company proved enlightening, it hadn't furthered her search for Oliver other than to eliminate the dreadful Foundling Hospital. Beth was all but despondent now, and Delilah worried her maid would fall so far into depression or become so dependent on laudanum to numb her pain, she'd never recover her cheerful nature.

Guilt and regret settled over Delilah in a now familiar tremor of emotion, and she forced herself to initiate conversation with her aunt, anxious to pass time during their travel to the Earl of Mumford's estate.

"It's difficult to don a fancy dress and slippers when such a large part of my heart breaks for Beth and Oliver."

"I know, dear, but it's best we keep up appearances." Aunt Helen nodded sympathetically. "I wouldn't wish for unseemly gossip to taint your arrival in London. As difficult as it may be, we need to paste on our smiles and perpetuate gladness. Try to find a little enjoyment in the evening. You may dance with your future husband tonight. One never knows when Fate will intercede."

Delilah turned toward the window so Aunt Helen wouldn't see her displeasure. A husband was the last thing on her mind. Her thoughts wandered as the silence stretched. Had Mr. St. Allen not chased after her and pummeled that vile miscreant in Seven Dials, her present state would have been even more horrific. A shudder rippled through her.

"Are you chilled, dear? Have you brought your shawl?" Aunt Helen had a penchant for meandering conversation. "Your gown is lovely, though I wonder if the modiste misconstrued my order. Paris designs are not wholly acceptable in London's ballrooms. Your neckline is more ambitious than I expected. Albeit this is a formal gathering and apparel will be under a speculative eye, I wouldn't want gentlemen or ladies to question your chastity."

"Aunt Helen!" Delilah covered her bare neck with her palm, acutely aware the gown revealed more skin than she was accustomed. Aside from being neat and respectable, she knew little of city style. "While a bit daring, this gown is fine. If needed I'll keep my shawl about my shoulders. Please don't give it another thought. Thank you for filling my wardrobe with dresses and accessories. You've been generous and caring without fault."

"You are my only niece and dear to me beyond words. I want to see you happily settled." Aunt Helen smoothed her gloved hand atop Delilah's. "It would be my worst failure if I didn't provide you with proper introductions and the come out you deserve."

Delilah only smiled in answer. She knew her aunt placed high value on appearances, took great pride in her pristine reputation and uncommon wealth as a respected societal widow, but Delilah experienced no hurry toward the altar and held the same opinion even before the tragedy of Oliver's disappearance. It was one of the reasons she was hesitant to leave Birmingham after her father's passing. That said, Aunt Helen's heartfelt sentiments were well meant and to be appreciated.

Delilah wished she could remember her mother more clearly, but her memories were nothing more than wishes, the yearnful longings of a soft voice and comforting touch to accompany the blurred image of her mother's face. Aunt Helen was trying to fill the void left by maternal absence. Her actions were cosseted by good intention.

Tonight, Delilah would play the appropriate role, but it would only be to repay her aunt's generosity. Matters of the heart were far from her mind and she preferred them left in the background right now. It didn't matter that the memory of Sebastian's kiss lingered on the periphery of this vow. She had no time for romantic ideas. She wondered now if it was another of his ploys of distraction, like his quick change of subject or random comment meant to derail her questioning. She hadn't been fooled for a moment. Julia had spoken to the point when she'd suggested men often weren't capable of relinquishing control.

It would be good to socialize this evening and sort her feelings come morning. Music, dancing, and a spell of lively conversation might alleviate the sorrowful burden in her heart. Her mistake in losing Oliver was unforgivable.

"My lady."

"St. Allen. I hardly recognized you in your dashing evening attire."

"I don't believe you. You have a gift for perspicacious detail. That's how you're able to turn gossip to a client's favor with expedient credibility and exactitude."

"Is that a compliment?" Eva laughed. "If it is, I've witnessed a rare moment."

"One for one. My debt is paid." Sebastian offered his arm.

"How economical of you." She placed her gloved hand on his elbow and they approached the marble steps leading into the Earl of Mumford's estate.

"I received your message. I'm to become Lord Wintel this evening, but what's my history? Am I your brother?" St. Allen replied briskly, uncomfortable with the way Eva leaned into his escort, her perfume overbearing. He'd mentioned to her more than once his desire to keep their relationship strictly professional. Were her actions this evening meant to convey the roles they played, or another attempt to entice his interest?

"How terribly mundane of you." She squeezed his arm for emphasis. "I'm Lady Herron, affluent widow and world traveler, recently returned from Cairo. You're Lord Wintel. We met during my passage to England. I'm smitten and you're besotted. It's the perfect arrangement for this affair."

Sebastian clenched his teeth, aware of the double entendre and unable to voice the response that readily came to mind. It was with considerable effort when he finally answered, "As I said, you're attentive to details."

"But I haven't finished." Eva's eyes flared for emphasis. "Most importantly, we both dote upon our Pomeranians."

"If I owned a dog it wouldn't resemble a piece of lint."

"Of course not, but we're here for altogether different reasons." Without missing a beat, Eva picked up on his displeasure. "You should relax and enjoy this evening. You know an approachable attitude will make it easier for us to gather information."

They entered the ballroom. With the festivities already underway, no formal announcement was necessary. Several couples twirled across the dance floor in time to the orchestra's lively tune, which blended with the vociferous chatter of conversation and gay laughter.

Sebastian stopped short of the grand double doors. "I hold little fondness for this arrangement."

"Don't scowl. We're here to mix with the guests and extricate the information we're after. We'll hardly be successful if you frighten people away with your expression. Appear more agreeable, won't you?"

"I'll do my best, although it's a challenge among this crowd. Men and women who create intractable problems and ignore the consequences."

Was his father here among the crush? Dressed in his finest to match a pompous attitude. A faceless, titled, and arrogant man who believed himself better than everyone else in the room. Sebastian forced his anger to calm. He preferred life in the shadows. Light revealed every scar and ravaged emotion. Tonight his appearance was necessary. Otherwise, he would have employed a different approach to information gathering that had nothing to do with glittering ball gowns and the pretentious airs of London's most elite.

His tone communicated the end of their discussion, and Eva noticed. She did have a flair for intuitive detail. Nabbing two glasses of champagne from a passing tray, he offered one to Eva, whose smug expression mocked him openly.

"I thought you despised this set, darling."

"That doesn't mean I won't drink their liquor." He drained his glass and surveyed the room, relaxing into the role he portrayed, although Eva's use of *darling* irritated more than cajoled.

"I don't see the Duchess of Grandon," Eva noted as she scanned the dance floor and refreshment area inconspicuously.

"Let's take a stroll around the perimeter and survey the estate. The terrace doors seem to be the only exit, but that alcove behind the orchestra piques my interest."

"A lovely idea." Eva slid her hand through his arm and they began their perusal, chatting amiably about every subject suited to carry to those intent on overhearing conversation, though Sebastian's interest was all business. He noted several gentlemen eyed

Eva with appreciation. She'd dressed to impress, her slim figure clad in an elegant gown of pale blue silk. He recognized her floral perfume as one she favored because it made his eyes itch. Lemons were more to his liking.

And then his bemused thoughts materialized and Delilah stood not three paces in front of him. It was as if she'd been conjured straight from his imagination, the impact both startling and invigorating. Gone was the frightened, guarded female in a long black cloak and tidy hairstyle, replaced by a demure and deceptively tempting vixen, her shoulders bare and neckline daring. Her evening gown smoothed over her figure to hug each curve in a way that had him at a loss for words. And her hair . . . ringlet upon golden ringlet invited him to undo the pins and allow the lengths to tumble down around her shoulders. He wanted to skim his fingertips along the curve of her neck, to trail kisses—

"Why have you stopped walking?" Eva hissed her complaint while keeping her smile in place.

Sebastian cleared his throat, relieved Delilah hadn't turned in his direction. She remained oblivious to his presence. When he didn't readily reply, Eva persisted.

"I see the duchess. Let's insinuate ourselves into the conversation and gain an introduction. Ready?" She squeezed his arm with insistence.

"Lead the way." He slanted another glance toward Delilah where she stood in conversation with two older women. The three had affable smiles upon their faces. He hadn't expected to see her at this function, but then he'd not given it thought. What did he know about her other than her fine address? Delilah was part of the society he avoided, and yet seeing her like this, glowing with excitement under the golden hue of candlelight, she appeared so naturally suited to the surroundings it sparked anger inside him instead of appreciation. He purposely looked away.

Their meeting in Seven Dials and subsequent association was

within the boundaries of his domain. Had he decided she belonged there with him? Forgotten she was a refined member of the ton? When exactly had he taken notice on a personal level? Their kiss didn't signify. He was trying to calm her before she fell into hysterics. Fool that he was. *Liar that he was. He'd wanted to taste her just that once.*

Unaware of his struggle but ever observant, Eva steered them toward the duchess with another whispered reminder. "You're too tense. You're supposed to be enjoying yourself. Play along with my conversation." She raised her voice as she continued, "This ballroom is grand and the company engaging, but I can't help but miss Sugar. She's the sweetest Pomeranian I've ever owned, and having just returned from abroad I despise leaving her alone." Her voice was loud enough to carry to the group beside them, where she'd wisely aligned with the Duchess of Grandon and the four women who kept her company.

Sebastian quelled his immediate reaction and dedicated himself to the tale Eva spun. "I'm sure your pet will be happy to see you this evening when you return. Brutus is loyal to a fault."

"Brutus?" Eva laughed. "Such a ferocious name for such a small animal."

"He may be compact but he embodies the spirit of a warrior." He would have fun with the inanity. At least it kept him focused enough to resist looking for Delilah among the guests. And then, because apparently Fate had a sense of humor, the Duchess of Grandon let out an exclamation and turned to greet newcomers to her conversational circle. It was Delilah and the two older women he'd spied in her company earlier.

Instead of widening the group, several of Her Grace's companions melted into the surround and left the duchess to her newfound conversation.

He watched Delilah dip low in a curtsy that displayed too much of her bosom. The swells of her breasts tempted near the lacy edge of her bodice. A misplaced and maddening urge to step in front of her and prohibit any randy onlooker's view had him clenching his teeth.

"What's wrong with you?" Eva's hiss met his ear. "Your muscles are poised like you're ready to punch someone." She huffed a breath before she spoke again. "Ordinarily I wouldn't complain, but at this moment . . ."

"Never mind." He flexed his shoulders and forced himself to relax. Delilah was being introduced to the duchess by the older woman who'd accompanied her. It was time to act.

"How did Honey Blossom fare on your crossing from France?"

"I've just returned from Cairo, my lord, and my dear pet's name is Sugar." Eva widened her eyes and pressed her fingertips into his sleeve. "Although anyone who cares for canines is aware the Pomeranian breed is agreeable and easily appeased."

Being tall had its advantages, and Sebastian noted how the duchess paused midsentence, her head canted in their direction as if she'd heard a word that sparked her interest. He didn't dare shift his eyes to Delilah. If she called him by his name, their charade would grow more complicated. "Yes, I couldn't agree more." He inclined his head to ensure he was heard. "Between their docile temperament and regal bearing, I would think most any discerning pet owner would choose their breed. Pomeranians are the finest companions."

This last bit accomplished their goal and the Duchess of Grandon turned her attention to their conversation.

"Pardon." Her Grace looked down her nose at Eva and eyed Sebastian with a shrewd stare. Then she turned toward the older woman in her company and issued an order. "Helen, do find Mumford so I may gain a proper introduction."

The woman she'd addressed as Helen scurried away, leaving Delilah behind. He didn't have to match her eyes to know Delilah was surprised. He could imagine what she was thinking, but when Eva tugged on his arm, he remembered she stood beside him. Peering into Delilah's thoughts at the moment might not prove rewarding. His suspicion was confirmed when he heard her gasp, fast overridden by her surprised stutter.

"Mr. St.—"

To her credit she recovered before his name slipped out, but there was no mistaking the questions that danced in her lovely hazel eyes.

CHAPTER 9

Delilah managed to quell her initial reaction, though her head spun with myriad riddles. Was St. Allen here as an invited guest? Was he investigating Oliver's disappearance? Had he some clue to share? And exactly who was the beautiful woman hanging onto his elbow, wearing a decadent design that revealed too much skin and offered gentlemen an eyeful?

Sinking her teeth into her tongue, she'd caught his name before the words hit the air, though she speared him with her eyes, hoping to convey how urgently she needed to speak to him.

The Earl of Mumford arrived with the practiced timing of a theatrical. An introduction was swiftly accomplished, though Delilah hardly heard, her eyes on St. Allen. This earned the interest of the woman who'd won his escort. Whoever the beauty may be. She assumed they were both using fictitious names. At least St. Allen claimed to be Lord Wintel. Or was that his real name? Did he possess a title? Was he truly employed by the bookstore? Did he own the bookstore?

The Duchess of Grandon turned her attention to the pair, and in that moment, Delilah regained her composure and smiled graciously at her aunt, all the while wondering if St. Allen's attendance here was social enjoyment or secretive investigation, and if the woman on his arm was another of his associates, or mayhap, his mistress or paramour. She reminded herself for the umpteenth time she had no claim to his attention and would do well by remembering that fact.

"Did I hear you speak of the Pomeranian breed?" Her Grace tapped St. Allen's forearm with her fan, monopolizing his attention for the time being.

Delilah took to assessing his appearance in deference to her conflicted emotions concerning the lady clinging to his arm. He looked far more dashing than any gentleman her aunt had introduced this evening. Perhaps it was his commanding height and build or her intimate knowledge of the solid muscles beneath his evening coat, the memory of being tightly fitted against his body between two hackneys only last evening, a fresh and forbidden recollection. Her cheeks heated.

He was dressed all in black aside from a startling white cravat, which brushed his jaw in an elaborate series of folds that left her wondering if he had a valet or accomplished the feat himself. His waistcoat was sophisticated and didn't display the ostentatious embroidery favored by dandies, and while he wore no other distinguishing accessories, a stickpin or lace collar, he appeared more handsome than any other male in the ballroom simply by his presence. He was a man of control and strength, only overshadowed by his intuitive intelligence. Some strange sensation, unfamiliar and inspiring, rippled through her and reverberated straight into each nerve ending. It held a shock not unlike when she'd unknowingly dragged her slippers across the rug and was rewarded with a sharp reminder of carelessness, except this feeling was wholly pleasant. She didn't want it to disappear.

"May I present Lady Warwick and her niece, Lady Delilah. Lady Delilah has only recently joined our fair city from Birmingham." Her Grace smiled cordially as she continued the introduction. "Lady Herron and Lord Wintel are also owners of Pomeranians. I'm afraid it pains me to speak of my dear Cygnet. He holds my heart."

"Has he passed?" Lady Herron inquired, her tone gentled by sympathy.

"No, thank heavens." Her Grace's expression pinched with concern. "Though the circumstances are complicated and peculiar."

"He's run away?" Lord Wintel added with a nod. "I understand."

"Indeed not." The Duchess of Grandon eyed Wintel with piercing censure. "I take the very best care of my animals. Cygnet is never out of my sight. He has undergone a horrible calamity."

"I'm so sorry to learn of your distress," Lady Helen added. "London has been equally unkind to our family."

"Let's not speak of it this evening." Delilah touched her aunt's arm to draw her attention. "Lest we add to Her Grace's displeasure."

"I only chose to attend tonight because I can no longer bear Cygnet's absence when I'm home alone. I miss his company and the sound of his voice. I worry for his safety. He must be terrified."

"What happened?" Lady Herron whispered as she leaned closer.

"Cygnet was taken from me. Kidnapped, I believe." The duchess sniffed in an elegant manner as she retrieved a lacy handkerchief from beneath her fichu.

"Kidnapped?" Lady Herron repeated.

"Kidnapped?" Delilah looked at Sebastian with wide eyes.

"Ransomed?" Lord Wintel prodded.

"Taken from me by force." Her Grace sniffled in silence for a long moment before she continued. "There hasn't been a note as of yet, but I will pay any amount for his safe return. I cannot bear the waiting and speculating."

"I understand how that feels." Delilah spoke more to herself than the solemn group around her. She raised her eyes to Sebastian's and wondered if he could read her mind.

Sebastian settled his eyes on Delilah. He'd heard her delicate mutter despite the room was filled with jovial celebration. If he could speak to her alone for a few minutes he would explain how he wasn't here this evening socializing, but rather in an effort to find clues that helped locate Oliver. He should tell her that. *To ease her mind.*

Eva had successfully drawn the Duchess of Grandon into an involved conversation about their beloved canines, and from what he could decipher, Her Grace was recounting the events of the afternoon Cygnet was taken. Eva possessed a gift of persuasion that came in handy at times like this. It was another reason he kept his distance.

Delilah had fallen quiet and he could imagine the thoughts flitting through her mind, but she didn't remain preoccupied. A nondescript gentleman approached and interrupted, claiming Delilah for a dance he'd reserved on the card dangling from her wrist. Sebastian hadn't noticed it with all their maneuvering, and now his mind spun in calculation of how many slots were likely filled on that card and how many gentlemen would enjoy the pleasure of holding Delilah within their arms. She intrigued him, and that alone kept her ever present in his thoughts.

The next conclusion came fast on the heels of his struggle. He would dance with her next. It provided the simplest way for them to converse privately. His eyes shot to the darkened corner at the far end of the ballroom where a pair of terrace doors let to an extending balcony. It remained vacant. A smile nudged his lips, although it quickly disappeared as Delilah whirled by, her expression bright and eyes fixed on her partner. The fellow must have said something amusing. Her laughter tickled the air as she passed.

"I'm for the retiring room." Lady Warwick interrupted his mental complaints. "If you'll excuse me, Lord Wintel."

The older woman didn't wait for more than a nod before she left. He'd behaved rudely. With Eva and the duchess involved in an exclusive conversation, responsibility for niceties had fallen upon him, and instead of providing light conversation, he'd watched Delilah on the dance floor with a spike of irrational jealousy and in turn ignored her chaperone. He wasn't born for this atmosphere and despised how easily it belittled him. He hated it all the more for that fact.

His anger dissipated in beat with the orchestra's melody and he exhaled thoroughly to rid his ill mood as Delilah returned. Her escort bowed and expressed his gratitude. It was good the man took his leave and didn't think to linger.

"Did you enjoy your waltz, Lady Delilah?" He stepped closer, hoping they could share a few words before her aunt returned.

"Yes. Thank you, Lord Wintel." Her eyes twinkled when she spoke, as if she enjoyed their shared secret.

How different she appeared now, surrounded by glittering chandeliers instead of skulky shadows and moonlight, though she was no less beautiful. Her skin glowed and her hair tempted him like a clutch of gold coins too precious to possess. Her slender brows rose in expectation and he realized she still waited for him to continue their conversation.

"Give me your dance card." The request came out in a brusque tone he hadn't intended.

"There's nothing for it, I'm afraid. Every slot has been re-served." She lifted her gloved wrist and wriggled it slightly so the card swayed with the motion. "My aunt prides herself on making introductions, and my evening's entertainment was claimed soon after we'd arrived."

As if waiting for some signal, a stout gentleman in a lilac em-broidered waistcoat approached with a friendly smile, his eyes on Delilah as if he wondered whether or not to believe his good for-tune.

"My lady." He bowed politely. "As reserved, the upcoming waltz is mine."

"The lady has other plans," Sebastian interrupted. His swift response held a note of warning.

The gentleman appeared startled, as did Delilah, and her at-tention volleyed between them.

"I'm sure I am correct," the man persisted, though he still wore a smile.

Sebastian shifted his shoulders. The subtle movement did nothing more than solidify he wasn't changing his mind. With mastered efficiency, another word wasn't needed.

"Although I could be mistaken, Lady Delilah. My apologies." The gentleman stepped away; his head bowed as he made his leave. "Another time perhaps."

"That was truly unkind of you." Delilah wore a light smile despite her words were meant to chastise him.

"Unkind? I did you a favor."

"A favor?" She bit her lip, perhaps realizing she'd echoed him.

"I spared you the awkward task of making polite conversation with that dandy."

"He's not a dandy. Why would you label him so?"

"It could be the purple flowers on his waistcoat."

She smiled up at him and amusement replaced annoyance. He matched her grin.

"You may call it a favor, my lord, but I do so enjoy dancing the waltz. I am disappointed."

Little room was left for debate after her comment. He bowed low and extended his gloved hand. "Then by all means, allow me to discourage any unwanted emotion."

Delilah grasped St. Allen's gloved fingers and walked beside him to the dance floor. From the corner of her eye she noticed Aunt Helen had rejoined the duchess, who continued her discussion with Lady Herron. A prick of bald curiosity reminded her St. Allen had appeared this evening with another woman on his arm. Although Delilah was the one he escorted to the tiles now and she wouldn't waste the opportunity to have a few questions answered, especially if it helped locate Oliver.

"I didn't expect to see you this evening."

He stepped to the side to allow her to pass and his sleeve brushed her bare arm. A thrilling wave of anticipation and excitement moved through her. They took to the dance floor, where he gathered her into the proper frame, one hand at the small of her back, the other tightly wrapped around her palm. Her foolish heart twisted in her chest, and for a moment it was difficult to breathe. What was she thinking? This wasn't romance. She needed to find out everything he'd learned about Oliver's abduction in the span of one song.

"Nor I, you."

The music began and when she glanced to his face, she noticed he did not meet her eyes. Was he angry? He'd bitten out his reply and his jaw looked rigid, as if he clenched his teeth. They moved through the swirling rotation and his expression eased. As wonderful as it was to be held in his arms, she didn't wish to miss the chance to speak privately.

"You're an accomplished dancer." She dared the compliment, though were her aunt to hear it, she'd earn a reprimand for the impropriety of speaking so openly.

"You're a lovely surprise, Lady Delilah."

She wasn't sure what to make of that, but when he peered into her eyes her heart thudded so hard, she feared it would fracture her ribs. Who was this enigmatic man dressed in impeccable eveningwear, as much at home in a ballroom as a dark alley in London's most dangerous slum?

Was he a rogue of shadows who sought to rescue lost children with no heed of his own personal safety? Or the handsome intellectual who guided her through her worry and concern below a rudimentary bookshop? Was he dashing Lord Wintel, a dog enthusiast and respected member of the ton? Was St. Allen even his real name? Which identity was his true self, or was he a combination of all four?

In truth, her heart didn't care a fig at the moment, lost to the thrill of his possessive touch, the pressure of his hand upon her lower back, the enthralling captivity of his pale blue eyes.

She gave herself to the dance, letting go of worry for a brief moment. She'd already invited too much darkness into her London visit. A temporary reprieve on the notes of an elegant waltz wouldn't be her downfall. More so, a tiny indulgence, considering the bleak sadness of the last few days.

"Are you husband hunting?"

His direct question pierced her musings and left nothing but confusion in their wake.

"What? No." She took a deep breath and cleared her mind. "My aunt wishes to see me well connected. We both agreed a night out would help to restore hope in our household. Since Oliver's disappearance there's been little happiness. The distressing consequences of the predicament are with me always."

"I want you to give me your word you won't sneak out to Seven Dials and attempt to thwart the dangers there." His hold on her tightened for several beats before it eased again.

"I mean to find Oliver." Her reply came easily. She was resolute in her vow.

"I have the experience, strength, and resources to work on your behalf while you remain safely at home."

Suspecting he worried for her welfare, she couldn't allow it to anger her, but his general dismissal of her involvement confirmed her resolve to venture to the Wycombe and Company building come morning. She could never change his mind any more than he'd change hers. Still, quarreling over the fact would spoil the dance and she thought it better to be gracious and broach a different subject. Whatever information he discovered could only help in the effort. "Thank you. I appreciate your thoughtfulness."

"Lady Herron is gathering facts this evening for an incident of interest. I believe it's a connection worth investigating in regard to finding Oliver, so I agreed to assist." His said this without hesitation, though he didn't explain further.

"And have you learned anything new?"

That question went unanswered as he swept her from the tiles and through the double doors at the corner of the ballroom. The swift removal from the dance floor into absolute darkness disoriented her at first but she quickly realized they were alone on the marble terrace. He led her farther away from the estate and around a narrow corner. Unsure what he intended, she followed until at last they stopped, cloaked in complete darkness, the area far from the lighted windows of the ballroom.

For a moment, neither of them moved. She took a deep breath and waited until she was compelled to break the silence. "Are we here so you can tell me what you've discovered?"

His breath was at her ear, his hands guiding her backward until he pressed her gently to the smooth stone wall and eclipsed her with the broad width of his chest.

"No, Delilah." His words whispered against her lips. "We're here for this."

Chapter 10

The first press of his kiss sent a pleasure rush through her so intense she all but forgot to breathe. He placed his hands at her waist and quickly removed them, aware he would wrinkle her gown beyond repair. He cradled her nape and tilted her head to better fit their mouths together, capturing her lips at a different angle, only to abandon his hold, unwilling to muss her hair.

His thinking seemed clearer than hers.

The only thoughts marching through her brain were primal monosyllabic demands. *Yes, more, now, there.*

When he settled his palms against her cheeks and deepened their kiss, she murmured her pleasure and he grunted his approval. Perhaps he was as disoriented as she. Regardless of the reactions, she was lost to the sounds of it all, the orchestra's romantic melody the perfect backdrop to her bliss.

Sebastian clung to the last thread of control, desperate to squelch the raw desire heating his blood. It was inevitable. Or so he told himself. Once he saw her, caught her fresh lemon fragrance, experienced the sharp prick of jealousy, he'd no other course of action. But even in this confusion, he acknowledged that lie. He was drawn to Delilah by an unmanageable force, unlike any other.

Every aspect of his being was composed of strength and control. He could afford no weaknesses. Not even a woman with petal-soft lips and hair like the first rays of morning sun. And yet, he recognized a strength beneath her delicate layers, a core of determination and courage unlike so many other females.

He relished the sound as much as the pressure of her touch, tentative and bewitching as her palms slid up his chest to grip his shoulders. She hung on tightly as if she too grappled with control.

He needed to end the madness before they were discovered— or worse, he changed his mind and forgot propriety altogether. It would be easy to change his mind.

Maybe just another minute longer.

Lost to want, he licked across her mouth, begging entry, and she gasped, allowing him to stroke inside. She froze, confirmation she'd never been kissed in such a manner, but she eased against his chest in surrender soon after. Slowly she opened to him, her tongue at first curious and shy, but then emboldened. She tasted better than he'd imagined, sweet, soft, ripe, and with each twine of his tongue with hers, each rub and caress, a shock of desire like nothing he'd ever experienced reverberated in his soul.

The other evening he'd kissed her to settle her nerves, nothing more, but *this* kiss, this kiss was slow and deliberate, a message expressed without words, a wonderful madness of their own creating. It was as if he couldn't drink enough of her and yet he was fast forgetting they stood near a ballroom filled with judgmental aristocrats anxious to prove he was of lower status and therefore unworthy.

For over two decades he'd worked at improving himself and demonstrating to anyone who took a moment to observe, that he was a better man because of it. But the ton considered one aspect of birth above all others. This thought provided the clarity he needed, and with reluctance and regret, he withdrew.

"St. Allen?"

Her whispered plea was hot against the corner of his mouth and

he almost leaned in to capture another kiss. What was this undeniable pull, this otherworldly spell she'd cast on him? The lady
posed a danger to his sanity. He hadn't released her yet.

"Sebastian?"

"The song is nearly over."

"Yes." She shifted as she inhaled a deep breath. "Of course."

He stepped back to allow her the room she needed.

"Follow my lead and I'll have you back in the ballroom with
none the wiser." He clasped her hand and squeezed it, anxious
now to return them both. He wanted to take his leave.

The brightness of the ballroom might cause her a moment of
confusion, so he waited until the throng of dancers crowded the
corner where they lurked, and then swept her into the waltz as
if they'd never missed a step, his hold on her secure. The music
continued gaily, the rush of silk and satin a garden of color and
texture, but deep within his chest, his heart thrummed a beat
that had nothing to do with dancing and everything to do with the
lovely and dangerous lady in his arms.

"Delilah, dear." Aunt Helen greeted her with a mixture of relief
and concern. "I lost sight of you for several turns. You gave me a
scare."

"It was very crowded on the dance floor and with the set in a
whirl, I imagine it would be easy for all the gowns and colors to
blend together." Delilah hoped the flush she'd experienced on the
terrace with St. Allen, *Sebastian*, would be construed as nothing
more than exertion. She turned toward her escort and offered him
a secret smile. "Thank you, Lord Wintel."

"Indeed, it was my pleasure, Lady Ashbrook."

He sounded unaffected, while she could barely form a coherent thought, her lips still warmed by his kisses, her tongue newly
educated. Good heavens, his kiss was divine.

Lady Herron had finished her conversation with the Duchess
of Grandon and now stepped toward Sebastian and slipped her
hand through his elbow. The action brought with it the unpleas-

ant reminder that circumstances weren't as simple as she'd like to believe. Lady Herron stared at her directly, perhaps with the same questions Delilah possessed. Something about Lady Herron seemed familiar. Was she in the tavern last evening? Delilah couldn't decide with certainty. Sebastian stated Lady Herron was here to gather information, but that didn't mean they weren't involved beyond the task.

"We'll leave you to the festivities."

Delilah noticed how Lady Herron pulled slightly on Sebastian's arm.

"It was lovely to make your acquaintance," Aunt Helen added.

Delilah had yet to find a suitable rejoinder. She mustered a quiet reply, her mind and body at odds. "Enjoy the evening."

"And you as well." Lady Herron turned toward Sebastian as she continued. "We should go."

Sebastian didn't reply to Lady Herron at first. His eyes lingered on Delilah's face, settled on her lips, and she knew he was recalling their kisses. This mollified her traitorous heart, though the organ had no right becoming involved. They shared a strange association, a waltz and a few kisses. She'd be every kind of fool to believe their collection of moments meant anything more to Sebastian St. Allen, or even Lord Wintel, than an interesting pastime.

"So, what did you find out?" Sebastian settled against the cushions of his carriage and waited for Eva to begin. He needed a distraction. Something to shift his attention; otherwise he'd rap on the roof, return to Mumford's ballroom, and claim Delilah's mouth right there in the middle of the dance floor. His body heated from the inside out, his blood simmering hot. She was a fiery mix of determined intelligence, proper lady, and innocent seductress, who'd shaken him to his soul with a few stolen kisses. She was more dangerous than any secret he pursued in the darkness.

"There's definitely more at stake here than a little white dog. From what Her Grace shared, I'd surmise the child was a victim of circumstance. The duchess was surprised to hear a boy was taken and believes his abduction wasn't the intent of the thieves. It will be interesting to discover if it's Cygnet's ransom or his priceless diamond collar that provoked the attack. However, there are a few incongruent details that need to be aligned. Her Grace mentioned her nephew wished to borrow money. She's denied him several times, their relationship strained from his efforts. She described the man as a wastrel. That's a lead worth pursuing. Additionally, she's hasn't had a note with demands for Cygnet's return. It causes me to think the thieves were solely after the gems and her poor Pomeranian was a complication easily remedied."

"As with Oliver." Sebastian voiced this in a low tone, the idea of a child being taken and silenced for someone's greed too reprehensible. That aside, they'd made progress and there was no reason to assume the worst until it was proven in fact. "It's only been three days."

Eva dared to laugh softly. "You know as well as I, most heinous crime is immediate." She shifted on the seat as the carriage maneuvered through a deep rut in the roadway. "Your waltz with Lady Ashbrook was an unexpected development." She let the implication dangle in the air between them.

"There was no way for me to speak privately, with her aunt hovering at her side. The dance was nothing more than a convenient ruse." He stared straight into Eva's eyes, daring her to call him a liar, because he wouldn't invite her opinions or her interference.

"It's not every day I witness one of London's most elite operatives charming a proper lady across the tiles." Something changed in her expression, a sharpening of her attention.

"Life is full of unexpected surprises." The carriage rocked to a stop and he exhaled fully, in want of the quiet it offered. "It's the nature of our business, isn't it?"

He rapped the roof and the driver was quick to extend the steps. He should walk Eva to her doorstep. But in actuality, she didn't need his assistance. She could deal with any poor fool who thought to provoke her this evening.

"Good night, Sebastian."

Her reply was tinged with strained emotion. Had she expected something to transpire between them? He hadn't given her a reason to believe it would, and instinct told him not to question it further.

"Keep me informed about the Her Grace's nephew and anything else that may be tied to Oliver's disappearance." He nodded and reached to close the door. With a knock on the roof, he set off for home.

"At least we've forced our thoughts to a more pleasant place for a few hours." Aunt Helen relaxed against the cushions. It was after midnight and exhaustion claimed both of them.

"I hope and pray this situation will resolve soon. The longer Oliver is missing . . ." Delilah couldn't finish that sentence, the words too horrible.

"I think Lord Wintel took a liking to you. He's certainly handsome, though I don't recognize the surname. It's too many years since I've paid attention to the bachelors of the ton." Her aunt faced her with a gleam in her eyes that bespoke of determination to explore the subject. "There were several other gentlemen who showed interest in you as well. I believe this evening went swimmingly."

"Thank you." Delilah didn't wish to discuss marriage prospects this late at night. Not anytime, actually. And the mention of Sebastian's appearance, his rugged good looks and commanding strength, only served to bring back a rush of sensation. Her thoughts returned to that darkened corner of the terrace where they'd kissed . . . *and kissed*. "But there's no need to hurry."

She moved the curtain aside to assess their progress through the streets, anxious to be free of their conversation. Was Sebastian home now? Did he haunt Seven Dials in search of thieves and lost children? Or had he pursued a different kind of distraction? Was Lady Herron in his arms? His bed?

She laced her fingers in her lap as if the action could control the unbidden images flooding her brain.

"Are you feeling unwell, dear?" Aunt Helen gathered the curtain from her side and peered out the window. "We're approaching Berwick Street now. Just another few minutes."

Delilah nodded, grateful for the vacant streets and efficiency of the driver. At the curb, she disembarked first and Aunt Helen followed. She gathered her aunt's hand in her own as they walked silently toward the town house. Life would never return to normal until Oliver was returned home and Beth could once again hug her child. She wished to appease Aunt Helen, but at the same time Delilah felt horribly she'd enjoyed a social event this evening. She'd never overcome the guilt of Oliver's disappearance, even though she'd caused it inadvertently. And what of the other children? The youngsters Sebastian sought to save?

Distress threatened to climb up her throat and she hurried her aunt along toward the steps. They were inside a moment later and Delilah made for the stairs immediately. Too many emotions crowded in, quick to blot out the glory of Sebastian's kiss and remind she had further work to do. Tomorrow morning, she would meet with Julia, Phoebe, and Diana to further investigate Oliver's disappearance. The disturbing prod of knowing so many children were stolen and suffered a tragic experience, never to be returned home and mayhap never surviving, reminded she needed to do more. Perhaps, once Oliver was found, she could work toward improving the outcome for others. There had to be more she could do.

Sebastian paced a hard line in front of the hearth in his bedchamber. He was exhausted, wrung out, but sleep evaded him with the same succinct efficiency as the abductors he sought. It was nearly half two, and yet his mind raced with unanswered questions, ugly memories, and the lingering remembrance of Delilah's lush kisses.

What was he doing besides breaking his personal rules? Too many of them, too quickly. It proved selfish to kiss Delilah tonight. Indulgent. Divine. *Maddening.*

He raked his fingers through his hair in frustration. Everything about the lady contradicted the man he embodied. She was pure. Unspoiled by time and circumstance. She represented the proper societal miss, while he was an outcast, an anomaly who'd learned survival in the streets and was better off left there. Overriding logic, an unrelenting pulse of anticipation reminded he wanted to see her again, learn her secrets and evoke another of her smiles. Her fragrance was so fresh and light it made him believe in hope and contentment, two qualities he'd long ago abandoned due to life's cruel treatment.

To follow that path was most dangerous, and not just for the inevitable outcome. The ton were a cold and calculating lot. His father the worst of them all. He clenched his eyes closed and drew a deep breath.

He couldn't explain why he wished to exhume old memories and haunting realities better left buried this evening. Perhaps he was in need of a reminder. A rush of unpleasant emotion spiraled through him and fueled his restlessness whenever he considered his father. His mother was nothing but a kind remembrance, a vague childhood recollection at best. The world's darkness had blotted out any goodness he'd attempted to salvage from all those years ago.

He was only a lad of five when his mother thought to better his situation. She dressed him in his cleanest clothing and had him delivered to his father, a nobleman and stranger, with a note expressing her desire for him to attend school and receive the proper education he was due.

But that was not to be. Sebastian remembered the moment his life changed with startling clarity. His father, a man he knew for only one day, enticed him with a ride in a fancy carriage. The carriage took them beyond London proper into the slums, where his father opened the door and shoved him out.

"You're a bastard. Best you learn your place at an early age."

Peers had a way of keeping their personal shame and scandalous regrets private. Sebastian was discarded like garbage in the streets. Considering the horrid conditions, the filth and vermin he'd endured and subsequent tormenting years, he was surprised he'd salvaged any memories at all. Some circumstances stayed with a person, no matter the atrocity.

At first, he'd simply attempted to survive. That time comprised tales of depravity and desperation, sadness and fear. He'd roamed the streets of London through his youth into early manhood, living as a street urchin and beggar, enduring the harsh realities that plagued the homeless and hungry. Weather was the least of his concerns. He'd escaped sexual deviants, sickness, depression, and those who derived pleasure from inflicting pain. He'd survived starvation, freezing temperature, repeated theft, and beatings, by use of his cunning, fisticuffs, and sharp intelligence.

As he aged, the desire for vengeance fueled him, and the thirst to reciprocate and incite retributive pain kept him strong. But as time passed and his life improved, he'd changed. Much the way water erodes stone, he used his pain to forge him into a better man. The best revenge was knowing he'd risen above where his father believed him to be. He'd thwarted the old man.

In that, his abusive history made him an ideal candidate for his work with the Crown. He had no family to recognize him. He knew the slums and crime to be found there like he knew up from down. He'd learned how to fight and survive and had honed those skills to a lethal level. Now he worked to better the streets and bring justice where it was due. That was his finest reward.

A ready image of Delilah came to mind when she'd looked to him for help, the aching worry and desperation to find her loved one clouding her eyes. Oliver wasn't even her son and she'd risked her own safety in Seven Dials and then again in the tavern, all to find the child.

What a fool he'd become? To be reduced to fanciful wishes in the middle of the night while sequestered in his chambers? He needed to right his mind and ignore the primal pulse of lust in his blood. Clear thinking was his most efficient tool and as of late it had all but abandoned him.

CHAPTER 11

Morning light filtered through Delilah's bedchamber curtains and reminded of her important appointment this morning. Hurrying to finish the last of her breakfast tray, she quietly moved down the hallway and out to the corner, where she hailed a hack for hire. She instructed the driver to Cavendish Square, squaring her shoulders with renewed resolve as she took the steps to the Wycombe building.

The ladies greeted her with cheerful smiles and they walked to the corner together, set to initiate further investigation while all of society viewed them as a foursome of friends out for a daily constitutional. It invigorated Delilah to believe she hid in plain sight. How freeing it was not to be questioned at every turn.

"So, we're off to Dorset Street."

"In Spitalfields?"

"Why?"

"Pawnees and nippers."

They climbed into the waiting hackney and Julia directed the driver.

"Children lost to the street. Mostly the worst cases."

"You think Oliver could be among them?" A beat of panic matched Delilah's words.

"Perhaps." Diana clutched the seat as the hackney gained

speed. "Or else someone there may know what happened to a clean, well-dressed lad who recently fell into the wrong hands."

For several minutes nothing interrupted the silence except the rotation of wooden wheels on crushed gravel, but within that time span the atmosphere changed and peripheral interruptions transformed. The lively commerce and sound of everyday London surrendered to a more cynical tone. The air quieted, heavy with a sense of ominous instability.

Trees became sparse and in their place, dilapidated blue-gray tenements lined the streets. Delilah was immediately pulled back to her sojourn into Seven Dials and the man she'd met there, a powerful, handsome man who'd saved her, protected her, and offered his help.

Although, the niggling irritant that he wished to exclude her was a blemish to her fond memory. He might seek to keep her safe, but at the same time he clipped her wings and labeled her weak and incapable.

"We're here." Phoebe was the first one out, and with a curt nod she motioned toward a narrow lane to the left.

The hackney sped away as if fleeing the gates of Hell, no matter it was the light of day. Delilah followed behind the ladies. An uneasy feeling, almost a sense of being watched, invaded her confidence as she walked.

"Why don't you visit the pawn houses?" Julia waved for Delilah to move to her side. "We'll circulate and see if the urchins know something."

"I've a pocketful of candy." Diana patted one side of her skirt. "And another full of coins."

The ladies split up and Delilah followed Julia as she maneuvered through the byways lacing the area. To the unsuspecting eye, the lanes appeared desolate, but as Delilah grew closer and looked with more focus, she realized it wasn't true at all. The farther they walked into the Spitalfields slums, the more each tenement breathed life, almost as if a secret city existed behind a deceptive disguise.

Women nursed their babies on the front steps. Barefoot children chased each other through the street, their steps silent on the broken cobbles, their clothes torn and oversized, the wind catching pockets of threadbare fabric like billowing sails, each frail body no more than a skinny mast inside.

Some children, hardly old enough to walk surefooted, wandered about unattended. Delilah saw a man, gin soaked or sickened, crumpled in the corner of a building. Two other men argued with no mind to foul language. Through it all, Julia walked with confidence, though Delilah's heart beat a nervous tempo. It might be early afternoon, but the surrounding circumstances brimmed with danger. It was daunting and at the same time, invigorating.

"Here." Julia rounded the corner and they stopped near a soot-covered tenement with two broken windows. A one-eyed cat lounged on the sill. "You should come inside. That way, if Oliver is among the others, you'll be able to identify him immediately."

Gathering her skirts, Delilah followed Julia through the narrow door and down a dim hall. They exited the rear of the structure into a small graveled yard. Several street urchins filled every corner. Some sat in the dirt while others leaned on a broken wooden fence. A lopsided gate at the rear remained unlatched as children came and went, most of them boys, although here or there Delilah discerned a female child. The entire lot of them were dressed in raggedy clothing and filthy from head to toe, their hair matted and unkempt. It wasn't altogether easy to distinguish age or gender for that matter.

"What is this place?" Delilah uttered, her voice filled with a strange mixture of surprise and dismay. There wasn't an adult in sight. Were these children completely unattended?

"London's Lost Yard." Julia waved her hand and they moved farther into the area. "Street urchins, orphans, nippers, and pickpockets, they've made their own community here. No one bothers them much. Uppers ignore the problem, and anyone else who cares to make a difference is soon dissuaded of the idea by the magnitude of the situation."

"But how do they eat? Sleep?"

"They care for each other and at the same time survive on their own." Julia paused and indicated a boy who stood a head taller than the others. "Jack will know if anyone new has surfaced, even if Oliver just passed through briefly."

"You know him?" Delilah absently checked the small dagger in her pocket.

"I bring food here whenever I can, cast-off clothing and other necessities the children find useful. For all their neediness, most still have pride and it causes them to resist help or reject charity. With that in mind, I just leave whatever I bring and walk away."

"You don't wait for a show of gratitude." Delilah understood. Julia was kind and generous. She didn't need a display to validate her benevolence. She performed these tasks for the goodness they allowed others. How unlike the ostentatious acts of charity perpetuated by the ton.

"Let's have a little chat with Jack." She flashed a smile. "He likes sweets despite he'll tell you they're for chits and babes."

Julia started toward the lad but Delilah hesitated. Across the yard, between two tenements, she noticed a figure—a tall, wiry fellow—who quickly reminded her of the driver she'd seen in Seven Dials. Not wanting to interrupt the conversation Julia had started with Jack, Delilah moved purposefully through the area, anxious to pursue the niggling feeling she might discover something important.

And she was right. Even at the lengthy distance, she discerned the stranger was the same man. Returning to Julia would mean losing sight of the driver. Her heart accelerated; still she followed after him, careful to tread lightly and at the same time move as quickly as possible. Her skirt hems skimmed along one wall after another as she barely touched the filthy bricks beside her. Indeed, Phoebe had the right idea wearing trousers. Disregarding her surroundings, she locked her eyes on the lanky man who walked several yards ahead.

At last, he entered an unremarkable building similar to the

others which lined the street. Delilah paused, uncertain how to proceed. Her pulse beat a furious thunder under her skin, urging her to act, but she remained motionless, with her hand in her pocket clasping her dagger. The sharp tenor of harsh voices and a dog's bark claimed her attention a beat later. Cautiously she drew back and moved around the corner, mindful the tenement where the driver entered was now behind her.

Recognition caused a wave of shock to ripple through her when she spied Sebastian involved in an altercation across the intersection of alleyways. He stood in profile and in front of him, a thug of questionable intent wielded a menacing weapon, possibly a crowbar or length of pipe, the glint of metal unmistakable in the sunlight. He swung at Sebastian, who avoided the attack with a swift dodge, though the thug came at him again right after. To worsen matters, a large dog snarled and growled near Sebastian's legs. Unsure how to intercede, she watched in horror as the mongrel leapt. It clamped down on Sebastian's leg and Delilah jerked into action. She withdrew her dagger and ran full speed across the broken cobbles.

Sebastian lunged to the right and blocked the oncoming strike while his shoulder took the brunt. The impact shuttled through him. His head already throbbed from the blow he'd received at the onset of this unexpected robbery. It would appear the thief wasn't satisfied with a purse full of coins and a gold pocket watch. He meant to steal Sebastian's boots and mayhap the clothes off his back before he and his ferocious dog finished.

A blur of yellow flittered in Sebastian's peripheral vision and then Delilah appeared out of nowhere. He shook off the dog, who'd sunk his teeth into the thick leather protecting his calf, but the beast came at him again. At the same moment, the thief raised his weapon and moved in for another strike.

With unexpected daring, Delilah leapt at the attacker's back, her tiny blade quick to bury into the thief's shoulder. His clothing blunted the intensity of the wound but her appearance served as sufficient surprise. The thief spun and grabbed a fistful of hair, hauling Delilah against his person, the metal pipe angled beneath her chin to press on her delicate throat.

A savage rage shot through Sebastian. He reached down with his bare hand and collected the dog's fur, the animal soon shoved to the side. Then he rushed forward, white-hot fury blinding him to anything aside from Delilah's safety. Using the left side of his body as a shield, he shouldered into the stranger and connected a solid punch. The man's head jerked back, loosening his hold on the pipe and allowing Delilah freedom. She didn't miss the chance. Unable to check on her well-being, Sebastian set to work finishing the encounter. Grunting his anger, he pummeled the man until he crumbled with a half-hearted swing as he collapsed, the metal pipe hitting the cobbles with an empty echo.

The dog's sharp howl snapped Sebastian's attention to the right, where Delilah sat on the ground, her knife buried in the dog's flank. She pulled it free and the mongrel ran off limping.

For several moments they remained quiet, looking at each other, until at last his shoulders relaxed and he readied for her inevitable tears. Instead she rose from the ground, the bloody dagger still in her grasp. She quirked a tight grin before she spoke.

"Not just for apples and cheese now, is it?" She waved her knife before she let it go. When she raised her eyes, she looked pleased with herself.

Relief coursed through him. Every interaction with Delilah proved a revelation. He breathed easier. "What are you doing here? It's like you're drawn to danger, Delilah."

She moved toward him, her expression all at once transformed into concern. He turned, alarmed the thief had regained consciousness or the dog had returned, but no, it wasn't what he'd expected.

"You're bleeding." Her voice was a mixture of worry and anger. She reached up to his temple and pushed aside the hair on his brow.

"It's nothing."

"Not to me." Her fingers probed the bruise left by the thief's initial strike.

He caught her wrist and brought her palm to his cheek. They stared into each other's eyes for longer than was wise.

"You're clever and courageous and beautiful." He exhaled deeply. "Why would you take such a chance with your safety?"

"He meant to hurt you."

She'd answered so quickly, she could only have misinterpreted his question.

"Had I not become distracted I never would have received a blow to begin with, but I thought I saw the driver from that first night in Seven Dials."

Delilah smoothed her palm across his jaw before lowering her hand. She took a deep breath. "I did as well. That's what lured me away from the Lost Yard."

"Whatever the reason, you shouldn't be here." He scowled down at her. "It's not safe for a lady such as yourself."

"Because of men like him?" She craned her neck to look around his shoulder.

"That gutter-wolf got less than he deserved."

"I'm more woman than you realize."

No, he realized far too much. Heat flared through him as he matched her crystalline gaze. It was neither the time or place for lustful thoughts and gestures, but he wouldn't allow logic to intrude. Perhaps it was the blow to his head that caused him to lean in and brush his lips across her temple, the bridge of her nose and gentle sweep of her cheekbone. Or perhaps it was madness. That same insistent pull of desire that refused to be ignored. He lowered his mouth to her rosy, ripe lips and deepened his kiss when she willingly met his request.

CHAPTER 12

Delilah nestled into Sebastian's warmth, the wool of his great-coat a buffer to the cacophony of emotions clanging inside her like church bells. Alarm, panic, anger, and excitement combined now with relief and the heated rush of desire, the latter coursing through her rapidly to dismiss the others. He considered her weak, but it was she who'd run toward violence in an effort to help him. She'd acted on instinct, the same as she did now.

Another breath and his kiss decimated all sensible thought, the press of his lips quick to ignite a fiery whirl of sensation high in her chest before it dipped down into her belly like the tail of a kite caught aflame. He growled, and the effect of that deep, throaty noise reverberated through her. When he nipped at her lower lip and licked across her mouth, she opened, anxious to taste him with matched desire. Something about the man made her forget every principled lesson she'd learned and toss caution to the wind, whether in regard to safety or worse, her heart.

His hands settled on her waist, where his thumbs traced over the edge of her bodice and skimmed the shape of her breasts with gentle pressure. Another shot of pleasure spun through her, although this time it began and ended at the peaks of her breasts. Her skin grew sensitive under her clothing, her awareness keenly

focused on every sensation, most especially the wicked exploration of his tongue tangled with hers.

He pulled her closer, tucking her against his broad chest with
a rough tug that kicked her pulse higher. He stirred up emotions
both daring and safe, and the opposing nature of the contradicting
notions intrigued her like no other. She curled her fingers into his
coat, holding tight, unwilling to end what had only just begun.

But it was he who pulled away.

"This isn't the place . . ." He glanced to his shadow on the
ground as if measuring the time. "It's getting late." He didn't continue even though there seemed more to say. They took a moment to right themselves.

"I'll walk with you." He indicated the path to their left and she
nodded, unsure if he'd asked or simply stated what was to be.

It was all for the best. Her mind hummed with a pleasurable
delirium brought on by his embrace. Her lips still stung from his
kisses and her skin tingled.

He accompanied her as far as the broken gate, where he could
both see her to safety and disappear into the adjacent alleyway.
She knew they couldn't share a proper goodbye, not even a touch,
and she watched with a pang of regret as he melted into the tangle
of shadows and light.

On the gravel path ahead, Julia stood with Phoebe and Diana,
the three ladies apparently in wait of her return.

"Are you all right?" Julia arched a brow and Delilah wondered
exactly what her friend perceived.

"I thought I saw the driver from that first evening," she offered
in way of explanation.

"Wandering off without a word is never a good idea."

This admonishment came from Phoebe and caused Delilah
to choose her reply carefully. "Sound advice and duly noted, although sometimes help appears at the most unlikely moment."

Now if that wasn't true of her rescuing Sebastian as much as he
rescuing her, nothing else needed to be said.

* * *

It was hours later, after enduring a tiresome social event with Aunt Helen when their carriage finally pulled to the curb and returned them home. Delilah had suffered through the evening, distracted with worry over Oliver's disappearance and her lack of progress in the search. The boy named Jack at the Lost Yard hadn't shared any useful information with Julia. Still another part of Delilah's thoughts was composed of misplaced and inconvenient reminders of the warm security found in Sebastian's arms and the searing heat of his kiss.

What did it all mean?

She disembarked from the carriage and assisted her aunt before they took the walkway to the front door. As they neared, a white bundle became visible at the doorstep. The shape resembled the canvas sack used by the criminals in Seven Dials. Delilah shrieked with alarm, startling her aunt into doing the same. Stumbling in her rush, Delilah regained her balance and took the stoop where she dropped to her knees, heedless of her gown and slippers.

"My goodness, what is it?" Aunt Helen stood over her, puffing each breath from her effort to hurry.

Removing her gloves with haste, Delilah picked at the rope, the knot difficult to untangle. Whatever was inside the bag was heavy and motionless. Her heart squeezed tighter and her fingers shook. Aunt Helen became a shadow over her shoulder and Delilah shifted to allow ample moonlight to aid her effort. Another tug and the rope loosened. Inside the sack, something stirred. And then the cloth bag took on a life of its own, the frantic squirming and wriggling inside making it near impossible for Delilah to keep her grip on the rope. Both the driver and footman had approached, anxious to lend help if needed, but she waved them away, her nails catching the last loop of the knot and at last freeing the bag's cord.

"Oliver? Oliver!" She believed she screamed the words but belatedly realized it was no more than a sobbing whisper, her fear too great.

Two small fists punched their way through the narrow opening at the top of the sack and she clasped onto the stubby fingers, a cry escaping before she could think better of it. The footman had gone inside and now returned with two lanterns. All the while Aunt Helen hovered over her, whispering a prayer. Delilah tugged feverishly at the cloth and at last widened the hole enough to see the lad, his wrists bound and mouth gagged. With tears stinging her lids, she yanked the rags from his mouth and pulled him into her arms, her eyes overflowing with gratitude and relief.

"Come inside. Both of you." Aunt Helen leaned down to their level, her voice overwrought. "Let's all go in now."

Ever concerned with society's scrutiny, Delilah didn't object, equally as anxious to be safely indoors. "Please go wake Beth."

Her words sounded broken. Too much emotion clogged her throat. When Aunt Helen rushed away, Delilah released Oliver and held him at arm's length, abashed she'd not loosened the ties at his wrists yet. She set to work on the task, grateful when the driver leaned in with his knife to slice through the bindings neatly.

"Thank you." She stood with Oliver balanced on her hip in a pose reminiscent of years ago when he was only a toddler. She wouldn't let him go. Not ever again.

"I'm better now." Oliver's shy reassurance was her utter undoing and she hugged him even tighter as she carried him inside.

Oliver's reunion with his mother was tenfold his reception on the stoop. At first Beth believed she dreamed, but Oliver's kisses and laughter were quick to prove he had indeed come home.

Despite their celebration, drinking chocolate and munching on too many biscuits, no one broached the subject of how Oliver came to be inside a sack on the front step or what had transpired during the four days he'd gone missing. Delilah was anxious for all the details left unanswered, but Oliver looked measurably better than when he'd emerged from that wretched canvas, his face stricken and pale, his eyes wide and frightened. Now, his infectious grin had returned and a rosy hue colored his chubby cheeks, whether from excitement or his mother's kisses Delilah couldn't decide.

She would contact Sebastian in the morning and tell him all

that had transpired. Hopefully he would be available to see her at the bookstore. She had no other way to find him. Undoubtedly, he would have dozens of questions, but as of yet Oliver hadn't produced a single comment concerning his harrowing experience, and everyone had seemingly decided not to ask in an effort not to upset him upon his return.

At Delilah's request the footman had collected the sack and lengths of rope for further examination, but from her brief perusal, the items appeared unmarked and ordinary. She wasn't trained to understand clues or details in the same light as Sebastian might be. The man himself posed an interesting riddle. Exactly who was he and how did he find his way into an earl's ballroom without question when he worked in the cellar of a bookstore? Now that Oliver was safe, would she never see Sebastian again?

A squeal of laughter interrupted her contemplations and she turned her attention to the lovely scene before her. Never mind her troubles. She should have none to complain about now that Oliver was home.

The next morning brought Delilah to Gilbert Street. The Last Page Bookstore opened at ten o'clock. With hope, St. Allen was a punctual employee. Delilah watched from the corner as a worker unlocked the door and raised the shades, a signal the establishment stood ready for customers. Was Sebastian already inside? Had he accessed the store from the lower level and the maze of corridors which somehow connected to his home? Her brows rose with this consideration. She'd forgotten that fact until this moment.

Careful to avoid a puddle of muck near the curb, she crossed the street and aimed for the bookstore as a rehearsal of pleasantries played on her tongue.

Good morning, St. Allen.

Yes, right, I'm to use your Christian name.

Good morning, Sebastian. Thank you again for all your help.

Oh, the kisses. Of course, I remember now that you mention them.

Her pulse quickened with the suggestion. His kisses were branded on her brain. Alive in her dreams. Amused with her imagined conversation, she startled as the bell atop the door announced her entry.

"Good day." Delilah greeted the clerk cheerfully, disappointed the elderly man she'd encountered during her last visit wasn't present today. "I'd like to speak to Mr. St. Allen, please."

She bit her tongue at the mistake. Hadn't Sebastian corrected her a few times already? The clerk noticed her discomfort and his eyes narrowed keenly.

"Have you his card?"

She hadn't considered the point, not that she had one of Sebastian's cards to offer anyway.

"No, I haven't, though I believe St. Allen will talk to me if you alert him to my visit."

"Perhaps you might call again another time." Seemingly finished with the discussion, the clerk nodded politely and stepped away, his dismissal as efficient as his denial.

Delilah drew a breath of frustration, stalled motionless by the unexpected circumstance, but only momentarily. She remembered where the door to the downstairs level was situated. Would it be so terrible for her to slip below while the clerk was occupied elsewhere? Sebastian would want to know of Oliver's safe return, otherwise he would waste precious time better served helping someone else.

With a sidelong glance beyond the geography section, she affected an avid interest and trailed her gloved fingertip over the spines of the nearest books on the shelf as if in search of the ideal volume. Once she reached the end of the aisle and confirmed she was obscured from view, she rose on the toes of her boots and did her best to move silently toward the far wall.

But to her confusion, when she reached the corner where she was certain a single cherrywood door stood, a golden oval colophon above it, she came nose-to-shelf with dozens of brown leather-bound books, neatly arranged, row after row.

She turned in a slow circle to reassert her bearings, confused and curious. Had she walked to the wrong corner? It was possible. She'd been overcome with emotion and worry the first time she'd visited the shop. But her memory never failed. There was something more to the bookstore and its neatly disguised corners.

Intrigued, she strode along each wall, disappointed to discover only more of the same. Books, books, and more books. Nothing but reading material lined the perimeter. How could that be?

Determined now to find the young clerk and insist he announce her visit to St. Allen, she smoothed her skirts, pressed her lips in a grim line and started toward the counter on the other side of the store. She could only see him in profile. A large display featuring books of art and culture partially blocked her view and she couldn't tell if he was busy or assisting another patron. She finally gained his attention when she was only two strides away. He met her gaze with an expression of annoyance, his eyes narrowed in what she perceived as unwarranted irritation. Good heavens, the clerk seemed insufferable.

Before she could voice her contempt for his less than hospitable reception, St. Allen appeared from behind a tall rack of periodicals, as silently as a shadow in that wonderfully mysterious way of his. One minute she approached the clerk with the intent to assert her demand, and the next the one man she wished to speak to emerged from nowhere.

CHAPTER 13

"Lady Ashbrook. It's a pleasure to see you again." Sebastian nodded to the clerk before he turned toward the lady. Indeed, it was an unexpected pleasure this morning.

"Hello, St. Allen."

Her cheeks were flushed with the rosiest hue and he wondered if she'd hurried in her walk to reach the bookstore. What could have caused her impatience? Had she come to her senses and sought to rail at him for taking liberties last evening? The memory of her kisses had kept him restless through the wee hours.

"What brings you to the store today?"

"I have good news to share." Her face lit with delight. "Oliver is home. Safely returned late last evening. There's still much we don't know, but I didn't wish for you to trouble yourself any longer on my behalf."

"Returned?" It was his turn to become the echo in their conversation. Abductors of children and thieves of any sort didn't usually return the items they'd stolen. Something else was at work here. "Why don't we sit down and discuss this? I'd like to hear every detail."

"I'm afraid I don't have too much more to tell, but I thought perhaps . . ." She hesitated and dropped her voice to a whisper. "If you'd like to visit my address and speak to Oliver, it could prove helpful in capturing the awful people who've perpetuated this act."

"Yes." He needed to speak to the boy and Delilah had thought it through intelligently. It would be good if Oliver remained with his mother in familiar surroundings when Sebastian questioned him. "If you could arrange the visit, I would appreciate your help." He also lowered his voice in consideration of the impropriety of their discussion.

"Of course. It's the least I can do after your diligent assistance." Delilah looked toward the front of the store and back again.

Was she checking for customers or workers to ensure she wouldn't be overheard, or was something else on her mind? He watched her adjust the buttons on her left glove and realized the moment would become awkward soon if one of them didn't speak.

"We could walk a bit and find a nearby tea shop. If you can spare a few minutes, I'm interested in hearing whatever you can share about what transpired last night." There. His request sounded entirely businesslike and not at all like he didn't want to lose her company.

She wore a becoming day gown in celery green that complimented the sparkle in her eyes. The pink embroidery work at the neckline was delicate and demure, while her pristine white gloves completed the image of a proper lady. She was nothing at all like the women he'd given his attention to in the past. Yet he was drawn to her with an undeniable yearning he hadn't deciphered. He wasn't ready to let her leave after only just finding her here this morning.

"What a pleasant idea."

She flicked a glance to him as if to measure his reaction. Did she feel uncomfortable? He would ease her mind.

"Strictly in a professional sense." That should do it.

"I understand." She straightened her shoulders and accepted his response with cordial agreement.

He could only assume she didn't feel the same tug of attraction, not after their dance or heated kisses, and in truth, why would she? He'd learned long ago the lines of aristocratic status were rigid and unyielding, always harsh in consequence. He valued his independence and the freedoms he'd created by hard work and loyalty alone.

The scuff of bootheels brought his mind to the present and he led Delilah to the front of the store and out onto the pavement, forcing himself to keep his expression casual, though he wondered if he were to lean closer, would he be able to catch her fresh lemon fragrance. He wanted to place her hand on his arm, offer protection against any wayward jostling as the thoroughfare sprang to life with shoppers, but logic warned it was the wrong decision despite desire dared him to act.

"There's a quiet tea shop one block over." He indicated the direction ahead. "It will provide us the refreshment and privacy we seek."

Delilah nodded and they started forward. It wasn't like him to be so out of depth and he sought conversation as a means to create a more amiable mood.

"I can only imagine the rush of relief that swept through your household once Oliver was returned with nothing more than a terrible scare." No truer statement had ever been made. His father's household had never experienced the same jubilation.

Unaware of his personal struggle, Delilah smiled, her animated words rising above the din of the crowd around them.

"We all feel thankful and incredibly lucky." As lucky as she, a woman of four-and-twenty years who was having tea with the handsomest man in London. With Oliver safely returned, her mind *and heart* were much lighter and driven to fanciful imaginings. Everything seemed better and brighter this morning.

"The shop is just ahead."

She Reads Tea Leaves was a squat building clad in weathered wooden shingles and bright red shutters, sandwiched between a cobbler and tobacco seller at the middle of the arcade on Burlington Street. Once they entered, they were greeted by a corpulent woman who swiftly ushered them to a corner table before she rattled off a list of available beverages and disappeared into the kitchen. A younger girl came to accept their order only a few minutes later as they both removed their gloves.

"I'd like a lemon verbena tea with no milk or sugar, please."

"And something to eat?" the young server asked.

"The glazed currant buns are very good. I know from personal experience." Sebastian's eyes sparkled as he offered the suggestion.

The shop was busy and the serving girl cleared her throat, impatient in her work.

"A deliberation this serious should be explored fully," Delilah agreed.

He turned his attention to the serving girl, who suddenly seemed much happier to wait tableside. "We'll each have a currant bun and I'll have a cup of Ceylon tea."

Delilah launched into the retelling as soon as the girl stepped away. She sighed as she finished, reliving the moment she'd hugged Oliver and confirmed he was well. "If only Aunt Helen and I had left the event earlier, I might have seen who placed Oliver on the stoop. If anything, I would have relieved his discomfort that much earlier."

"You shouldn't chastise yourself. The situation has proven unpredictable and surprising since the onset."

Delilah stared into his eyes, searching his face and finding compassion and sincerity. Her gaze dropped to his lips, her brain quick to replay the press of his mouth to hers, stroke of his hot tongue, and growl of desire barely leashed. She pushed it out of her mind. "In any matter, thank you for your help."

"I'm not sure how much I contributed to Oliver's safe return, but hearing the details would be helpful as I pursue the criminals further."

"Yes, of course."

The service arrived and for the next few minutes they busied themselves arranging the table in silence. They both reached for the jam pot at the same time and his fingertips brushed against hers. Ignoring the warm tremor his touch evoked, she sought safe conversation. "I hope you don't mind that I visited your workplace today. I had no way to reach you and it was imperative you knew Oliver was returned."

"Does your bedchamber face the street?"

"My bedchamber?" She took a hurried sip from her cup and attempted to understand his unexpected inquiry. She immediately burnt her tongue, the tea too hot. "My rooms are located above the wrought-iron terrace on the left side of the town house."

"You mentioned you had no way to tell me of Oliver's return. In the future if you need me, to speak to me," he amended, "leave a lantern on the left side of your windowsill. I'll contact you discreetly as soon as possible."

If she did as he asked, he would know exactly where her bedchamber was situated. The very idea was wicked. Not that it mattered. But it seemed intimate, even if Sebastian would never understand that his having the knowledge pleased her on an elemental level.

"You'll have my aunt's property watched?"

"I have since that first night in Seven Dials."

"But how? Why?"

"There was no way for me to know if the criminals intended further harm and whether Oliver's abduction was premeditated or mistaken identity, possibly a victim of circumstance." He took a hearty bite of his currant bun and the action brought her eyes to his mouth again. A smudge of sugar laced the curve of his upper lip and more the pity, she noticed. He'd kissed her thoroughly with those lips. Exceptional kisses. Not that she had an inventory of comparison. Still, a delicious ripple of sensation undulated through her with the secret knowledge. Would he lick the errant trace of sugar away?

Much to her disappointment, he raised his napkin and cleaned it away before she'd even completed the thought.

"Oh." Her sigh of disappointment caught them both by surprise and provoked his explanation for something he had no idea existed.

"I meant no offense." He paused and stared at her directly, his tone edged with an emotion she couldn't readily identify. "I only meant to keep you under a watchful eye. My man is dependable and confidential."

She raised her palm to ward off further discussion. "I'm sorry, St. Allen. That's not it at all."

"But you should understand, the streets of London are no safe place for a woman alone, most certainly not at night or in areas which breed danger along with vermin."

"You make it sound terrifying."

"Because it is."

She drew her shoulders back, all at once remembering the incident in the dark alley and the magnificent rescue Sebastian initiated. Although her assistance in stopping his attacker in the Lost Yard affirmed her self-reliance. "I hope you realize I won't take any unnecessary risks."

He didn't appear convinced, so she offered him a brilliant smile. Men always seemed more assured when a lady punctuated a sentence with the same.

How could taking tea in the middle of the morning prove so sensual? Sebastian steeled himself against the onslaught of forbidden thoughts poking at his brain. Delilah looked more inviting than the delectable pastry on her plate, her expression sweeter, her rosy lips more tempting. And her hair. She had it neatly secured at the back of her neck but all the style did was serve as a reminder he should undo the braids and pins so he could fan the lengths around her slim shoulders.

She was brandy in a teacup. All prim and proper on the outside but able to heat his blood with one taste. And so much more too. Compassionate, generous, dedicated . . . *fearless*. Delilah possessed a unique vibrancy often snuffed out of refined ladies by overbearing nannies and finishing school. When had he become so aware of her every gesture? Damn if she wasn't looking at his mouth again. Had he said something wrong? Spoken his thoughts aloud?

He raised his napkin and wiped his chin as a means of stalling their conversation and regathering his concentration. No matter, he liked the idea of knowing where her bedchambers were situated even if he would never visit them.

"I will speak to Beth and Oliver and arrange for you to call. Then, if you'd like to stop in during afternoon hours, with my aunt present to keep propriety, you can hear whatever Oliver has to share."

Delilah easily accepted the rules he disdained. Just another difference between them. He didn't give a damn about society's opinion, but then again, he spent most of his time being invisible. The rules for a young woman hoping to make a match could hardly compare.

Was she really considering marriage? She'd only just arrived in London.

"I wouldn't wish for my aunt to draw any incorrect conclusions."

She'd lowered her voice to a clandestine whisper, as if the patrons at the next table worked for the London *Times*. Or maybe there was more to it than that? Could she possible view their meeting in a different light? That she wasn't so unaffected by his kisses after all?

He'd only just arrived at this satisfying suggestion when a narrow shadow fell across their table.

"Lady Herron." Delilah's surprise was evident.

"Good morning." Sebastian ground out his greeting. Was it necessary for Eva to interrupt? How did she find them anyway?

"May I join you?"

Eva didn't wait for an answer and moved a chair beside his on the opposite corner of the table. He was wise to her actions and wondered if Delilah perceived the same. Eva was staking a claim with silent intimidation and he didn't like it.

"How did you know where to find me?" He gathered his patience. Business discussions were conducted at one of the agency's offices. Nothing of relevance could be shared at a tea shop, and Eva knew as much.

"Pressman overheard you and shared the location."

"Pressman?" Delilah asked, her slender brows raised.

"Pressman is the lanky clerk you spoke to at the bookstore this morning. The same man who will be looking for employment tomorrow." The newly hired worker had failed in his ability to make intelligent decisions. First in his refusal of Delilah's request, and now again, by repeating information he'd gained by eavesdropping.

"Don't be so harsh, St. Allen. I charmed him into it." Eva grinned, her face showing no regret.

The table fell silent for a beat before Delilah spoke.

"Lady Herron, did you enjoy the festivities at Lord Mumford's gathering?"

Sebastian eyed Eva in an attempt to read her expression. Was Eva here to make havoc when Delilah sought friendly conversation?

"Thank you for asking, but I was working. St. Allen was assisting in the matter. There's no fun to be had until after hours." Eva's smile grew wider as she turned in his direction, the implication clear despite it was entirely false.

"Indeed." Delilah sat up straighter, her monosyllabic reply able to communicate that Eva's aim hit the target perfectly.

"Why are you here?" He didn't attempt to hide his annoyance.

"I thought the two of us should discuss developments connected to our mutual interests."

Having had enough of Eva's misleading innuendo, Sebastian pushed back his plate, the half-eaten currant bun a reminder of what a pleasant time he'd shared with Delilah before Eva had intruded. He swallowed the last of his tea and worked to keep his voice even toned. "I'll be in touch soon, Lady Ashbrook. Please feel free to finish your refreshments. I'll wait out front to escort you to the hackney stand whenever you're ready." Then with an exhale composed of tolerance and exasperation, he turned to Eva, but Delilah rose before he could express his displeasure.

"Please don't trouble yourself on my account." She glanced to her half-eaten bun and he knew she regretted the interruption as much as he. And maybe not for just one reason.

CHAPTER 14

Delilah walked beside St. Allen and Lady Herron as far as the hack stand on the corner. Her farewell was curt, despite a number of questions that burned on her tongue hotter than her unfinished tea.

She might be new to the city and not altogether worldly within London society, yet there was no misreading Lady Herron's veiled insinuations. Had St. Allen spent time with the lady once he'd left the earl's estate the other night? Was he involved with her on a personal level? Kissed her only hours after Delilah and he lost themselves on that darkened terrace? He hadn't looked pleased with Lady Herron's comments, but was that because they were exaggerated untruths or simply shared out of turn? Lady Herron's fondness for St. Allen evoked an immediate response Delilah recognized as petty and unkind.

She rubbed her temple. When had she become so invested in Sebastian's emotions? He'd come to her rescue and had worked to find Oliver and deliver him to safety, but that matter was settled now. Perhaps it was time her heart realized the same. She'd arrange for him to meet with Oliver. She'd place her lantern on the left sill and wait for Sebastian to contact her. Then, when he gathered all the information he needed and left, she'd do her best to distance herself because, as unexpected as their meeting, it was unlikely their paths would cross again. It was as she'd already surmised. London held too much disappointment and as of yet, it hadn't offered the life she'd imagined. The hackney encountered a rut in the road and she gasped as she slid precariously on the seat. Indeed, it was time for her to set her life to rights again.

Sebastian and Eva went below the bookstore to one of the rooms used for interrogation. He wanted to hear what she'd gathered from her conversation with the Duchess of Grandon, but he still stewed from the obvious allusions she'd dropped when conversing with Delilah. He wondered if Delilah believed the worst.

"What was that all about?"

Eva didn't pretend innocence. He doubted she ever regretted an action or word.

"I was doing you a favor. We're friends, right?" She splayed her palms as if no answer was necessary. "I couldn't sit there and watch Lady Ashbrook grow more and more moon-eyed. You've told me often you want no part of personal entanglements. I only thought to help you out." Eva reclined against the cushioned chair in a pose that declared she was completely comfortable with her decisions.

"I need no assistance, though I appreciate your thoughtfulness." His tone expressed the opposite. If Eva wished to play a game, she'd created a situation she could never win. Obviously, if she worked toward warding off females and perpetuated his assertion he wanted nothing of relationships, she needed to adhere to the same rule. "It's reassuring to know you understand I have no intention of becoming involved with anyone." He stressed the final two words.

Although Delilah could be the exception to the rule. The idea had crossed his mind more than once since meeting her that evening in Seven Dials. *Or* she might be nothing more than a curious attraction. Only time would tell.

Either way, he hoped Delilah arranged the meeting with Oliver promptly. Not only would it do well for him to speak to the boy while details remained fresh in the child's mind, but by spending time with Delilah again he could gauge whether Eva had upset the natural ease they'd developed or succeeded by instilling doubt. He didn't believe Delilah would draw unsubstantiated conclusions. She'd need proof, and since there wasn't any, he doubted Eva's interference was significant. That singular thought eased his anger. Best he get back to Eva's report and then dispatch a message to his man near Berwick Street.

"So, what do you have to share? Has the duchess received a ransom note for her jewels?"

"Events have taken an interesting turn." Eva sat up as she warmed to their discussion. "Wait until you hear this."

Delilah blew out a resigned breath as she approached her aunt's town house, the earlier elation she'd experienced at calling upon St. Allen and sharing the news of Oliver's safe return now cast in shadow by the weighty doubt instilled by Lady Herron's comments. It didn't signify to Delilah's heart or other attached emotions that Sebastian's attitude shifted noticeably when Lady Herron approached their table. Was it disappointment at her intrusion or an uncomfortable reminder of their previous night's dalliance that caused his gruff attitude?

And why did it matter anyway? Delilah wasn't so countrified she believed a kiss equaled a promise. A kiss wasn't a vow.

Lost in her disgruntled musings, she made her way through the house and into the kitchen, following the delightful sound of Oliver's laughter. Her mood immediately brightened and her tension eased with each step nearer.

She crossed through the doorframe and into a cloud of flour. Everything seemed to be coated with a light dusting of white powder, and the usual order of the room was in blatant disarray.

"Good heavens. I leave for one morning and the entire kitchen is turned upside down. What's happening here?"

Cook stood by the pantry, her arms overfilled with ingredients. A small sack of flour was open on the counter. Dusty handprints were evident on the work slate and cutting board. A small pool of melted butter dripped over the edge of a saucer onto the floor. But Oliver's grin was worth the mess. An immediate smile found its way to her mouth.

"We're trying a new recipe for Mama's birthday cake. Cook says we can bake three different kinds and decide which we like best. Then next week we'll have the most perfect cake to celebrate the day."

The mention of Beth's birthday threatened to bring back the horrific memories of what happened when Delilah brought Oliver to purchase his mother's present, but she refused to allow the thoughts to ruin what could only be a joyous result. Despite this effort, her heart squeezed tight. What of the other children? The ones who never returned to hug their families or resume a normal way of life. How many were lost to the streets? St. Allen sought to fight back and single-handedly bring these brutal miscreants to justice, but it wasn't enough. She wished there was some way she could help as well.

"How clever of the two of you." Delilah hemmed her lower lip. Should she mention Sebastian's request to speak with Oliver? No, she would speak to Beth first. Still, with Beth's birthday approaching there were gifts to be bought, and the cyclical tangle of the events were a difficult knot to resolve. "And of course, we'll need presents. If you tell me what you would like to give your mother, I'll be sure to have it delivered."

As silly as it sounded, she wasn't ready to take Oliver shopping again. Not even if a footman accompanied her this time.

"Thank you, Delilah, but I've already the best gift I could ever hope to give Mama." His smile grew bigger, his cheeks as round and shiny as apples. "It's very special."

"As are you, young man." She ruffled her fingers through his hair and then brushed a fingertip across his mouth, dusting away the sugar. "Your safe return to us is the very best gift of all."

Cook placed a few more items on the table and Oliver began to open each bag, his curiosity as eager as his grin.

"Is your mother upstairs, Oliver?"

He nodded his head in the affirmative, though his attention was still captured by the display of ingredients and sweet treats. He popped a few dried dates in his mouth when he thought no one was looking.

"Thank you." Delilah addressed Cook next. "See that he doesn't spoil his appetite too much or invite a stomachache. I'll be upstairs speaking to Beth if you need me for anything."

"So—" Eva emphasized the last of her retelling. "It's about breeding."

"Isn't it always?" Sebastian laid his palms flat on the tabletop, equally intrigued and inured by the odd collection of facts Eva had gathered.

"Maybe." Eva gave an aborted laugh. "But not usually the canine kind."

That was true. Duchess Grandon was sincerely concerned about appearances and was reputed to be quite obstinate when her mind was made up.

"Someone hired a few commonplace miscreants—" Eva continued.

"Unreliable miscreants," Sebastian interrupted. "to steal the Duchess of Grandon's dog with the purpose of having it mate with a female Pomeranian."

"One bitch in particular," Eva added with laughter in her voice.

"The dog owned by the Earl of Yardley?"

"Yes." Eva stifled another snicker. "When Oliver hung onto Cygnet's cut leash and wouldn't let it go, the fools panicked and picked him up along with the dog. They dashed away in the carriage, only they had no orders to abduct a child and no idea how to care for one, so they panicked. When they made contact and received word from Yardley, he only wanted Cygnet. The thieves were stuck with Oliver and few options, and so they decided to return him. Thankfully he's safe now."

"And Her Grace's diamonds? The collar fashioned out of countless valuable gemstones?"

"Missing." Eva shook her head as she went on. "The story is a little muddy there. The buffoons that carried out the plan don't have the gems and neither does Lord Yardley. Or so I was told. It does make one wonder what happened to that fortune. Apparently Yardley promised the thieves a portion of the take, and they're left having done the job with little compensation."

"And Cygnet?"

"He's still with the earl . . . or with the earl's bitch." Eva's expression showed amusement again. "I can't believe this conversation."

"Why wouldn't Yardley go about this more openly?"

"He'd already approached the Duchess of Grandon multiple times with generous offers for the stud, but Her Grace treats Cygnet like a child and believed Yardley's female wasn't a pure breed. In the duchess's refined opinion, the bitch wasn't good enough to bear Cygnet's offspring and therefore the duchess held hostage her dog's ability to reproduce."

"And here I thought the marriage mart was dangerous."

"Her Grace has more than a few secrets to hide." Eva leaned forward. "She recently participated in a torrid affair with Yardley, but when he continually pestered her about the stud, she broke things off and likewise broke his heart. It's a bit of a love triangle."

"With Cygnet as the third party."

"I guess. Yardley tried to make amends, but Her Grace said she could never trust him, not knowing if his vows of affection were true or just a means to get his hands on Cygnet's future offspring."

"And Oliver was in the wrong place at the wrong time," Sebastian concluded. "What a cock-up."

"You have that right. The thieves wanted nothing to do with a child."

"So, they got more than they bargained for," Sebastian murmured. He had too, when he'd chased Delilah down that alleyway.

"And so did the earl. He was enraged, or so I'm told, and once he secured the dog, he left disposal of the child to the fools he'd hired. They were at rights with kidnapping a dog, but not abducting a child."

"I'm not sure if I should feel relief or anger. Relief at their ignorance or anger that the child experienced a scare because of their ineptitude." He shouldn't be surprised at hearing yet another peculiar predilection of the aristocracy. Uppers protected their own, willing to weave a tapestry of crimes if it kept their lineage pure, their heritage respectful, and secrets hidden behind closed doors. He could never return to that life. He was his own man who made his own way. Keeping to the peripheral shadows of life was a comfortable existence and afforded him freedom to make his own choices.

Eva had accumulated a wealth of answers, but all the pieces didn't fit yet. "So then where do we stand? And how did you come by this abundance of information so quickly?"

"After you left me off at home, I was restless." Eva shrugged, her expression indecipherable. "The duchess hadn't confessed anything directly while at Mumford's gathering, but a few of her comments, her expressions, didn't seem true, or at least not as honest as she wanted me to believe. So I took my questions where they should have been asked from the start."

"The servants."

"Exactly." Eva knocked on the desktop.

"That explains some of what you've told me, but not everything."

"Right." A mischievous smile spread across her face as she continued. "I knew if anyone would have insight, it would be her driver. Naturally he would be the one who brought her to clandestine meetings, delivered messages and the like."

"And you charmed him too?"

"I prefer to think of it as planned persuasion, and let's not discount you left me in that state of restlessness. You might have come in for a drink, or at the least, a discussion of the transpired events, but your carriage pulled to the curb and that was the end of our night together."

"You have an uncanny way of phrasing things." Sebastian exhaled, refusing to be pulled into a personal conversation.

"Do I?" Her smile dropped away but her eyes still gleamed with knowing agreement. "I haven't noticed."

Sebastian was determined to keep their discussion strictly business. "I'm planning to speak to Oliver soon and see if he can lend insight into where he was held. Uncovering one band of thieves often links to the next." He didn't share how he hoped this whole absurd dog situation would help him locate the miscreants he'd seen in Seven Dials, because even though the logical side of his brain told him that as fast as he snuffed out one ring of criminals, another likely formed, the more intense and definitely angrier side demanded he continue his search. To force justice onto those who stole it from the innocent.

"There's still plenty of holes in the story that need to be filled," Eva continued, her voice drawing him from the darkness of his thoughts. "Until Cygnet is returned, the duchess will have no peace. She doesn't seem worried about the diamonds, although that singular fact is debatable. No one can be that blasé about losing priceless heirloom gems."

"I wonder if this is nothing more than entertainment for them. Yardley, the disgruntled lover, and Grandon, the coy mistress who holds all the cards at the moment."

"Not all the cards." Eva stood, a signal she knew their time was coming to an end. "I don't think she takes Cygnet's disappearance lightly."

"True." Sebastian strode toward the door, anxious to message his man at watch near Berwick Street. "A visit to the Earl of Yardley's residence later tonight might shed some light on things. Keep me up-to-date and I'll do the same."

CHAPTER 15

Delilah moved away from her dressing table, reminding herself any further fussing over her appearance would indicate she'd developed a personality flaw. She wore her finest muslin gown with her hair in a simple twist at her neck. No jewelry or fancy slippers were necessary. Sebastian was calling on the house for a visit. Everyone would be present in the drawing room and his questions would be meant for Oliver or Beth.

Still, listing these facts didn't make the swarm of butterflies in her stomach stop their fluttering. He was handsome. There was no denying it. His dark hair and pale blue eyes spoke to her without words. She couldn't stop thinking about his kisses. It was as if she could still feel them on her lips. The press of his mouth against hers, the slide of his tongue. She wrapped an arm around her middle and squeezed in an effort to force the butterflies into obedience. They didn't listen any more than her foolish, hopeful heart. Since when had she become preoccupied with thoughts of romance? It was as though she had no control over her own mind.

The clomp of horse hooves and a slowing carriage brought her to the front window. She watched through a slit in the drapery as Sebastian stepped out of a sleek black barouche. It was decidedly cloudy and the sky set to storm, yet she could discern his broad shoulders and strong profile. He possessed an elegant grace that belied someone who worked in a bookstore. Mayhap he belonged to the night, better suited to the dusky shadows that revealed so little.

Last evening she'd placed the lantern where he'd asked, and just as he'd promised, a messenger arrived to receive her note. The meeting was set without effort. She wondered at his ability to make events happen so seamlessly. There were a great many things she didn't know about him, whether he presented danger to her heart—or fulfillment, for that matter—and yet just the thought of him set her pulse to racing. If the butterflies didn't cease their flight, she'd hardly be able to converse downstairs.

Ambivalence wasn't in her nature. She was decisive and thought all matters through to completion. Yet in regard to Sebastian, nothing seemed to make sense. Being of common birth, she could never welcome him as a suitor, and regardless, he'd never indicated he wished to become one. A few stolen kisses hardly amounted to evidence of emotion. Certainly standing at the window peering down at him accomplished nothing more than agitating her further.

Sebastian spoke to his driver and then turned, his eyes gliding upward to linger on her window. He could only have paused to look for the lantern. Nothing else. She hurried away and made for the stairs.

Below, Delilah watched with fascinated amusement as Beth colored crimson upon being introduced to Sebastian. Aunt Helen was abovestairs with a megrim, which solved Delilah's problem of explaining how *Lord Wintel* was here and why. Was that St. Allen's real name? She'd forgotten to ask him at the tea shop and only remembered this afternoon as she'd reviewed the events of Mumford's social. Yet this evening he'd presented his card and the Wintel name was printed on it. Blast, the man was confusing.

"Let's all settle in the drawing room with refreshments." Delilah nodded toward Beth, who hurried Oliver along. The child's eyes hadn't left Sebastian, and Delilah wondered if Oliver felt scared or was simply impressed with their guest's compelling presence. For a man who spent most of his time behind bookshelves, he certainly spent a coin on tailoring. Tonight he was dressed in charcoal gray, so dark a shade one might mistake it for black, but having studied his wide shoulders and how his coat tapered to his trim waist, Delilah decided her first impression was correct.

Being they were home, she'd forgone the formality of gloves, so when Sebastian took her hand in greeting, his strong fingers wrapped around hers, her breath hitched, caught unaware by the rough caress of his fingertips coasting over her palm, for he hadn't worn gloves either. She immediately accepted the tea Beth offered, anxious to regain her equilibrium.

"Oliver, Lord Wintel is here to talk to you about what happened on Jermyn Street," Delilah began. "He would very much like to find the people who treated you so cruelly."

"And Cygnet too," Oliver added. Beth stroked her son's arm, a mixture of pride and protectiveness on her face.

"If you could start at the beginning and tell me everything you remember, no matter how small a detail, it would be helpful." Sebastian took a plate and two biscuits off the silver tray on the oval rosewood table. This seemed to signal a casual mood and Oliver complied without pause.

"Delilah took me shopping so I could choose a birthday gift for my mama." Oliver leaned over on the chaise and whispered in a not-so-quiet voice to Sebastian, "Her birthday is almost here." Then he resumed in his normal speaking tone as if she and Beth weren't in the room and hadn't witnessed the latter. "Once we were out of the coach, another came down the street. It was the fanciest carriage I've ever seen. The horses were huge, four true high-steppers, and they had ribbons in their manes. Everyone stopped to watch and I did too." He swallowed thoughtfully as he hesitated.

"Go on." Sebastian prodded.

"I just wanted to see a little closer and I would have returned straight after."

"It's fine, Oliver. I'm not angry," Delilah reassured from where she sat on the other side of the room.

"I let go of Delilah's hand and squeezed between the people on the walkway. Everyone was trying to see the fancy lady who exited the carriage. She had a fluffy white dog with a sparkly collar and a long black leash. I wiggled my way to the front and the lady with the dog saw me. She introduced me to Cygnet and invited me to pet him. He was very soft." This was said in a gentle, almost mournful tone, and Delilah wondered if Oliver saw something untoward happen to the animal while they were both in captivity.

"Tell what happened next, Oliver, and make sure you include every detail," Beth encouraged.

"I was petting Cygnet when two men rushed through the crowd and pushed the nice lady to the ground. She dropped Cygnet's leash. I didn't want her dog to get scared and run away so I picked up the lead and held tight. One of the men tried to take it from me but I kicked him in the leg good and hard. I didn't let go and before I could run away he cut the leash, but I held on to Cygnet. The man cussed. He picked me up with the dog and pushed his way to the street. I was thrown in a carriage. I had to let go of Cygnet. They put a sack on my head after that. I struggled at first but one of the men gave me a whack and I stopped." Oliver's voice dropped lower, his excitement dimmed by this part of the retelling. "It was terribly hard to breathe. I yelled at first but little threads made me cough and I had to stop or they said they would strike me again. The carriage was already moving and I was bumping on the floor. I might have hit my head. I don't remember." He stopped and fidgeted a little with the edge of the seat cushion, the room eerily quiet until Sebastian placed a hand on Oliver's shoulder.

"You're doing a brilliant job." Sebastian removed his hand, though he leaned closer. "You are a brave lad."

Oliver nodded and matched eyes with Sebastian before he continued. "They took me to a dark room. When I woke up, the cloth bag was gone but my mouth and hands were tied. I could hear Cygnet barking but I couldn't see him. The floor was damp and everything smelled like rotten fish."

Oliver wrinkled his nose and Beth grasped his hand in hers. Delilah experienced the same desire to comfort Oliver but knew it wasn't her place. Besides, she didn't wish to distract him.

"Is there anything you recall about the two men who took you? Did you see what they looked like or hear anything they said to each other?" Sebastian probed for more information.

"One bloke was called Bert, and I don't think either one of them were very learned. They drank and cussed a lot and they were angry to have me there. They said I was a problem they had to fix." Oliver huffed a deep breath. "Sometimes I heard a sad bell ringing. Like the kind we hear near the waterman's wherry, Mama."

Beth looked across the table with a slight smile, encouraged by that clue. "Is there anything else you remember, love?" She smoothed her fingers over the top of his hand, but Oliver wriggled free from her grasp and helped himself to another biscuit. His resiliency was inspiring, though Delilah wouldn't discount the child had no idea of the horrific events that might have happened were the kidnappers of a different disposition.

"They told me I was nothing but trouble and belonged at the bottom of the Thames where the fish would eat my eyes. When one of them took off the rags so I could have water, I bit his arm. That's what I did." Oliver beamed with satisfaction and the corner of Sebastian's mouth twitched.

Delilah's chest tightened at the retelling of Oliver's suffering. She had foolishly believed he was returned mostly unscathed, but the memories and nightmares of his experience would weigh heavily on her conscience for many years to come.

"Well, you're home now." Sebastian replaced his teacup on the table. "And you've helped me greatly. I'm proud of you."

The latter comment caused Oliver to sit up straighter, a bright gleam in his eyes. "They put me back in that sack and dumped me out last night. I didn't know where I was, but I was dry and there weren't any rocks in the bag. I kept thinking about the man who wanted to drop me in the river. They meant to get rid of me, but I needed to see my mama again. I kept my fingers crossed even though my arms were tied. I kept wishing."

Another unsettling quiet enveloped the room.

"And then I must have fallen asleep." His normal cheeky smile in place, Oliver stood up as if to prove he was fit as a fiddle. "Until Delilah opened me up!"

"Well done." Beth scooped him up and wrapped her arms around him tightly, though he wriggled free not two beats later.

"Yes. You did an excellent job of recalling the events." Sebastian stood. "I won't trouble you any longer. Thanks to Oliver I have several new clues to investigate."

"Please let us know if you capture the men who harmed my son." Beth placed her hands upon Oliver's shoulders and squeezed lightly as a reminder.

"Thank you, my lord." Oliver was all business as he extended his palm forward for a handshake.

"Thank you for allowing me into your home at this late hour."

Delilah followed Sebastian out into the hallway in hope they could speak privately for a few minutes. All of a sudden it was as if sand flowed through an hourglass and her chance to be in his company and experience the shimmering thrill of his pale blue attention was nearing its end. What could she possibly say and not appear too forward? Aunt Helen would suffer an apoplectic fit were Delilah to extend another invitation to a bachelor in their home.

"I hope Oliver's information assists you." *Foolish. Obvious. Redundant.* She was wasting her last chance with inane niceties.

"I'm sure it will, although the matter of the dog and his gemstone collar are still an issue I've yet to riddle out."

"The matter you're working on with Lady Herron?" *Perfect, Delilah. Remind him of the woman who has a transparent attachment to him.*

"Yes." He stalled near the front door and turned. "Today at the tea shop, she purposely misrepresented our relationship," he replied as if their thoughts were interwoven.

Delilah considered this carefully. Why would he tell her this unless it mattered? Could it be that *she* mattered? Even a little? She assumed he was a private person. It would take a lot for him to speak openly of personal relationships. But then, they had shared those heart-stopping moments in the darkened corner at Mumford's ball. He was all strength and brawn on the outside, but she sensed something else, something on the inside she couldn't yet decipher. She breathed deep and was rewarded with the scent of his spicy cologne.

"Thank you for that." She watched his expression closely, looking for answers in his eyes. "And for working so diligently to protect Oliver and help us find the men to be punished."

"You have no need to thank me, Delilah."

His voice dropped low and silky when he said her name, as if they revealed secrets instead of expressed common gratitude. A race of goose bumps sped over her skin. Watching his mouth proved the greatest test of her endurance.

"If you should ever need my assistance, you can put the lantern out on your sill."

"Now that Oliver is safe, I would never dream of troubling you." Somehow, she'd moved closer to him. Only inches separated them despite they stood in the hall, the staircase at her back where Aunt Helen or any servant could easily view their exchange. Her pulse thrummed with an insistent tempo.

"You're not trouble. Quite the opposite, actually." He reached forward and tucked a loose tendril of her hair behind her ear, his bare fingertip tracing the curve with the tenderness of a lover's touch.

She leaned a hairsbreadth nearer. What was she doing? Inviting him to sin in the foyer?

"Sebastian . . ." His name was a breathy exhale on her lips.

"Never wonder, Delilah." His voice was no more than a husky murmur. "I will see you again."

And then he turned and left, his sudden departure causing her to sway unsteadily. She grasped the newel post at the bottom of the landing in an attempt to steady her emotions and stared at the closed door for several minutes afterward.

Sebastian poured himself brandy and walked to the far side of his bedchamber. He gazed out the window at the night and considered the recent series of events. He lived comfortably in a town house close enough to Mayfair to be considered valuable real estate and far enough detached to keep one boot firmly planted in his past. He thought that was the way it should be, but perhaps the time had come for him to choose his future. Straddling the lines of society was doing nothing but forcing an insistent fracture to his peace. He was a bastard, and he best remember it. Wasn't that what his father had said? It didn't really matter how expensive his clothing, the truth prevailed.

Delilah looked lovely tonight. The thought of her warm hazel gaze and delicate touch ramped his ardor another notch. Whenever he was near her, he found himself in a state of persistent arousal and it was becoming an uncomfortable habit. Cursing beneath his breath, he took a long swallow of brandy. He wanted her. Not in the usual sense a man aims to relieve his physical needs with a woman. No. *He wanted her.* Period. He wanted to keep her. Wanted to make love to her. Learn her likes and dislikes. Hear her laughter. Bring her smiles. All that ridiculous rubbish poets and painters poured into their compositions and he usually dismissed out of hand.

What did Delilah want from life? He had little more than a collection of random comments to form his opinion.

He needed to remedy that. A distant voice reminded he was breaking yet another of his rules.

Oliver's information was helpful, but Sebastian believed the child had more to tell. It would offer him another reason to pay a call. First, he needed to share what he'd learned with Eva and investigate a few aspects of the story by himself, but then he would send Delilah a message and arrange another visit.

Lately he'd neglected his usual pursuits. He needed to check in with Vane and Darlington too. He'd become distracted, but thankfully the other members didn't ask questions. They didn't prod him, because he relentlessly sought those who sold children and beat the pulp out of each when caught. They viewed it as a valiant cause.

What would Delilah think were she to learn of his past? The immediate assumption, that she would distance herself with haste, caused him to finish off the brandy in his glass.

Delilah represented everything he usually shunned in better society. Still, some part of her called to him. Some deeply buried yearning inside of him answered that call. It wasn't merely a physical desire. She made him feel something, when he'd been numb for so long.

He cursed again and set his glass on the bedside table. What were all these emotions suddenly brought to the surface? Why was his past asserting itself into his present?

As was his habit, he'd only lighted one lantern. Everywhere he looked, darkness pervaded. Did he live his life in shadows, unwilling to face what couldn't be ignored? Lately he'd grown tired of being invisible.

One more week and that same date, the single day that had altered his entire life, would reoccur and remind him of all that he'd lost. Perhaps this year he should enact a change.

Skimming his eyes over the blue-black profiles of the street below, he raised his attention to the stars and exhaled deeply. It was a futile mission to believe he could rid London of child predators by stalking Seven Dials and running in and out of shadows. He'd be better off writing a petition to his superiors at the Crown and urging they enforce stronger laws, better patrol, and harsher consequences.

Sebastian turned from the window and began to undress. With each article, he abandoned another of his concerns. He sat on the edge of his mattress and removed his boots, then stood to shed his trousers, shirt, and smalls. Were Delilah waiting in his bed, he'd have moved with greater anticipation, but with only the haunting images of his past poised to greet him, he took his time before climbing between the sheets.

CHAPTER 16

"This way." Malcolm Vane's low command melted into the dank fog lingering across the vamp of their half boots. Sebastian advanced in the opposite direction, intent on circling to the back of the dilapidated fishing shack before Vane reached the front. Closer to the water now, the expected odors of rancid fish and rotted wood were quick to evoke eerie reminders of another time, when Sebastian wasn't nearly as wise, when he was composed of nothing more than an odd mixture of fear and determination. Now he shoved those memories behind a locked door and focused on the task at hand.

Oliver's retelling of a man named Bert and the clang of a mournful bell in the distance had triggered Vane's memory when Sebastian mentioned it at the offices. Vane had worked on a problem that required he mix with the lowest element of humanity. He recalled a twosome of petty thieves who fancied themselves smugglers but were little more than fools for hire. They went by Bert and Sullivan.

It could result that the overlap between the two facts shared nothing in common, but Sebastian never abandoned information until it either proved useful or useless. Same as the evenings he'd spent waiting in Seven Dials. No clue was too small to investigate when attempting to save lives and right wrongs.

Tonight, veiled by humid mist and murky cloud cover, he pursued justice. Too many loose threads and peculiar aspects of the events on Jermyn Street persisted. It would be good to locate one of the thugs who'd aided the earl. Thieves knew all the goings-on of other thieves, their loyal network more steadfast than an agreement in the House of Lords. To that point, criminals respected each other on a level inconceivable to common man because each decision made could possibly be one's last.

With enough of the right kind of persuasion, Sebastian was confident he could extract information linked to the ruined sale of a child in Seven Dials. Had Delilah not startled that transaction, he might have caught the men involved. More importantly, he would have rescued the youngster trapped in the canvas sack. That thought alone sparked rage. Horrible circumstances awaited the children who were stolen. The automatic assumptions of chimney sweep, pickpocket, mudlarker for a child's fate were hardly the worst. Those were trades of the lower classes. But sexual deviants and abusive miscreants were at times the same titled men who graced ballrooms and drank imported cognac at White's.

Shaking away the maudlin reality, he summoned a ready image of Delilah to mind. Never a hard task. He wouldn't discount her courage. Or her beauty. Nor the fact that, had she not been there in Seven Dials, he'd never have found her, saved her . . . *kissed her.*

A rat scuttled across the slick stones ahead outlined in silver moonlight, and banished fanciful notions of affection and romance. He was dockside near Blackfriars Bridge in the southwest end of the city along the shipping yards of the Thames. Far enough from Tooley Street where as a child he'd been kept in a rickety shed, the sour smell similar to his surroundings this evening. This was where he'd left his childhood, his innocence and belief in decency, never to be reclaimed. He hadn't returned to Tooley Street in ten years since he'd visited the ramshackle tenement where he'd been held, and burned it to the ground. He'd left his past life in the ashes and embers of that fire. If only he could extinguish the conflagrant memories.

* * *

"Now that our household is returned to normal, I hope you're not bothered I've accepted this invitation on your behalf. It's time to change our focus to a more enjoyable subject. Your future, dear." Aunt Helen beamed with expectation from her seat across the carriage. "I've spoken fondly of you for so long, it's only natural my closest friends feel anxious to make your acquaintance."

"It will be my pleasure." Delilah truly didn't mind. An outing would be good for her spirits. It held the potential to inspire her to believe she'd find happiness here; and, too, it would disperse her restlessness, provoke her to cease thinking about everything she wasn't doing. She needed to visit the Wycombe building this afternoon. She had an idea to share. Still, she couldn't allow Aunt Helen to become curious about her silence. "It's a wonderful feeling to have everything restored to rights."

"Indeed," her aunt continued, unaware Delilah's smile was prompted by something else entirely. "I'm encouraged by recent events. Now that you call London home, I want you to be content in all ways. Lady Bridley will be most curious as to your interests. She has a bachelor son, mind you, who has recently expressed an interest in marriage."

At times Aunt Helen was more transparent than glass. But she meant well. Delilah didn't comment and her aunt hardly noticed.

"With the season in full swing I'm sure there will be many proposals to fill the gossip pages. Just imagine the excitement if you're one of the lucky ladies."

Delilah turned to look out the window. Marriage was the farthest thing from her mind, although memories of Sebastian's lingering gaze and enthralling kiss haunted her, most especially in the evenings when she climbed into bed. She missed him. Knowing their paths would likely never cross again was a difficult thing to accept. If Aunt Helen intended to play matchmaker, Delilah would only disappoint.

The carriage rocked to a stop, and by virtue of brilliant timing Delilah was saved from having to explore the topic of marriage further. They were soon ensconced in Lady Bridley's salon, a congenial room with quoined windows framed by vibrant fringed draperies of celadon green trimmed in poppyseed. There were several overstuffed chairs in scattered pockets about the interior and seemingly situated to encourage private conversation. The walls were covered with silk paperhangings in a flocked damask pattern to add to the cozy mood. Across the room a fire crackled in the hearth, providing warmth and just the right amount of ambiance.

The butler announced their entry in a discreet, austere tone and Aunt Helen clasped Delilah's hand with a squeeze before they linked arms and made their way around the perimeter. Her aunt took great pride in each introduction. Delilah flit her gaze from one guest to the next, surprised to see several gentlemen in attendance. Aunt Helen had described the afternoon visit as a lady's friendly gathering, but a prickling of ill ease suggested perhaps Delilah had misunderstood. Regardless, she did her best to partake in social niceties and polite conversation. It wasn't until three-quarters of an hour later when she'd settled on an inviting cushioned chair that she acquired a moment of calm. She spent a few moments taking inventory of the circulating crowd. Several ladies appeared unescorted, their fans and lashes aflutter as the gentlemen present meandered from group to group, initiating polite discussion. Exactly what type of congregation was this? Delilah had never seen so many unattached people mingling together where conversation shifted with such frequency and alacrity. It was as if they continually changed partners in a lively dance.

"Aunt Helen"—Delilah hesitated as she leaned closer, prepared to ask a delicate question—"how did Lady Bridley describe her gathering when she invited us this afternoon?"

"Lady Bridley and I have known each other for decades." Aunt Helen patted Delilah's knee in reassurance. "She's regarded as an effectual matchmaker. I daresay she's brought together several young couples and has earned herself a glowing reputation."

"So, we're here because you wished to introduce me to your friends or . . ." Delilah left the remainder of her sentence, *the unthinkable*, unsaid.

"It harms no one to be seen in an advantageous light, dear," Aunt Helen continued. "While you may not seek a husband with the same earnest dedication as some, one never knows when a fortuitous introduction will turn your eye or speak to your heart. I want only what's best, and here you will meet a wide selection of available gentlemen who are vetted specifically by Lady Bridley. Men of fine history and reputation. Blue-blooded and highly respected."

"If they're so regarded, why *are* they here?" Delilah regretted the bold inquiry, but it seemed only logical. Surely gentlemen with so many distinguished qualities wouldn't need the assistance of a matchmaker.

"Only a young person would ask such a thing." Aunt Helen tutted her tongue before she continued, promptly dismissing Delilah's question. "As I've told you, the horrid experience with Oliver has opened my eyes to the many threats within London. Danger takes many forms and I wouldn't wish for you to be swayed by the wrong sort. I've heard horrid stories of proper ladies who have cast aside their fine breeding, all because a scoundrel whispered in their ear. A lady should never become susceptible to a rogue's wicked influence. It can happen quicker than one might imagine."

It was no small coincidence a ready image of Sebastian came to mind. Delilah breathed deeply, a bemused smile on her lips. No gentleman had ever caused her heart to pound, pulse to rush, or blood to simmer in the same manner as he. She skimmed her eyes across the room. No one's shoulders were as broad, hair as dark, eyes as light, voice so intriguing it caused a rush of gooseflesh . . . the list was endless. No one compared to Sebastian. Was that an affliction she would need to overcome, or an uncompromising fact she needed to pursue? Only time would tell.

"But there's no hurry for me to become engaged." Delilah tried her best to keep her voice even. "I've only just relocated to London."

"Exactly." Aunt Helen's eyes took on a determined gleam. "Being new to the city affords you a mysterious quality that will enhance your overall appeal, but only for a brief time, so we must take advantage."

"Still, I—"

"I know what you're going to say."

There really was no way Aunt Helen could fathom it.

Nevertheless, her aunt kept speaking.

"Again, I remind you this nasty situation with Oliver has awakened me to how quickly circumstances can change. London is more dangerous than I originally believed. It's fraught with peril, and a delicate female needs the strength and guidance of a proper gentleman. There are invisible, forbidden forces at work. Unseen danger lurks in dark corners, and as genteel ladies we're all but powerless against it. Scandal"—her aunt's face paled at the mention—"now that's truly the worst of it all. You're in need of protection."

"I understand your concern, but—" Delilah gentled her tone, though a beat of panic danced in her chest. Aunt Helen was highly motivated now.

"The sooner you decide upon a husband, the better for all of us. I don't like to consider my mortality, but only a fool would leave the future in the hands of Fate. Naturally I'll do my best to ensconce you in the marriage mart and provide proper introductions, but it should not be ignored that one of my dearest friends is adept at handling these matters."

"So, all of these ladies are here in hope of making a match?" With this new knowledge, Delilah viewed the guests scattered about the room.

"And the gentlemen too." Aunt Helen nodded vigorously. "It's a lovely arrangement, isn't it?"

Delilah hemmed her lower lip in thought as her aunt's hushed voice continued.

"While many feel a formal ball offers opportunity, what can truly happen between a man and woman when under the speculative eye of hundreds of guests?"

One can be swept into a dark corner and kissed senseless.

Delilah stood up as a pang composed of revelation and longing arrowed straight through her. Aunt Helen joined her, dedicated to pursue the subject.

"Excellent. You've decided to participate, and might I remind you Lady Bridley has the right of it. A quiet, collective effort where everyone is aware of the stakes and participates without censure or pretense seems more the expedient path." Aunt Helen bobbed her head in approval. "How clever of her to take on this social responsibility."

"Very well." The two words were all Delilah managed before an amiable, sandy-haired fellow approached. She pasted a smile on her face. "I will do my best to become acquainted with the kind gentlemen gathered here, but in the future, Aunt Helen, please allow me to have a say."

"Of course."

The gentleman had reached them now. He bowed at the waist while she curtsied in greeting just as Aunt Helen took her leave.

"If you'll both excuse me, I must ask Lady Henley about her recent trip to Rome."

And with premeditated efficiency, much to Delilah's chagrin, she realized her aunt played a fine game of matchmaker too.

Lord Hibbett was of medium build with a friendly smile and warm brown eyes. They fell into conversation with immediate ease and Delilah welcomed the reprieve.

"I understand you've not always called London home," Lord Hibbett began.

"That's correct. I'm fond of the countryside, but in time I believe I could come to enjoy city life."

"We have that in common, my lady." Lord Hibbett nodded

thoughtfully. "I've resided here for the past six years, but I'll always consider Birmingham my true home."

"Birmingham?" Delilah shot a glance around the room, surprised by how loudly her voice sounded and wondering if her aunt watched. But no, Aunt Helen was engrossed in her own conversation. "This cannot be happenstance. I'm from Birmingham. Surely my aunt must have told you."

Lord Hibbett stifled a chuckle. "No. I assure you no one informed me, though perhaps our kindred spirits called to each other."

"It is a clever coincidence." Delilah didn't suppress her smile. Lord Hibbett was affable company. "My father's country home was lovely. The crowded town houses of London are a distinct transition. Everything seems so closely pressed together here."

"I understand. It does take time to become accustomed to the lack of endless grassy fields and wildflower-edged roadways. My familial home, Hibbett Manor, is in southeast Birmingham, not far from the River Trent. It's a dashing estate, but I shouldn't go on. You'll think I dislike London when I intended to welcome you here instead."

"I thought nothing of the kind, my lord. There's no saying we can't like both country and city life. Isn't that true?"

"Indeed, it is." Lord Hibbett searched her face as if he was deciding on the right words or deliberating them with great care. When he spoke again, his tone acquired an appealing tone. "Would you allow me to call on you tomorrow afternoon? I'd like nothing more than to show you a few noteworthy sights in the city."

"Thank you, yes." Delilah swallowed past her immediate urge to decline. She needed to regard London as her new home even if it took a bit of audacious effort on her part. "I'd like that very much."

Lord Hibbett appeared reassured by her acceptance. "I suppose Lady Bridley has the right way of it. Had I shared a rigorous quadrille or lively country dance with you, I'd never have uncovered our shared commonalities. I expect as we become better acquainted, there will be more of the same. One never knows what will arise from a risk taken."

A swift image of Sebastian's cool blue eyes right before he captured her mouth for his sinfully delicious kiss proved that theory correct, but Delilah only nodded her agreement.

CHAPTER 17

"Son of a bitch." Sebastian overturned the wooden table that rested against the far wall of the fishing shack. Vane entered a moment later, his jaw tense, alarm sparked in his eyes.

"I thought the goal was to remain invisible."

"No one is here." Sebastian slanted a glare to his friend. Anger had a strong hold on him. "I found a docket of sorts."

"All kinds of cargo enters and leaves these ports. A manifest doesn't seem unusual."

"It lists requests for children."

"Children?"

"Street urchins and orphans. Young girls mostly." Sebastian put the booklet in his inside coat pocket and gestured toward the door with a curt nod. "It all depends on the disturbing appetite of the person who placed the order. The lucky ones become chimney sweeps, sometimes house maids who clean after those who believe themselves above it. The others . . . their future is too reprehensible to discuss."

Vane didn't say more and it was for the best. Sebastian's heart thrummed with such intense rage he wondered if it would ever return to normal. Better London, people with the means and power to enact change, cared little for children sold into dreadful conditions, all perpetuated under society's long aristocratic nose.

"Let's get out of here and find a tavern." Vane's suggestion broke through Sebastian's hold on the past. "I sense you have more to share."

Sebastian didn't reply. This time he followed his friend out to the alleyway labyrinth leading away from the docks. They walked a long while before he calmed enough to speak. Eventually they advanced beyond Falcon Draw Dock and entered the first tavern in their path. By the time they'd settled in a corner and ordered tankards of ale, Sebastian's temper had cooled considerably, but the docket in his coat reminded him, no matter how hard he worked against the evil forces who stole children from the streets, it was an unending battle. One he could never win.

"We never discuss how each of us found our way to the Crown." Malcolm took a hearty taste of his ale as soon as the serving girl set it down on the table. "For the most part I believe the service finds us. Outcasts, for our own reasons and histories, but bound together nonetheless because something in us is not the expected."

"Agreed." Sebastian surmised the same even though no one in their group shared anything aside from mutual respect of each other's privacy.

"You looked like you would have destroyed that shanty, burnt it to the ground with the flames in your eyes."

"Selling children, stealing them to force into unthinkable situations . . ." Sebastian brought his ale up for another long swallow.

"Did you lose a child in that way?"

It was a natural assumption, he supposed, but Sebastian shook his head in the negative. Should he confide in Vane? Malcolm was his closest ally at the agency. Eva liked to believe she was, despite Sebastian did his best to discourage her flirtations. Without effort his mind drifted to Delilah. He flicked his eyes to the front of the tavern and out the grease-covered window into the street. What was she doing now? Reading by the fire? Safely tucked into her bed, lost to a pleasant dream, no doubt. She belonged to the daylight. She was meant to be seen. His life was too crowded full with darkness and shadows. Still he wondered, did she think of him even one tenth of the times he thought of her?

Vane's tankard scraped against the scarred wooden tabletop and forced Sebastian's attention to the present. There was no doubt he already knew what Sebastian hesitated to share and only sought confirmation, or perhaps thought to encourage the opportunity for Sebastian to come to terms with it.

"I was one of those children. Lost to the street. Abandoned, barely five years old, and too young to defend myself."

Vane nodded, understanding in his eyes.

"It wasn't pleasant," Sebastian murmured, though it was loud enough for his friend to hear over the din in the tavern. "It made me a different person. I made choices I wouldn't have, had I a family or life away from the streets." He finished the ale in his glass. "Regardless, I'm the man I am today."

"Were you abused?"

It was an inoffensive question. The reply obvious. The depth of that answer hinged on how much Sebastian wished to reveal. "The emotional damage far exceeded the physical." He clenched his teeth. Having his arm broken in two places meant little when compared with the assault on his mind and heart.

"And so you wish to single-handedly dismantle London's reprehensible underworld trade, a perverse business more lucrative than smuggling imported India silks and French brandy."

"It didn't begin that way." Sebastian stood and tossed several coins on the table. "I only sought vengeance. But now I don't know what I want." The thought of revenge had forged him into a survivor. It had nurtured him when he was sick and emboldened him when he was scared, but he learned as he grew older that it would poison his soul if he didn't let it go.

He motioned toward the door and Vane joined him. "One thing holds true: I find it conducive to my well-being whenever I exorcise my anger and pummel the assorted miscreants who cross my path."

"Indeed." Vane chuckled. "I've found the same release quite therapeutic."

The next day Lord Hibbett appeared at the town house with fastidious punctuality. He carried a bouquet of assorted flowers in shades of pink, yellow, and white. His cordial smile and amiable nature were well received by Aunt Helen. Delilah greeted him warmly and they left with haste.

With Beth settled beside her, and Lord Hibbett's driver atop the boot, the open-air landau provided everyone a clear view of the outing and ensured propriety as well as a good amount of gossip fodder for onlookers.

"I thought it prudent to have a driver today. Aside from wanting to give you my full attention, a few popular locations are usually crowded with visitors and I wouldn't wish for you to miss out if I couldn't find an appropriate place for the carriage." He indicated the driver at the reins with a wave of his hand. "This eliminates that concern."

"How thoughtful." Delilah relaxed against the leather bench at her back. The landau was well made and immaculate. Lord Hibbett could only be deep in the pocket if such a luxurious vehicle and handsome team composed just one of his conveyances. "I'm looking forward to learning more about the city I now call home."

"Then you'll especially enjoy our first stop."

The carriage jerked as it maneuvered over a series of uneven cobbles. Lord Hibbett extended his gloved hand as if to reach for her and ensure she remained steady on the cushions, but his hand froze inches away from making contact. Indeed, the man was a true gentleman. Delilah wondered for a fleeting moment if she would have experienced the same frisson of energy that overtook her whenever Sebastian touched her, but she dismissed the fanciful thought and focused on the scenery. She would likely never see St. Allen again. That fact alone was enough to force the subject away. She turned and viewed Lord Hibbett beside her and they rode on in comfortable silence until she was compelled to dispel the silence.

"We couldn't have hoped for finer weather."

"London's fickle skies have turned sunny in your favor, Lady Ashbrook." He gave her a wide grin, his teeth straight and even. "Soon we'll approach Temple Church on the right. The original Round Church portion was consecrated in the year 1185."

"I've read of the history. It's fascinating." Delilah leaned closer and peered over the side of the landau in anticipation. "Is it true Shakespeare composed some of his works here?"

"The church is featured in *Henry VI*, so it very well may be fact. At the least, Shakespeare was inspired and I can understand why. I've passed by a few times when the organ is being played. The music sounds angelic."

"I imagine so." She glanced at Lord Hibbett and he nodded in answer. "It's lovely."

"We won't disembark at this location, but I've instructed my driver to slow the horses so you can have a long look at the church."

"Thank you." Awed by the magnificent marble columns and round domed construction, Delilah appreciated the historic landmark and hoped someday she might hear the organ play as Lord Hibbett described. She settled back against the bolster when she'd had her fill.

"Now that we've touched on history, we'll ride to Kensington Gardens and take in the Long Water of the Serpentine River. Does that please you?"

She nodded, her interest piqued. "Yes, very much so."

The ride to Hyde Park took some time but their conversation never failed, though it lacked any true depth. Delilah didn't mind, simply enjoying the carefree day spent out of doors. Lord Hibbett was pleasant company and he didn't pepper her with questions or try to force conversation for the sake of interruption.

Once arrived, they walked at a leisurely pace through the colorful gardens, their easy chatter exploring topics of all areas and subjects. Lord Hibbett seemed genuinely interested in her opinions and kindly tipped his hat to other couples who passed on the pathway. The sun had climbed high in the sky and it was decided soon after they would enjoy refreshment at Gunter's Tea Shop as an end to their perfectly proper afternoon.

Once on their way in the landau, though, Delilah's mind wandered far from the respectable and into the sinful. For no reason she could fathom other than a need to compare gentlemen, she imagined Sebastian as she'd last seen him, her face nestled in his strong hold, his mouth crushing down on hers and hot, seeking tongue as it slid between her lips again and again, each time deeper, more insistent.

"And we've arrived."

Lord Hibbett startled her. His expectant expression caused her to feel more the despicable guest by way of her wandering recollections.

Gunter's Tea Shop in Berkeley Square was busy with patrons of all ages anxious for a taste of their famous flavored ice on this seasonable day. The driver led the team to a shady area across the thoroughfare, where he secured the reins, opened the door, and extended the steps. Lord Hibbett exited the interior first and offered his hand. Delilah took hold and noted she experienced none of the sensations she'd wondered about.

She was anxious for the promised refreshment and she smiled at Lord Hibbett, took his elbow and ventured across the street into one of the ton's favorite gathering places. Customers milled about in front of the tea shop with their flavored ices, while other couples and clusters of friends sat inside enjoying the sweet treat. She wondered idly at the perception of the onlookers. How socially acceptable it was for her to be here with Lord Hibbett. Would she be equally as accepted if she'd arrived with St. Allen? His cool, enigmatic stare could easily belong among the chilled desserts, but his arresting good looks and hot, fiery kisses would leave nothing but melted ice in their wake. Truly she was a despicable person to be on the arm of one gentleman and preoccupied with thoughts of another. She forced herself to attend the conversation with Lord Hibbett as they enjoyed their refreshment.

But much later, after Lord Hibbett returned her home and escorted her to the door, when Delilah was finished bathing and dressed in her night rail, readied for bed, she allowed herself the freedom to reflect on the day without censure.

Lord Hibbett had mindfully planned a day to please her, but despite her best effort, remembrances of Sebastian and his wickedly wonderful kisses eclipsed the outing. Frustrated, she fell back against the bed pillows and closed her eyes tightly, as anxious as earlier, with thoughts of Sebastian, and no better for it.

CHAPTER 18

The dull scrape of wood against wood and the distinct rustle of heavy fabric roused Delilah from sleep. Did someone call her name? A rich, velvety voice, powerful enough to evoke sensation, begged her to awaken while a prickle of energy coursed over her skin. The hour was late. Reluctant to release the lazy vestiges of slumber, she urged her lids to stay closed as the room fell silent again. Surely, she dreamed.

That sound.

His voice.

Sebastian.

She calmed by degree until an unbidden skitter of awareness stole over her despite the fine linen sheet and counterpane draped across the bed. With a strict mental reprimand, she forced her mind to dismiss concern and ignore distraction. She needed sleep. Intent on this goal, she drew a deep breath and her pulse spiked immediately. Spicy notes of Sebastian's cologne water permeated her consciousness. No matter she clung to the drowsiness of her dreams, her body quickened, her breath caught, and she opened her eyes. She sat up quickly and grasped the covers against her breasts.

It took only a blink for her vision to adjust. He stood near the foot of the bed, one with the shadows save the waning flames in the hearth that limned his wide shoulders and commanding height in an ethereal glow. She would have believed her imagination at work. He'd originated out of nowhere. How could he be here in her second-story bedchamber? Except an insistent throb of awareness, *desire*, swirled in her abdomen and lower, between her legs, to assert she was wide-awake and he no invisible illusion.

"You're here." Her voice sounded breathy, as if she'd run a long distance to reach him.

He nodded, the sheen of firelight offering her a quick glimpse of his handsome profile.

"How?" She lowered the sheets from where she'd gathered them. "I don't understand. I didn't put the lantern on the sill."

She sensed more than saw his mouth twitch and suddenly she wanted nothing more than to be in his arms. With an exhilarating flare of daring spirit, she flung her legs over the side of the mattress, straightened her night rail, and stepped closer to him.

"I needed to come here."

"Oh!" A pulse of excitement went through her. "Do you have news? Did you find the men who took Oliver?"

"No." He let out a long exhale. "And you shouldn't think about them or let it trouble you."

"But it does. What's happening on the streets of London, what happened to Oliver, isn't to be ignored."

"No, of course not. It just shouldn't be your concern."

Delilah didn't know how to respond to that. As much as she appreciated Sebastian's desire to shelter her from life's ugly truths, she was never one to sit idly and not act. He meant to protect her, but his actions also excluded her.

"You had a caller this afternoon."

His tone held an edge of emotion she couldn't label. How did he know of Lord Hibbett's visit?

"You still have someone watching the house?" Incredulity laced her question.

"Of course, I do." He cleared his throat and his posture shifted slightly. "For your safety."

* * *

For my sanity. Sebastian blew out a slow breath and willed his heart to stop hammering. Delilah appeared like a midnight vision, her skin warm and rosy from her bedcovers, her hair unbound around her shoulders. He wanted nothing more than to reach for her, kiss her, claim her. But he couldn't act on these impulses. He'd only wanted to see her. That was, until he'd called her name, hoping to awaken her.

"Well, I'm safely tucked into bed. No one can get me here. But it's very kind of you to check on me. I appreciate it."

She shouldn't say things like that. Things that made him think thoughts best left outside a lady's bedchambers. Thoughts that made him believe she might feel an affinity with him. This was madness. He'd climbed into a second-story window of a quality town house. What was he doing? Since when was he driven by need and not purpose? He'd abandoned all the rules he'd made for himself. Visiting the wharf had unearthed buried memories, and now he sought comfort. Nothing else. And it was Vane's fault too for churning up ugly emotions from the past.

"I wanted to ensure you were safe." He would never have believed that explanation, were someone to have told him the same.

"Yes. You mentioned that, and I am. Aren't I?" She canted her head with the curious question, her slender brows arched high.

"You are." *At least from outside forces. The biggest threat to you this evening stands before you in your bedchamber.*

"I didn't know if I would see you again."

"I'm here now." He couldn't stay away tonight, no matter how many times he'd told himself it was a poor idea.

"I still have so many questions."

"What do you wish to know?"

"I'm not sure at the moment." She moved to the foot of her bed and grasped one of the ornate posts, her slim fingers wrapped around the wooden column tightly. Did she wish to hang on for support or did she also fight her will?

A rush of misplaced possession surged through his veins. He clenched his fists at his sides. She wore a simple night rail. Demure in its simplicity, and yet his cock hardened as if she were dressed in provocative silks, his insistent arousal a damnable nuisance since he'd put his boot in the trellis outside her window and hoisted himself onto the balcony. Her delicate perfume hung in the air to further entice him. He needed one kiss. And then he would leave.

Maybe.

"Do you trust me, Delilah?" His voice lowered to a husky tone and he waited for her answer.

"I—" She acted as if she didn't know what to say. "Yes. I trust you." She released the post and moved before him.

She longed for him as much as he longed for her. At least, he wanted to believe it. He didn't wait for her to change her mind, and gently tugged her forward. He brought his mouth to hers with unerring accuracy, the kiss meant to be gentle though it left no doubt he'd waited too long to claim her lips.

She was everything he'd remembered. Warm, soft, willing, fragrant, and perfectly formed. He skimmed his hands from her shoulders to her waist, his thumbs brushing over the sides of her full breasts. She shivered against his touch. His cock twitched with impatience. She didn't stop him, the silky fabric of her night-clothes no barrier to every delicious curve beneath. He explored the hollow of her mouth with his tongue as if in search of secrets, anxious to quell any objection and at the same time, eager to collect her soft moans and heady whimpers. She participated with enthusiasm, her tongue twined with his, the erotic rub and slide a mimicry of what his body craved. With desire on a short leash, he resisted the urge to rock his hips against hers.

Instead, because he had to move in some way, he walked her backward to rest gently against the bedpost before he reversed their positions. Then he widened his stance and brought her between his knees, her hips encased by his legs, her body nearly flush with his. She placed her hands on his shoulders and squeezed. Again, he wondered if she solidified her balance or meant encouragement.

Unwilling to take what she didn't offer, he broke the kiss and waited, though it pained him to do so.

Her breath brushed against his jaw in teasing invitation.

"You kiss very well."

The words weren't what he'd expected and he managed a slight grin. She amused him.

"A lady as lovely as yourself must have experienced several kisses by comparison." It was a devious ploy to discover what he truly wished to know.

"Well, no." She hesitated. "Not exactly."

This information pleased him and he held her tighter. "Do you still trust me, Delilah?" He'd asked her before and her answer seemed unsure.

"Yes." She nodded her head in the affirmative to confirm he believed her.

"Let me show you pleasure tonight." He wanted to devour her. Kiss her senseless and taste every inch of her body. Claim her. Make her his. But he couldn't do any of those things. Not now at least.

"You have. I like your kisses." She stroked her fingers across his cheek and down along his jaw until one fingertip traced over his lips.

His cock grew harder still. He wouldn't have believed it possible.

"Come to the bed." He loosened his hold and stepped back so she could move more easily. "I want to give you something to remember me by."

Her expression went through a series of emotions, dimly lit by the firelight, but she didn't speak and moved to the mattress, where she sat obediently on the edge.

"Are you nervous?"

"No." She raised her eyes to his, dark aside from the dancing light of the flames.

Several beats of silence stretched between them, their mingled breaths heated with anticipation.

"Lie down." He captured her mouth for another long, lingering kiss and lowered her to the sheets, his hands guiding her as she moved backward. "You're so beautiful, Delilah. Let me touch you, inside and out."

She watched him closely and he wondered if she understood how he meant to bring her pleasure from his first caress to the gratifying pinnacle of her climax. He ignored his own satisfaction because as much as he yearned to bury himself inside her soft heat, he would never disrespect her. He cared too much to act selfishly and take what could never belong to him.

Delilah lay still on the bedsheets, her mind racing almost as fast as her heartbeat. Sebastian had sprung to life from her dreams. It was the only explanation that made sense, though it seemed too fanciful to be true. Yet, even though her pulse thrummed and she struggled to make sense of his appearance, she couldn't regret he stood in her bedchamber. A thrilling, scandalously wonderful tremor wracked through her. If trousers offered freedom, then this, *this choice to indulge in pleasure*, represented the ultimate act of liberation. The freedom to choose who she shared her body with, when and how it was done. Every action empowered her to understand her newfound strength on another level.

She wanted to touch him everywhere, stroke over his hard muscles and explore the ridges of his perfectly formed physique. The gruff whiskers at his chin abraded her face when they'd kissed and she relished the sensation of the sensitive burn, wanting more, needing more.

The mattress dipped with his weight and she slit her eyes to take in his shadowy form, one knee bent as he leaned over her and captured her mouth in another heated kiss. What did he intend? She knew undoubtedly he would never hurt or harm her. Her body quivered with anticipation and wild curiosity. He settled on his side next to her, his gaze fixed to her face as his fingers smoothed over her outline and memorized her figure.

"You're so very lovely. I could spend all night looking at you, learning the way your skin feels and tastes, finding the sensitive places that bring you pleasure."

"I could do the same, Sebastian."

He smiled slightly, seemingly pleased with her honesty before he traced the ends of the ribbon holding her bodice closed. He slowly tugged the bow loose. Her night dress fell open to reveal her bare skin, and the cool air combined with his heated touch caused a shot of sensation so strong she gasped. He eased away her trembling with another long kiss, his hands settling on her shoulders, then lower, taking the thin cotton night rail with them to expose her breasts.

He murmured something and she strained to hear, but her pulse pounded too loudly in her ears. Every type of restlessness, anxious satisfaction, unanswered yearning, and painful insistence bombarded her simultaneously. She shifted on the mattress, her legs agitated, and a deep, burning desire to feel more, experience more, urged her to do something. She reached up and grasped his shirt, wrapping her fingers in the linen to anchor herself to him.

He nuzzled a path from her neck to her shoulder, his heat and weight against her side a pleasurable accompaniment. Everywhere he touched her she tingled. She had no idea what tomorrow would bring, but she wanted this, now, tonight. It was as though she was cast into a dream and she didn't dare question it too much for fear it would evaporate.

The first touch of his tongue to her breast caused the conflict inside her to intensify. Impatient with lying still, she threaded her fingers through his thick hair, holding him to her heart, his tongue hot against her, stroking over the tips of her breasts and causing an undulating tremble through her entire body. This was insanity. To awaken in the night and find St. Allen in her room. To allow him in her bed. Invite him to touch and taste her as he wished. She'd never felt so alive and acutely aware. She exhilarated in it, this feeling of absolute power. It was dangerous and at the same time indescribably fulfilling.

As if perceiving her inner thoughts, he pulled away, his eyes darkened by shadows and not their usual cool blue.

"Are you all right?"

His voice was gruff, his hair disheveled from where she'd threaded her fingers and clutched him to her chest.

"Yes. Please. Continue."

He couldn't stop. Not now. Not when it seemed as though every cell in her body had awakened with his touch. She'd not done so much as touch another man's bare hand before Sebastian. But now, now she found she wanted to know every heady pleasure he promised. She wanted to master all the wicked knowledge he had to share. No matter it was daring, she welcomed the opportunity.

He stroked over her cheekbone, his fingertip tracing a line down her jaw and chin. Then he shifted on the bed and placed his palm on her thigh, the fabric of her night rail useless against the heat and pressure.

They didn't speak as he gathered the hem and bared her skin to the chilly air. She couldn't manage more than appreciative sighs and whispers anyway, so she bit into her lip to keep quiet. Everywhere he touched her shimmered with sensitivity. He trailed tender caresses over her calves and behind her knees, drawing little circles to stir a maelstrom of feeling into a whirlwind low in her belly, deeper, as if he touched her from the inside out.

He skimmed his palm up her thigh, his thumb paused at the seam of her legs. She clenched her muscles in reaction.

"Softer than the finest silk. More precious and pure." He exhaled and the heat whisked across her skin. "Let me show you pleasure, Delilah. Let me touch you."

"Yes, Sebastian. I want this."

She heard his growl of approval and she parted her thighs slightly, her night rail gathered over her belly. Her pulse raced in anticipation as her body grew impatient. She wriggled her hips in answer.

His heated breath teased her inner thigh and she startled, in wait of the touch of his fingers, unprepared for the divine pleasure of his kiss. The first stroke of his tongue against her sex sent a shock of sensitivity through her so sharp she believed an arrow pierced her heart. She couldn't breathe for a moment, caught in a timeless moment of carnal bliss.

And then it came again. And again. Each pass of his tongue over her flesh evoked unbearable yet exquisite pleasure. She trembled from the force, rejoiced from the divine ecstasy. This. *This.* This was madness. Glorious madness.

And just when she managed that startling realization, he pressed deeper, his tongue stroking over her core, tight and tense, until she lost hold on everything but sensation, her climax too much to bear.

CHAPTER 19

Sebastian watched with satisfaction as Delilah reclaimed her normal breathing. She'd lost herself. Fallen apart and become undone. He marveled in the beauty she'd displayed during the throes of pleasure he'd offered. She'd shown her innate poise as a proper lady and her bravery and strength in the face of adversity, but in this she was truly magnificent. She'd given him trust and bared her vulnerability, and she'd never appeared more beautiful.

"I . . ."

Her lids fluttered open and she made quick work of adjusting her gown and the sheets around her.

"Yes?" He wondered at what she would say.

"I didn't know I could feel that way."

Her honest confession struck him unaware. For no apparent reason, the middle of his chest hurt and he only kept from rubbing away the ache by busying his hands with the bed linens. She seemed compelled to talk despite he'd remained silent.

"It was wonderful and powerful. I never felt so weak and yet so strong . . ." She picked at a loose thread on the coverlet. "What time is it anyway?"

She scanned the area over his shoulder where he sat on the edge of her mattress. He still carried her scent and that singular fact aroused him further.

"Late enough so I should be leaving." He stood as he spoke, not wishing for her to ask something he couldn't answer, although one question remained that had prompted his visit in the first place. Granted, he looked for any excuse to see her again. "Who was the dandy who escorted you about town today?"

"Lord Hibbett?"

When he didn't respond, she elaborated. He found most people interpreted silence as a need to supply details.

"He's a fine gentleman. Quite kind, actually. Polite. Most polite." She paused as if choosing her words with care. "We had a nice afternoon."

"Nice?" He leaned down and tilted her chin upward, leaving her no choice but to abandon her torment of the threads on the counterpane and match his eyes. "And this evening?"

He ran the pad of his thumb over her lower lip, kiss swollen and tempting. "Was this evening just as nice?" He tensed, unsure why he'd asked the question. Unwilling to acknowledge how much her answer mattered. How much he needed to claim her in some way.

"Not at all."

He released her chin and exhaled deeply. Glancing to the window, he readied for escape.

"Tonight was incomparable, Sebastian. It still is." She rose up on her knees, spoiling all the care he'd taken to tuck the blanket around her legs properly. "Now kiss me goodbye and vanish into the night so I can return to sleep and continue this precious dream."

This time he didn't wait for her to elaborate. Dipping his head, he captured her mouth. Then did as he was told and became one with the darkness.

Peculiar, how a good night's sleep could change one's perspective. Delilah awoke with more than a pleasant remembrance of her intimate interlude with Sebastian. Of course, she remembered each wicked kiss and indelible touch with remarkable intricacy, but that wasn't why she awoke with emboldened resolve. Plans, ideas, and questions that needed to be answered bombarded her. She couldn't wait to begin the day and walked into the breakfast room with her effervescent mood.

"It's almost your birthday, Mama." Oliver was seated at the table, his chubby cheeks sticky with fig preserves, the white damask tablecloth in front of him littered with crumbs.

"Never mind about that." Beth did her best to encourage her son to eat over his plate, but it seemed a battle she couldn't win.

"What do you mean, never mind?" Delilah joined them at the table. "Where's Aunt Helen?"

"She went into the kitchen to speak to Mrs. Dunn." Beth picked up her napkin and began to clean Oliver's face. "She hardly allows me to complete a task since I've arrived."

"Oh, I wouldn't give it too much worry. You walk the fine line of being my maid but also my dearest friend. You're more like family. When we first arrived, Oliver's disappearance claimed our immediate attention. I'm just relieved everything resolved peacefully." She cast a glance to Oliver, who was busy licking his fingers despite his mother scrubbed at his cheeks. "I think a celebration in your honor is exactly the right antidote to erase the dreadful memories we met upon arriving in London."

Without effort her mind conjured images of St. Allen. Her collection of memories was vivid and interesting, all different and intriguing. His dark, threatening presence in Seven Dials, his bookish and rugged handsomeness at the Last Page Bookstore, his polished appearance at Mumford's social, and last night, when he materialized like a wicked vision from her dreams. Were there more to come?

How silly that she'd checked behind the draperies and upon the window ledge this morning as if he was perched there waiting for her.

"Delilah? Delilah?"

Delilah shook her head briskly and poured a cup of tea from the pot in front of her. "I'm sorry. My mind wandered for a moment. What was it you were saying?"

Oliver found her befuddlement amusing and his laughter prompted her to smile as well.

"Cook and I have decided on a cake. Now I'll only need one last thing. Will you help me, Delilah?"

Considering what Oliver had experienced and the guilt she still carried, Delilah couldn't deny the child anything, but it was more so his precious wish to please his mother that had her agreeing before she knew the circumstances of the situation. "Of course." She reached across the table and squeezed his sticky fingers. "I'd be happy to assist in any way needed."

Aunt Helen returned and the conversation advanced to social news and upcoming events. When at last they'd finished breaking their fast, Beth rose to help clear the table, even though Mrs. Dunn objected. Oliver darted off to the kitchens behind the two of them.

"How was your outing with Lord Hibbett? Did he give you any indication he plans to call again?" Aunt Helen dabbed at her mouth with a linen napkin.

"He was very kind and thoughtful. We visited some wonderful sights around the city and ended our visit with a trip to Berkeley Square for flavored ice."

"How lovely." Her aunt's approving grin widened. "I've taken the liberty of asking my friends for their insight. I only want the best for you, dear, and we can't make a misstep."

"A misstep?" Delilah didn't like the idea of her aunt posing questions on her behalf, most especially when she harbored no feelings for Lord Hibbett. He was a pleasant gentleman and she appreciated his consideration, but that was all she could muster regarding emotion. She hardly knew him. Sebastian, on the other hand, had drawn her in with nothing more than his piercing blue-eyed attention and confident charm.

"Delilah, dearest, are you listening?"

"Yes." She blinked rapidly to refocus on the conversation.

"Shall we invite Lord Hibbett to dinner sometime soon? I

understand he has impressive connections and is well respected by the ton."

"Oh, no." Realizing her objection sounded too assertive, Delilah softened her tone. "It's too early for such a personal gesture. After only one meeting—"

"You did speak to him at Lord Mumford's," Aunt Helen corrected.

"True, but we shared only one dance and while our afternoon was delightful, I have no idea when he'll call on me again."

"We'll give it a bit of time then."

Disliking her aunt's liberal use of the word *we'll*, Delilah nodded in the negative and her words confirmed her feelings. "Indeed, some time is necessary."

This seemed to mollify Aunt Helen, who busied herself with fetching a copy of Debrett's Registry of Peerage from the writing desk in the drawing room, apparently intent on researching Lord Hibbett's lineage.

"Are you in such a hurry to marry me off then?" Perhaps a little levity would lighten the morning mood. Delilah wished Oliver would scamper back into the breakfast room. Any type of distraction would be welcomed.

"Of course not." Aunt Helen took her chair again and settled the registry on her lap. "I wish to take advantage of opportunity. Nothing more."

Aunt Helen dedicated herself to the pages in front of her and Delilah interpreted that as a sign their conversation had ended. Excusing herself, she walked to the front hall where Oliver sat on the bottom stair, his face and hands clean now and his shirt replaced.

"What has you looking so down in the mouth?" Delilah settled beside him.

"Mrs. Dunn scolded me." Oliver's unabashed affront was endearing.

"Did you try to sneak sweets from the pantry again?" Delilah attempted a stern yet understanding tone.

"No." Oliver exhaled wearily as if he carried the weight of the world on his narrow shoulders. "She saw me enter the garden. She said I'm not allowed to pick any of the flowers there, but I wasn't going to take them. She scolded me and startled me straight into the hiccups."

"I see." Delilah bit the inside of her cheek so she wouldn't betray her solemn empathy.

"I sat here to rest and now, finally, my hiccups have gone away."

"Sometimes the littlest things can be such a bother." She smoothed her palm over Oliver's back in comfort.

"I suppose, but Mama's birthday is almost here and I want to give her flowers with my gift. The garden in the back of the house has lovely flowers, but Mrs. Dunn won't let me even look at them."

"I suppose Mrs. Dunn worried you might step on the plants or pull the flowers out too roughly. She didn't mean to upset you, I'm certain."

"Maybe. All I wanted to do was look."

"Why don't we take a little walk, just you and I, to Redman Square. There's a lovely public garden there and you can choose a whole bouquet to go along with the gift you have for your mother. I'm sorry our earlier outing didn't turn out the way we'd hoped. I'm only thankful you're returned to us unharmed." She slid her arm around his shoulders and hugged him tightly to her side. She was ready to move forward and refused to allow her inhibitions to rob her of further experiences with Oliver. Lately life had an auspicious way of reminding her time was precious. "I'm certain the gift you made for your mother is more special than any trinket we might have purchased at the shops on Jermyn Street. She will adore it most of all because it comes from your heart."

"Oh, I know Mama will love my gift." Oliver wiggled from her grasp and nodded with enthusiasm.

"Perfect, then." Delilah stood and smoothed her skirts with her palms. "Let's plan to take our walk on Friday morning. The flowers will be fresh and ready for your mother's birthday celebration later that day."

"Thank you, Delilah."

"It's the very least I can do, Oliver."

Delilah knocked on the door of the Wycombe building and waited in hope someone would answer promptly. She'd slipped out without her aunt's notice and left her maid behind. This conversation was meant to be had with the utmost privacy.

Julia answered the door with a smile and Delilah was reminded of the first time she'd visited and how welcoming the three ladies had been. She followed Julia up the stairs into the modest drawing room and began a conversation she'd itched to have for some time already.

"What else can you tell me about your remarkable group?" Delilah settled back in her chair, prepared to listen although her decision was already made.

"The four of us, including Scarlett, who's since left, came together by chance and opportunity," Julia began. "As a young widow with few family relations, I quickly learned females have little power or recourse. All control rests with men. As you're aware, as part of polite society, ladies are prepared for marriage and encouraged to live an ornamental existence. It's rather insulting and I've always believed I'm meant to do more."

"I agree." Delilah's opinion of Julia rose another notch. "All that wasted intelligence, ingenuity, and resourcefulness women are never allowed to share."

"Not to mention myriad other qualities females are instructed to hide or they'll be perceived as unbecoming or undesirable."

"How very true." Delilah said.

"Phoebe and Diana had their own reasons to join the effort, yet we all have a common belief: Women should be safe, treated as equals, and have parallel advantages in business, science, or other masculine pursuits. But beyond these values, we also want to help, whether it be children, women, or even the occasional gentleman. We don't expect anything in return, not even a mention or moment of glory."

"What you and the other ladies do is extraordinary."

"Thank you, but honestly we're following a calling from our hearts. We've found meaningful purpose in this group. We came together and formed the Maidens of Mayhem to assist where we can, educating some, saving others. It's completely voluntary. And as I already mentioned, Scarlett left us recently." Julia's expression turned expectant.

"The Maidens of Mayhem?"

"Yes, we fancy the name because we believe we bring a new perspective, a *female* perspective, to fighting crime and righting wrongs. We might stir up a bit of chaos in the process, but we always work toward establishing equity and justice."

"I find everything about your remarkable group intriguing." Delilah smiled. "Invigorating, more than I imagined. I have so many ideas to improve the orphan situation in Greater London, and not just at the Foundling Hospital. But the boys and girls at the Lost Yard too, and all the others who hide in alleyways and down near the riverbanks."

"You could contribute to established charities." Julia canted her head in wait of Delilah's response. "Many ladies of the aristocracy support noble causes."

"I have something much grander in mind."

"So why are you here, Delilah? Are you asking for our help?"

"No." Delilah stood as she answered, her voice strong. "I'd like to become a Maiden of Mayhem. Will you have me?"

"This isn't a decision to be taken lightly. You may be called on to challenge your fears and be strong in the face of danger." Julia's expression grew serious.

"I've discovered I act when there is peril, I don't run." And it was true. She'd been tested with Oliver's abduction and then when she'd spotted Sebastian in the Lost Yard. Her heart might thrum in her chest, but she embraced danger.

"If this is what you want, and you understand the commitment, we'd love to have you." Julia rose and embraced Delilah in a tight hug. "I can't wait to share this news with Phoebe and Diana. They will be just as delighted as I am."

Sebastian followed the dimly lit tunnel beneath London proper on his way to the King's Elbow. He'd received a message from Eva requesting he meet her there at half ten. No reason or indication was given, though no one who vowed loyalty to the Crown was foolish enough to put important details in ink.

He hadn't slept, restless and agitated after he'd left Delilah's bedchambers, and he didn't like the cause. He wanted something he'd never wanted before. A relationship. Permanency. Some kind of commitment he didn't know how to make. How to live.

So he'd forced his mind to whittle away at the scarce clues he possessed concerning the abductors. Something he might have overlooked, too distracted by Delilah's moonlight hair and rosebud lips. He'd found his way to the offices at daybreak and Eva's note arrived soon after.

He took the stairs and entered the tavern, the establishment closed to business this early in the day. Eva could have simply come to the offices. He wondered why she needed him to visit the tavern, but then he didn't waste any time on the consideration. Eva always possessed an underlying agenda.

"You're here."

"You asked me to meet you."

"I need a favor."

It was the type of exchange they'd had before. Members of their vocation didn't explain why their help was needed. They simply listened and completed the task. But Eva played games at times and he hoped this wasn't one of them.

"What's happened?"

"Somehow our problems have become further intertwined." She crossed her fingers and held them up as if he needed the visual. Either that or she was set on flirtation again. "It's Her Grace."

"The duchess and her dog. Another crisis of aristocratic breeding." He paused with less than three strides between them. "What do you need me to do?"

"Approach Yardley."

"About the stud?"

"About the jewels." Eva closed the distance. "Meet him tonight. Happen upon the earl in the darkness as he leaves his club. Become a buyer or a fencer. Someone who knows he has the diamonds but is also aware he's uncomfortable with possession. Offer to sell them because their value is worth more than he can imagine."

"To what end?"

"At first the duchess disregarded the loss of her jewels, eclipsed by emotion and overwrought with Cygnet's disappearance, but since then her pet has been returned, relatively unharmed. Someone left the dog in a box in the mews—"

"Unharmed?" Sebastian grinned. "I suspect the dog had a good time of it, actually."

"We could have a good time." Eva slanted a look at him that suggested more than her bold offer. "Better than good."

"Eva." He took a step back, shaking his head to be clear he wanted no part of a personal relationship. "Let's keep to the information update."

She didn't say anything at first, but then with a swift jerk of her chin she met his eyes and continued describing Her Grace's concerns.

"The duchess doesn't wish to involve the authorities. She has her own men working on it discreetly, but now that we've become involved there's no reason why we shouldn't give Yardley what he deserves. A lover scorned and set on revenge deserves a future ruined. If you pose as a fencer and recover the jewels, everyone walks away with what they want." She glanced away and back again. Her voice dropped to a disgruntled murmur. "Well, almost everyone."

"Since Oliver's return I haven't had the opportunity to pursue the matter further. Are you certain Yardley is behind the theft?"

"The duchess is. She'd rebuffed him repeatedly both in the bedroom and on Cygnet's behalf. Her Pomeranian was returned without his gemstone collar and she views it as Yardley's petty vengeance. Like I said, it's a love triangle."

"With a dog." His droll tone conveyed annoyance.

"Love is powerful and sometimes has a peculiar way of clouding one's judgment."

Sebastian was wise enough not to remark on Eva's comment, yet he wondered at the word, *love*. For so many years he focused solely on survival. A decade followed where he woke each morning with the singular goal of revenge. But when he'd burned that tenement down to the ground last year, he vowed to let it all go or he'd become so bitter he couldn't look at himself in the mirror.

With that all behind him, he'd never considered what his future held. Was it love? He'd happened upon Delilah and his perspective on things had shifted considerably. It was unexpected and yet he wasn't disappointed.

"So, will you help?"

Eva stared at him with such intense focus it was as though she could read his every thought.

"I'll let you know what I learn after I cross paths with Yardley."

"Thank you."

With nothing left to say, he turned and left.

CHAPTER 20

White's was crowded, and that pleased Sebastian as he approached the exclusive St. James's Street address. Carriages and drivers jockeyed for position at the curb, and the pavement streamed with gentlemen on their way in and out.

This was a world he didn't belong to, unless, like this evening, he initiated subterfuge. Dressed in a finely tailored black kerseymere tailcoat and well-shined hessians, he fixed an arrogant expression on his face and joined the back of a vociferous group of gentlemen already on their way through the door.

Some nights it was that simple. As easy as the life of an aristocrat. Until now he'd hardly considered the vast divide between the classes with any true interest, but meeting Delilah had caused him to contemplate facets of his life that seemed otherwise irrelevant until this point. He shook his head and dismissed his conflicted thoughts as he separated from the rabble-rousers who enabled his entry.

With a sweeping glance, Sebastian noted who'd imbibed too much, who engaged in a heated debate, and who sat in the infamous bow window, before he slid into the shadows. White's provided the ideal place to confront Yardley. The earl would want to avoid undue attention. The other men intent on gambling and other raffish preoccupations would provide Sebastian with the discretion and distraction he needed.

He waited and nearly an hour passed until the earl showed. The greetings the man garnered as he moved through the crowd was all the confirmation Sebastian needed. He followed Yardley to a dimly lit corner near the rear, where the earl met with a younger man, a privileged dasher by his appearance, and someone unfamiliar to Sebastian. He needed to find out the identity of the man and his connection to Yardley. Was he someone connected to the theft, or an exclusive fencer at the ready to sell off the goods? Aristocrats were wily when it came to their subterfuge.

Nabbing a brandy from a passing tray, Sebastian strode toward the men, angling his body so his shoulder connected with the young stranger.

"You there, watch where you're walking." The dandy appeared affronted, his face screwed into an expression of annoyance while the earl merely raised his eyebrows at the interaction.

"Excuse me, Harper, I didn't see you there. It was entirely my fault."

"Harper? You're mistaken." The young man brushed at his sleeves in an apparent effort to assuage his bruised attire.

"Come now, Harper. I meant no harm." Sebastian smiled, adding a short chuckle as if sharing a joke with the gentleman. And then, as expected, Yardley supplied the information Sebastian needed.

"This isn't Harper," Yardley insisted with exasperation. "This is Viscount Clayton, the nephew of the Duchess of Grandon, and you'd do well to apologize and be on your way."

Peers with their airs. It was all Sebastian could do not to let loose his opinions, but he'd achieved his objective, and insulting the cocky prigs here in White's would only complicate matters. He'd wait outside and confront Clayton in a more individual discussion.

"Indeed, this is my error." Sebastian raised his glass in a subtle gesture as he stepped away. "Excuse me, gentlemen. Enjoy your evening."

Delilah stared out her bedchamber window. The hour was late and the street below quiet. A bemused smile curled her lips as she recalled Sebastian's arrival through the very same window. The man was a perpetual surprise. She wouldn't mind a midnight visit again tonight. She'd leave the latch open just in case.

Aunt Helen believed in propriety above all else. She viewed life through her own modest upbringing, and while Delilah valued her virtue and would never compromise her future, she enjoyed the pleasure she'd experienced with Sebastian. Was it wrong? Perhaps. If viewed in a certain light. Was it wonderful? Most definitely. She wouldn't be ashamed of her feelings or her body's desire. All too often men had a claim on aspects of life and living that women were expected to pretend were nonexistent. She just couldn't accept that.

But Sebastian was a riddle she couldn't decipher. There was so much she didn't know about the man. And this intrigued her more than she cared to admit. No other gentleman, not Lord Hibbett or any other who desired her attention, made her heart stutter like Sebastian did. He caused her to think all kinds of things. Things one didn't speak of openly. Things left well to the late-night hours. It could only be a case of wanting what she couldn't have, like a child who wants dessert instead of dinner. Not knowing when she would see him again or how he viewed their intimacy complicated the matter further.

Sebastian seemed to understand her in some ways, but not others. He would never approve of her decision to join the Maidens of Mayhem, and yet she was never surer of her decision. No doubt he was out in the night right now, pursuing justice and proving her point. She doubted he would admire her initiative when he'd insinuated she should stay home like a precious collectible.

And really, why did it matter? Sebastian could never be more

than an acquaintance. Any romantic illusions were better abandoned before they instigated disappointment. She was born into
the gentry. The expectation she'd marry a refined gentleman existed before she'd drawn her first breath. The contrary positions of
her wants and reality weren't easy bedtime consideration.

Retying the ribbons of her night rail to waylay her frustration,
she raised her eyes to the sky. There wasn't a star to be seen amidst
the gloomy cloud cover. Lowering her gaze, she saw movement
on the lawn, but when she stared into the darkness she dismissed
it as a trick of reflected candlelight and shadow. She backed away
from the sill with a sigh. It was time for sleep. Oliver was safely
tucked into his bed. That's what mattered most.

Blowing out her bedside candle, she climbed between the
sheets, anxious for the cool linen to soothe her distemper as questions continued to buffet her. But a true sense of calm proved elusive even when her body began a slow surrender. Caught in the
ethereal whisper before sleep claimed consciousness, she wavered.

A heartbeat later, the scrape of wood against wood reasserted
acute awareness. Someone had raised her windowpane. The room
was drenched in darkness, but the sudden tension in the air and
her accelerated pulse warned she hadn't imagined the sound. Motionless, she waited. Would Sebastian speak before he approached
her bed, or would she need to light the candle to complete her
idyllic fantasy? She trembled and pressed her lips together, stifling
a smile even though the room remained blacker than soot.

A looming figure rounded the corner post of her bed. She
couldn't discern more than the shift of movement, but amusement
soon fell away. Something was wrong. Sebastian wouldn't lurk in
her chambers and frighten her.

Summoning clear thinking, she sat up and quietly moved to the
corner of the mattress away from the wall, unwilling to trap herself in an indefensible position. If need be, she could push away
the counterpane and run straight toward her bedchamber door.
But before she could form another thought, a hand shot out and

grasped her arm, hauling her through the bed linens, where she stumbled to gain footing. She was yanked to standing and shoved to the windowsill, the narrow casement cutting into the back of her thighs.

"Wipe the sleep from your eyes and fetch me the diamonds. That way no one gets hurt."

She couldn't see who held her, but his menacing command guaranteed he meant harm. "I don't know what you're talking about."

He tightened his hold, the unforgiving bite of his fingers through her sleeve stinging her skin. "Don't waste my time—"

"Delilah?" Aunt Helen's voice rang through the door, followed by an assertive knock. "Are you all right? I thought I heard a noise."

Delilah swallowed, unsure how to warn Aunt Helen and simultaneously keep her aunt in the hallway, away from the menacing intruder who held her captive.

"Tell her you're fine and send her away." His vehement tone near her ear caused her pulse to race harder.

She summoned another breath, her mind clamoring for an effective response.

"Do it." The vile stranger pushed her harder against the sill and pain shot up her legs. "I wouldn't want you to take a tumble through the window."

"I . . . I'm fine." She managed to sound reasonable. Perhaps Aunt Helen would think she'd just awoken and remained groggy from sleep. "Please go back to bed."

"Are you sure, dear?"

"One wrong word and the old lady suffers a terrible accident. I'll make sure she never sees another sunrise."

Panic rushed through Delilah, swift and sharp. "Yes, I'm fine. Please leave me." She'd failed at delivering any meaningful message but at least she'd kept Aunt Helen safe for the moment.

Another hard beat and the hallway grew silent. Inside her chamber the darkness became suffocating. Still situated in a painful position near the sill with her arms twisted at an irregular angle against her back, Delilah had no recourse, no ability to reverse the situation and retaliate.

"The next time we meet I expect the diamonds. Otherwise I'll send grandma to a permanent sleep."

The intruder shoved her to the floor before he exited out the same way he'd come. Delilah scrambled to the bedside table and lit the lantern. Rushing to the window she saw nothing outside, the man as fleeting as a ghost. She never despised the pair of trees and wrought-iron balcony outside her window as much as this evening. It offered anyone a path into the house, and while she'd only just mused how much she'd enjoyed Sebastian's visit, tonight she'd learned a much different lesson.

But what diamonds? She drew another shaky breath and pulled on her robe. She couldn't take any chances with Aunt Helen's safety. With anyone's well-being. They'd only just recovered Oliver.

Unable to sleep until she checked and secured every window latch and door lock, Delilah donned her slippers and took the stairs, where below she methodically moved from room to room, taking special care to be as silent as possible. When at last she was at ease, she made her way to her bedchamber and moved inside. She almost dropped her hand candle when she saw Sebastian standing beside the bed.

"But I locked the latch." She looked at the window and back again, questioning if she wasn't imagining everything. Mayhap she was caught in some wildly realistic dream. Hadn't she had the very same thoughts about his visit before climbing between the sheets?

"My man alerted me to trouble." He strode forward, his eyes narrowed as if working to decipher every emotion hidden in her eyes.

"I . . ." She struggled to organize her reply. Finding Sebastian in her bedchamber scrambled her thoughts even more so than a moment before. She shook her head and begged for clarity.

"What happened?" His tone was insistent. Best she get on with the retelling.

"I was in bed with the curtains drawn. I heard the window open and for a moment I thought . . ." She abandoned that sentence and started another. "A horrible man dragged me from the mattress. The room was black and I couldn't see anything. He demanded I give him diamonds. He seemed certain I had what he wanted, but I have no idea what he's talking about. He said when he returns, he'll harm Aunt Helen if I don't meet his demands."

She laced her fingers together, unaware she was shaking until she performed the motion. Sebastian must have noticed too. Another breath and she was hauled into his embrace, the solid wall of his chest more desirable than her bed linens.

"Did he say anything else? Did he harm you?"

"He didn't say more. Nothing of worth. Threats, mostly." She moved closer, but Sebastian pulled back, forcing her to meet his eyes.

"Did he harm you?"

The words were said in a tone so lethal, had the invader been present Delilah held no doubt Sebastian would have beat him senseless.

"He pressed me to the windowsill and threatened to push me out. I was frightened more than hurt, although I suspect I'll have a few unsightly bruises from his handling. I never thought to keep my dagger near the bed. I assumed here, more than anywhere, I was safe, but again I was proved wrong. I have a lot to learn."

The events this evening solidified her resolve to work with the Maidens of Mayhem. Females, children, most anyone it seemed, could be a victim of harm, even when safe at home.

A variety of emotions passed over Sebastian's face, not all of which she could label. When he finished processing her reply, he returned her to his arms and kissed the top of her head.

"When I find him, he will suffer for the harm he's done you."

It was a controlled statement and Delilah didn't wish to delve too deeply into the kind of *suffering* Sebastian intended. Besides, within her a rush of comfort and warmth was quick to override logic. A sense of safety, possessiveness, and belonging to someone's heart, now all mixed with the contrary feelings of the evening. She pulled away slightly and looked up at him, positioning her mouth below his chin, exactly in place for a kiss.

As usual, Sebastian proved dependable.

Sebastian lowered his mouth and embraced Delilah tighter as he deepened their kiss. What was this madness? The lady found danger at every turn. Yet she recovered almost instantly without tears or a need for smelling salts.

And what of the mention of diamonds? Why would Yardley or his henchman believe Delilah had the dowager's gemstones in her possession?

He wanted to unravel the intricate knot of these questions and understand how the two problems overlapped, but it couldn't be done with Delilah in his arms, with her sweet delectable lips beneath his, her lush breasts pressed against his thundering heart.

That was an impossibility.

And this was madness. What was he doing in her bedchamber again? Tempting Fate. Tempting the strength of his conscience. He'd like nothing more than to bed her here in her room, claim her virtue and make her his, even though the one thing he knew with certainty was that she never could be.

She would be an intriguing lover, anxious and curious, open to pleasure—the ideal mistress.

No. Delilah deserved better. Wanted better.

This was madness. Dangerous.

Dangerous, indeed.

She wrapped her arms around his neck and curled her fingers into his hair to keep him there, as if she was anxious to see where their kiss would lead. She played with fire, his thread of control practically frayed through, and yet he didn't pull away. Her fragrance seduced him even more than her delicate sounds of delight. He should end it all, here and now.

She shifted, pressing the weight of her slim figure to his and causing him to sway backward. He pulled her down with him, the two of them landing on the bedding, the dip of the mattress adding to the vertiginous force of their tumble. Her hair fanned across his face, the sensation far too tempting, the work of a seductress, though the lady had no idea what havoc she caused.

Instead, lust, that randy taskmaster, obliterated common sense and took control. He made quick work of lowering the lacy little sleeves of Delilah's night rail and filling his greedy hands with her perfectly formed breasts. Their ongoing kiss stoked the fire within his blood to an inferno that threatened to consume them both. She lay atop him and he nudged his hips higher, just enough to rub his ungodly hard erection against the soft welcoming sweetness of her sex. Bloody hell, what spell had the vixen cast?

He broke their kiss and rolled from beneath her, removing himself and his hands from the alluring temptation of her silky, smooth body in a desperate attempt at the right choice.

"Delilah."

"Yes." Her answer was no more than a whisper of breath between them.

"I should . . ." He stalled, fighting back an onslaught of randy impulses and summoning good conscience, but it all was for naught as soon as she reached for him.

Beginning at his chest, Delilah skimmed her fingers down his shirt, over his tensed muscles, the ridges of his abdomen jerking from her fleeting caress. She continued her inquisitive exploration until her palm pressed flat against his erection and his whole body throbbed with pleasure. What could this naïve, beautiful, seductive temptress mean to do now? He dropped his head back to the coverlet and resigned to allow her every freedom.

"You're so hard." Her voice held a note of triumph.

"You're very soft," he muttered in reply, at war with the insistent urge to react.

She rubbed her palm along his erection, firmly stroking the entire length, and he growled his approval, his teeth clenched in kind to the rest of him.

"This doesn't hurt." She spoke as she traveled her hand over him again.

"No." Was she asking or telling?

"I don't think you'll fit. You may be shocked, but I do know how this works. You put yourself inside me."

"Delilah." He choked back a groan. "You can't talk that way and expect me to . . ."

She rose up on the mattress and straddled his prone body, her hair tumbling down around her disheveled night rail, the single candle bathing her in an otherworldly glow. "I hope we can try." She shook her head a little and her breasts swayed softly with the motion, her thighs hugged his. "I'd like to try."

Having lost command of simple conversation, he nodded. Still, if the vixen meant to fit him inside her, she'd have to take control and figure things out by herself. Watching her would be almost as satisfying as when she accomplished the task.

CHAPTER 21

Delilah stared into Sebastian's pale eyes, the glint of candlelight alive there, mesmerizing. What was she doing? In an effort to gain control, she'd accomplished the opposite. The thrum of energy coursing through her veins might be brought on by her brush with danger, but it was now rechanneled into sexual exploration.

Perhaps the vulnerability and helplessness experienced at the hands of the intruder was too easily replaced by the protective security of Sebastian's embrace. She needed to reassert her self-reliance.

She drew a deep breath and searched his face for a clue to how to proceed, but the handsome scoundrel beneath her had closed his eyes, eliminating any chance she could seek answers anywhere besides her own heart.

She remembered too well the shocking pleasure of his attention in her bed, and tonight she meant to offer him the same gratification, yet somehow everything had spiraled into a sensual frenzy. Settled astride him and brazenly whispering wanton things wasn't what she wanted. She was bold. And daring. But she couldn't do this.

She shifted carefully and lowered herself to the mattress at his side.

"My apologies." She sounded foolish. Would he think she regretted the actions from the onset, or because she couldn't finish what she'd started?

"What?" His voices sounded gruff. Was it anger or disapproval that caused the husky tone?

"I honestly don't know how to explain myself. I got carried away in the moment, I suppose, and—"

"Delilah." His tone transformed and amusement replaced any earlier roughness. He rolled to his side and propped up on one elbow, his expression indecipherable.

She caught a faint trace of spicy bergamot and it soothed her soul.

"I'm sorry." Somewhat mortified, she attempted to recover a shred of misplaced dignity as she adjusted her sleeves. "I realize you must be uncomfortable." Her face heated as she darted her eyes to his lower half. She'd said much worse when she'd boldly stroked her hand over him, but now within their private chat atop her counterpane, she wished she could dissolve like the whisper of smoke from her bedside candle.

"I dislike finding you in the path of danger yet again."

Combined with the glimmer of seductive appreciation in his eyes, she wasn't altogether sure of his intent. Did he mean to protect her from herself? His seduction? The intruder? She touched her fingers to her collarbone and finished adjusting her disheveled night rail. The only danger threatening her at the moment was the safekeeping of her heart. She teetered on a precarious precipice.

If she fell in love with Sebastian—

"I cornered Viscount Clayton, the wastrel nephew of the Duchess of Grandon."

Clearly his mind was on other matters.

"Because you believe he's connected to Oliver's disappearance?"

"In some manner. He has pockets to let, and repeatedly pesters his aunt for a loan. He also keeps close company with Lord Yardley, who most likely perpetuated the theft of Her Grace's cherished canine and his expensive diamond collar."

"When Oliver was abducted."

"Unfortunately, yes."

"And you believe these gentlemen worked together."

"Yes." He reached across the bed linens and swept a loose tendril of hair from her forehead. "As more pieces of this predicament fall into place, it will become even more dangerous than currently. That's why I insist you stay home and out of harm's way."

Ridiculous request. But still charming.

And being together like this, atop her bed with him gazing across the coverlet and fixing her hair, bespoke of intimacy. However, no matter the unlikely bond they'd formed, she couldn't sit still and wait for him to flush out answers. But telling him about the Maidens of Mayhem would be a terrible mistake.

"I understand why you'd feel that way." She stated this knowing he would assume her compliance. "But I'm home. That horrible man climbed through my bedchamber window. I can't be more *home* than in my very own rooms."

"My associate was knocked unconscious." Sebastian muttered a curse. "I'll assign two men to watch from now on. This incident will not happen again, even though there's the threat of return."

"I appreciate all you're doing on our behalf." If only she could tell him of her involvement with the most remarkable group of women. Perhaps it would change his view she was nothing more than a helpless female dependent on his strong manliness. But she doubted that would prove true.

Instead, he might become even more insistent she remain in hiding. Her comings and goings would be under further scrutiny if he assigned another watchman outside the town house. She needed to act with haste, even though Sebastian wouldn't be pleased.

But his opinion didn't matter at the moment. She was proud of her decision to continue her relationship with the Maidens long after her personal matters were settled. Furthering their cause, to restore justice and fairness to London's less fortunate, was now her calling as much as theirs.

He shifted on the mattress and forced her to awareness. Then he stood and offered her his hand so she could do the same. His fingers wrapped around hers and he tugged her up, but not into his arms.

"I'll leave you to your rest."

She regretted her silence if he perceived it as a show of fatigue. She was hardly tired. A whirlwind of emotions swirled within her, all insisting to be heard. And she needed to learn what he'd discovered about the men who took Oliver. "When will I see you again?"

It was bold. So be it. She could be just as bold as he.

"I'll notify you if I learn anything useful."

That was hardly an answer to her question. "How noble of you."

Good lord, she sounded petulant, and yet he leaned down and looked directly into her eyes before he pressed a heated kiss to her lips to remind her, he was every bit the scoundrel.

He didn't remain. Instead he murmured her name and slipped out the window as silently as a shadow becomes one with the night.

"What do you make of all this?" Delilah had returned to Cavendish Square and now sat in the drawing room with the Maidens of Mayhem, each equally curious about the encroacher who'd crawled through the window last night and threatened her safety. The double entendre wasn't lost on Delilah, but she didn't share that portion of the evening's events, wanting to keep her relationship with Sebastian private. At least for the time being.

Whenever she remembered his lingering touch and sensual good-night kiss, her breath caught in her chest as if her heart expanded and she no longer had room for oxygen. It was odd and unsettling and altogether thrilling at the same time, until that pleasant realization was ruined by his stifling response to her interest in pursuing a resolution to the threat she'd received.

"This wasn't some random thug or depraved criminal out to rob our household. His voice was cultured, his words smoothed by privilege, and his slight build youthful. Yet while accustomed to an entitled lifestyle, he was ruthless," Delilah continued. "To that point, his request was specific. He only wanted the diamonds, nothing more."

"It's the threat he's left behind that has me most concerned." Phoebe tapped her fingertips on the tabletop. "Does your aunt leave the house often? Would this miscreant be so determined as to strike in broad daylight?"

"They did it once," Julia added. "Although however the events are connected, the abduction of Her Grace's dog was likely perpetuated through lowlife men for hire. I doubt an aristocrat would take any chance of being recognized in daylight on Jermyn Street."

"We'll need to keep an eye on the town house to ensure your aunt's safety."

Delilah opened her mouth to discourage the idea and inform the Maidens that Sebastian already had provided watchmen, but that would lead to further explanation she was unwilling to disclose. Albeit it was going to become quite crowded in the neighbor's hedgerow.

Transforming her expression into one of speculative interest, she modified her reply. "So what do we do now?"

"If diamonds are involved, a visit to Shadwell Street is in order." Julia placed her hands flat on the tablecloth, her fingers drumming a light cadence.

"There's a businessman at the docks in Wapping who knows every questionable jewelry exchange within the ton, as well as the transactions, legal or otherwise," Diana supplied.

"Is he a smuggler?"

"An astute assumption, Delilah, but no." Julia smiled. "He's a fencer, and sooner or later every valuable piece of jewelry passes through his greedy fingers. If someone stole the duchess's heirloom diamonds and meant to double-cross the viscount and monetize the gemstones, our man would be the likely choice."

"He's a shrewd negotiator. I've dealt with him on occasion and it's rarely an easy transaction." Despite her comment, Phoebe's grin indicated she'd enjoyed the confrontation.

"Phoebe and I will visit Wapping this evening. Diana, are you comfortable with surveillance?"

"Of course." Diana nodded. "I'm ready, however I'm needed."

Julia turned her attention to Delilah. "Would you rather stay home and help ensure your aunt's safety, or join us at the docks?"

"That's quite a choice." Delilah considered the decision. "If I go with you, harm may come to my unsuspecting aunt—"

"No one will attempt a thing without dealing with me first," Diana interrupted.

And too, Sebastian's men would be watching.

"If I stay home, I will feel useless and unsettled knowing all three of you are taking risks on my behalf while I sip tea by the fireplace."

Julia laughed before she sobered. "You're so unlike other aristocratic ladies. I've always known I'm somewhat different from the ton, and it's reassuring to find another proper lady who doesn't mind getting her boots dirty. You won't allow others to carry the burdens of society."

"Thank you." Delilah drew a deep breath. "That's a fine compliment. But if I stay home, I'd be doing just that. My view of London proper was dreadfully wrong and I'm embarrassed to admit I hadn't previously considered the plight of the unfortunate, or at least realized the depth and magnitude of the problem. Birmingham was different by contrast, but now my eyes have been opened in more ways than one. I insist on accompanying you to Shadwell Street."

"Then that's settled. Oh, I almost forgot these," Phoebe piped in as she rose and gathered a package from the side of the desk. She unwrapped the brown paper and held up a pair of black wool trousers.

"For me?"

"We'd hoped you would join us and went ahead and commissioned them for you. The waistband is completely adjustable, so you shouldn't have trouble slipping them on beneath your skirts and fitting them securely."

"How spectacular." Delilah accepted the trousers, her smile growing.

"Welcome, Delilah." Diana stood with her teacup raised as if making a grand toast. "You're officially a Maiden of Mayhem now."

The little round of applause and congratulatory encouragement made the memorable moment all the more special.

CHAPTER 22

Later that evening when the house had grown silent, Delilah slipped out the back door, down the steps, and around the side of the property to discreetly venture to the corner. She glanced across the street, but even though she couldn't see Diana, or Sebastian's men for that matter, she believed they were there as promised, overseeing the town house and Aunt Helen with vigilant surveillance.

Avoiding the lamppost and its generous light, she walked two blocks north and hailed a hack. She settled on the bench as a smile curled her lips. The trousers beneath her cloak were comfortable and convenient, never mind wickedly invigorating. They added a sense of daring and danger to an evening that already promised adventure.

She spared a moment to consider Sebastian's whereabouts, but then pushed all thoughts of him from her mind and refocused. Locating the gemstones and returning them to the Duchess of Grandon was the purpose of tonight's mission. She needed no other distraction.

As arranged, Julia and Phoebe met her outside the King's Elbow, a local pub near the Wapping docks and hardly a stone's throw from the jewelry shop the Maidens intended to visit. A few pedestrians congregated near the entrance and to the right of the building in a narrow alley, but no one bothered them other than an occasional glance. With their cloaks drawn tight and hoods shadowing their faces, they likely appeared a visage of haunting death rather than three ladies in disguise. In general, Delilah found Londoners to be a suspicious lot. Were anyone to interfere with their passage, they were prepared to call upon spirits and to spook whoever thought to bother them with morbid incantations predicting an early grave. That, and Phoebe carried a pistol.

Keeping to the eaves, they advanced down Shadwell Street, the narrow thoroughfare lined with shabby two-story tenements and dilapidated sailors' victuallers. When Julia stopped in front of a whitewashed wooden façade, Delilah assumed they'd reached their destination.

"The store is up ahead." Julia worked the ties at her chin to loosen her hood. "Knox will be there. He lives above the shop so he can be accessible at all hours. Smugglers don't always keep a convenient schedule."

"I'll go around back." Phoebe pulled her hood further over her brow. "I wouldn't want him to remember our last dance."

"Your dance?" Delilah waited, unsure what her friend implied.

"Our last go around." Phoebe grinned. "I'm sure I left him with a few bruised ribs."

Delilah didn't ask more questions and walked beside Julia until they reached the jewelry store.

"Follow my lead. Trust your intuition." Julia turned to her as she lowered the hood of her cloak.

"Your hair." Delilah took in Julia's new look. "How did you manage that?"

"You'd be surprised by the tricks I've acquired to change my appearance. A little boot black and water make a wonderful rinse when necessary. It's not so much for Knox's benefit, although I wouldn't want him to describe me in detail, but one doesn't know who may come into the shop while we're inside. It's better to not run the risk of having to explain ourselves. Since you're a newcomer, you'll be unrecognizable, although you should keep your hood up. Your hair is the color of sunshine. It's easy to remember."

Delilah tightened the strings at her neck and followed Julia into the fencer's shop. It was empty, aside from a middle-aged man behind a waist-high glass counter. He had a large book open before him, but he wasn't reading a novel or catching up on social news. It appeared to be a ledger book or journal of sorts, and when they stepped nearer, he marked the page, closed the book, and pushed it off to the side.

"Good evening, ladies." The man called Knox gave them his attention. "It's rather late to be visiting Wapping. I can only guess you didn't wish to be seen."

Delilah scanned the small interior, noting every detail and avoiding eye contact with Knox.

"It wouldn't do for my gentleman friend to find me here pawning the pretty bauble he just gifted me this morning. My companion was kind enough to join me." Julia twittered in a way that had Delilah biting her bottom lip. It would appear her friend was as practiced and capable as an actress on Drury Lane.

"Let me look at what you've got. It could be paste. I see it all the time. Ladies come in thinking they've earned a fortune only to discover their keeper was a liar and a cheat."

Knox tapped the glass in front of him and Julia moved to the right. She reached beneath her cloak to an inside pocket and placed a velvet pouch on the counter, a good distance from the ledger book. The way she fanned out her cloak and positioned her body offered Delilah the advantage she needed, and she didn't think twice.

At first, she feigned interest in a display of garish earbobs, but while Julia distracted Knox with flirtation and conversation, Delilah silently opened the journal and read over the marked pages.

She didn't need longer than a minute and a thorough glance to commit the words to memory. She'd have no way to know if she'd discovered anything helpful until later when she shared the information with Julia and Phoebe, but at least she'd put the visit to good purpose.

She closed the book and turned her attention to a collection of brooches, one of which was fashioned to resemble a ladybird, the ornate gold inset crowded with a cluster of glittering garnet gemstones.

"Come along, dear."

Julia's voice beckoned and Delilah fell in step behind her as they left Knox behind. Phoebe joined them as they passed the first alleyway and advanced farther from the fencer's place of business.

"How did it go?" Phoebe was barely visible. Her dark hair and black hood concealed her face completely. "Did your conversation reveal anything useful?"

Delilah would never feel reassured until the threat to Aunt Helen and the search for the missing gemstones was resolved. Everything seemed complicated and interwoven. She waited to hear what Julia revealed, anxious to share what she'd read in Knox's ledger.

"I showed him a sapphire choker my husband had given me. It's lovely and I had no interest in selling it, of course, but I feigned interest in trading my piece for a more valuable diamond necklace. I purposely underestimated the worth of the choker to tempt Knox's greed. Then I flirted and portrayed the naïve female to sweeten the conversation, but Knox didn't cooperate. Sometimes I think that man is a eunuch."

"Did he offer *any* information to help us?"

"He made reference to having a dislike for diamonds at the moment. I told him I needed to keep our dealings between the two of us and assured if he gave me a better price, I wouldn't speak a word of it beyond the shop, but he made a vague disgruntled comment about an overdue delivery. He said *Everyone's making promises these days that they don't keep.*"

"Do you think he was referring to the heirloom diamonds?" Phoebe asked.

"Maybe the gemstone sale was agreed upon, but with the botched theft, he's been left waiting on their arrival," Delilah suggested.

"It sounds possible." Julia indicated the King's Elbow on the corner up ahead. "We'll be able to nab a hackney here."

"Yes, I'm anxious to return home and check on Aunt Helen," Delilah added. "But first let me tell you what I saw in Knox's book."

"You read his ledger? How ever did you manage that?" Phoebe chuckled, her face still lost to shadows.

The three ladies moved away from the tavern windows and down along the side of the building.

"While Julia caused a distraction with her attempted sale, the ledger on the counter was blocked from view, so I took advantage of the opportunity."

"How clever you are." Julia touched Delilah's arm. "I'm so happy you've decided to become a Maiden of Mayhem."

"You're a natural." Phoebe nodded before she finally set her hood back and became visible again.

"Knox was reading the book when we entered and marked the page before he flipped it closed. His expression was one of annoyance right before he looked up to greet us." Delilah spoke quickly, aware they couldn't linger outside the tavern overlong. And too, she needed to see Aunt Helen and confirm nothing untoward occurred. No matter two or three people kept the town house under watch, she needed assurance of her own. "As expected, there were columns of entries, money in and money out. There were fourteen deposits and eight disbursements. Each line ended in a check mark and initials. Some of the initials were circled. And these entries were all the same. The initials were LC."

"Wait." Phoebe placed her hand on Delilah's arm to gain her attention. "You memorized all this from one quick glance at an open ledger?"

"Remembering things has always come easily to me." Delilah nodded. "I have a knack for recall, I suppose."

"She's more valuable than we ever imagined." Phoebe blew out a breath, seemingly impressed.

"I'm glad you think so," Delilah continued. "But getting back to Knox, I'm interested in those circled entries. They were all made by the same person, and that seems unusual. What would cause someone to repeatedly sell off their valuables?"

"It could be a smuggler selling his wares or a thief on a hot streak," Julia mentioned. "Although a gentleman in low water would also pawn trinkets and the like to keep himself afloat. Did you notice the dates of these entries?"

"Of course." Delilah smiled, happy she was able to contribute in a meaningful way. "Most of LC's sales were spaced by three weeks, but the last four entries were only five days apart."

"That sounds a bit desperate, doesn't it?"

Two men exited the tavern and drew the ladies' attention to the street.

"We should leave Wapping." Julia pulled her hood up and approached the hack stand, but there wasn't a cab to be seen in either direction of the roadway.

"I suppose we have a bit of a wait ahead of us," Phoebe murmured.

Heaving a breath of disappointment and impatience adding to her concern for Aunt Helen, Delilah moved closer to the windows alongside the tavern and peered discreetly inside in want of distraction. Customers overflowed from the back bar to the small tables that lined the perimeter of the room. In a far corner off to the right, her eyes settled on a table and her pulse raced even harder than when she'd flipped Knox's ledger open.

Sebastian and Lady Herron were seated there with another man dressed in a blue coat, although from the distance and dimly lit room, Delilah couldn't be certain. Patrons and waitstaff obstructed her view intermittently and caused her frustration to intensify. She didn't wish to be noticed but likewise couldn't tear her gaze away. The conversation appeared convivial, most especially as Lady Herron leaned against Sebastian's arm, her fingers at play on his sleeve, her bright red lips near his ear as she spoke. And it was the look in her eyes, the conspiratorial glance that communicated so much more than her words ever could. Lady Herron and Sebastian were equals, whereas she came from a different world entirely. She may have dismissed the way he sought to keep her safely tucked away, but she hadn't done the same for her heart.

"Delilah," Phoebe called. "We've got a hack. Let's leave this place before we overstay our welcome."

Delilah heard her friend's bid but didn't move, reluctant to leave without seeing Sebastian's reaction to Lady Herron's clingy affection. Hadn't the intimacy they'd shared meant something? Not just the physical bond they'd formed, even though Delilah treasured their stolen moments, but the personal conversation afterward? The tender kisses and precious caresses? It all seemed foolish now. Clearly it mattered little to him.

Glancing over her shoulder to where her friends waited at the curb, she nodded before turning to join them. Sebastian hadn't pulled free from Lady Herron's grasp. Delilah had seen enough this evening.

Sebastian clenched his teeth, irritated with himself for falling prey to another of Eva's conniving manipulations. He strove to maintain a sense of calm as she draped herself over his person.

He'd planned to send a message to Delilah and then travel to Berwick Street to confirm his men were in place guarding the town house, but instead Eva's message had arrived. Her note stated the Duchess of Grandon's driver had entered the King's Elbow.

As an agent of the Crown he had an obligation, above his personal desires, to resolve the situation of Her Grace's theft, but the evening had become increasingly more difficult as it went on.

Now he wondered why Eva needed his help. She'd already lured the driver to a private table and loosened his tongue with flirtation by the time Sebastian had arrived.

"Her Grace likes to keep her liaisons private, although I don't think his lordship feels the same way. He has me all about London sorting things out."

Sebastian eyed the driver. At last they were getting somewhere. "Where did Yardley need you to take him?"

Sebastian motioned to a serving girl to refill the glasses on the table, though he hadn't had more than a few sips all night.

"Right kind of you to spend so much of your coin on my pleasure."

"We're enjoying your company. You have such authority. I'm impressed someone so young manages so well," Eva answered. "You were saying Yardley likes to visit the pleasure gardens?"

"Nothing so scandalous, I assure you. Though there's nothing wrong with the bawdy houses now and again."

The young driver took another hearty gulp and his hesitation to continue reminded Sebastian of the first time Delilah had come to his study. Her reluctance to reveal where she'd visited in hope of finding Oliver had earned his respect more than his censure. Was she asleep now? In the middle of a fanciful dream? He hadn't heard from the two watchmen he'd stationed to watch the town house. All must be quiet on Berwick Street.

"He had me use a nondescript gig. Didn't want to be recognized, I suppose. Her Grace would cook my giblets if she knew I'd taken out one of her carriages anyhow. He asked me to keep his confidence and I told him how I'm trustworthy to a fault. I'm as good as my word." The driver took a breath and then continued, seemingly fine with the fact he was breaking the very rule he claimed to uphold. "He paid me a tidy sum to take him beneath the London Bridge to St. Michael Crooked Lane on Mile's Lane."

Eva pressed her shoe against Sebastian's boot beneath the table. "What use would Yardley have in Candlewick Ward? He doesn't seem the kind who goes for stews or cock fighting."

"You're right about that." The driver finished the last of his ale. "Never did know what he wanted with the place. Just needed me to take him beneath the bridge to meet with another carriage outside St. Magnus-the-Martyr. He left with the blokes and returned an hour later, madder than hell. He's normally a good sort."

Sebastian slanted a glance at Eva and placed a handful of coins on the table before he stood. "Good talking with you." He patted the driver on the shoulder. "Eva will make sure you find your way home safely."

And then he turned and left.

CHAPTER 23

Having found little sleep through the night, Delilah was short on patience when she arrived at the Last Page Bookstore a quarter hour after it opened. Concern over her aunt's safety held peaceful slumber hostage, and seeing Sebastian in the tavern with Lady Herron on his arm stole her serenity in equal measure. She needed to resolve both problems and one was undoubtedly easier to address.

During the hack ride to Gilbert Street she'd debated whether or not to confide in the Maidens about her connection to Sebastian, but swiftly rejected that idea. She didn't want them to think she was like so many other females who fawned over a handsome gentleman or relinquished power to the other gender instead of solving the issue independently. And too, she didn't know the Maidens well enough to judge how the news would be received. They might think she undervalued their help. She didn't want any misconceptions to form.

Besides, soon it wouldn't matter. With her goal for the morning, the infuriating man would no longer be her concern. She glanced to the sky and paid the driver. The weather echoed her mood as the clouds muttered their complaints and gathered with the threat of rain.

She entered with determination and made her way to the rear

of the store. Today she didn't need to ask for help or request an appointment with St. Allen. He stood in the same corner, near the cherrywood door with the golden colophon above it. He watched her approach with what could only be considered a pleasant greeting, but as she grew closer his expression became indecipherable.

"I need to speak with you," she said without preamble, pleased no emotion crept into her tone.

"Of course."

He opened the door and they proceeded downstairs. She reminded herself heartache spared no one, and he'd offered her nothing more than assistance in recovering Oliver. True, the recent threat to Aunt Helen kept them connected, but that too was a matter of business. Midnight visits and sensual kisses were never part of the plan.

They walked through the same tunnel as before, but this time he paused beside a modest room and gestured she should enter. A table and two chairs were inside, but she didn't sit. Instead she feigned a casualness she wasn't feeling. How dare he initiate intimacies between them and dismiss them in less than twenty-four hours as he dallied with another woman.

When he moved to the table and leaned a hip on the corner, she strode several paces away. Wrestling with her physical attraction would only undermine what she'd come to tell him.

"Is something troubling you?"

He folded his arms across his chest, his muscular shoulders outlined, and Delilah wondered at the strength of his tailor's handiwork. Best she begin before sentimental feelings overrode good judgment.

"You needn't bother yourself with my welfare any longer." She spoke in a terse tone and for a fleeting moment, he looked surprised. Then, as if he reconciled something, a slight smile edged his mouth.

"You were never a bother, Delilah. I wanted to help you. I still do." The conviction in his voice brought her pause.

She dismissed his reply. "Well, that hardly signifies now that Oliver is returned."

"And what of the threat made to your aunt? To you?" He stood and strode toward her. "What of the diamonds these thieves think you possess?"

She wanted to believe she heard tenderness and concern in his voice, but then why would she? She closed her eyes in a long blink and recalled the scene she'd witnessed last night, Lady Herron's lips against his ear, her wandering hands wrapped around his arm. Becoming involved with Sebastian had shown a deplorable lack of judgment on her part.

"I'm capable of protecting my aunt. I'll find a solution to the problem without involving you further." There. She'd said it again.

They exchanged significant looks.

"I think you underestimate the man who climbed into your window."

She aborted the scoff that wanted out of her mouth. A truer statement couldn't have been made.

"I should go." She turned and made for the door.

"Don't leave." He moved until only a stride separated them. "We should talk further about this perpetrator. I acquired some interesting information last evening."

A measure of frustration kept her silent. What would he tell her? He didn't know she'd stood on the pavement peering into that tavern where he'd likely gained the very facts he dangled in front of her now.

"Then please share what you've learned so I can pursue the matter."

"I don't want you put in harm's way again, Delilah."

He may have aimed for consideration, but insult edged his reply. Did he think her incompetent? Fragile and frivolous? She'd shown him time after time she was capable of protecting herself. She wouldn't remind him again.

"Why?" Her voice rose an octave even though she fought against it. "Do you even care? Don't pretend, when you and Lady Herron were twisted together at that back table in the King's Elbow."

She'd surprised him again, though he recovered just as quickly.

"You were in Wapping? It was nearly midnight." Censure and disbelief colored his words. "Are you trying to kill yourself?"

"I know how to move about unseen."

"Apparently." He laced his fingers in front of him, his thumb rubbing his palm as if he kept his temper on a short leash.

Good. He needed to see her as more than a proper lady. She was a Maiden of Mayhem now. He should be wary of crossing her.

"The miscreants, thugs, and criminals who call Wapping home also know how to move about and are more familiar with the surroundings than someone newly arrived in London."

"I wasn't alone."

This, too, took him by surprise.

"Who were you with?"

His growly question cut the air between them and she watched as he curled his fingers into a fist. She relished a misplaced beat of satisfaction for having frustrated him.

"Why does that matter?" she countered. "You were apparently otherwise occupied."

He ran his fingers through his hair and blew out a breath before he returned to the table and settled in a chair. "Eva and I—"

"Eva?"

"You know her as Lady Herron." He huffed loudly. "Eva and I were gathering information from the Duchess of Grandon's driver. Eva has a way of charming people into speaking freely."

"You don't say." Damn, she didn't want to sound like a tart. But, too, she'd shared herself intimately with Sebastian. Foolish, how she'd convinced herself it was meaningful when it was far from the truth. Seeing Sebastian with Lady Herron hurt on a level she wasn't ready to examine.

"That's what we were doing at the King's Elbow. Gathering information."

"Is that how you always conduct your interviews?" She followed this with an airy laugh. She refused to allow him to think she was emotionally affected.

"No. And I wasn't happy about her public display, but at the time, the most important goal was to keep the driver talking."

The mood in the room shifted. Clearly he was a man unaccustomed to explaining himself and yet he had done just that. Delilah took a few steps closer to the table, though she didn't sit. What he said made sense. Her emotions had gotten in the way of logic.

"I didn't like it." No doubt he could hear the truth without her saying so, but if she was going to make a clean break, she needed to speak her mind.

"Neither did I."

Sebastian wanted to pull her into his arms. He wanted to kiss her senseless and erase every silly notion she'd created about what she'd seen at the tavern. But he was smart enough to know he'd hurt her feelings, and trying to smooth over the misunderstanding with anything besides words would be a mistake greater than the one which caused their problem.

Delilah met his eyes, but remained quiet.

Again the urge to reach for her, lace her fingers with his and soothe away hurt was near overwhelming, but he forced it away. Moving had to be better than standing in silence. "Let's walk and talk. I don't want disharmony between us."

She nodded in agreement and he led them into the hall. When it came to Delilah, he had a primal need to protect her. It didn't matter that nothing could become of their relationship. He couldn't have anything happen to her. Especially not on his watch.

He indicated the hall to the left. "I grew up in the slums. Any day when I had something to eat was a good day." He couldn't confess the atrocities he'd endured, but he would share what motivated him to pursue runaways and stolen children. That much he could tell her.

Her reaction was immediate. She stared at him, eyes wide, as if she wished to see inside him. Her reaction affected him and he worked to steady the sudden unexpected emotion lodged in his chest. When she didn't comment, he continued.

"My path to adulthood wasn't easy, but it taught me many things I would never have learned otherwise. These qualities and my own desire to better myself led me to the work I do now. I'm employed by people who trust me to resolve problems and oversee the common good." He could never reveal he served as an agent of the Crown, but in fairness, he wanted to share a general description of his work in hope it explained why he fought so hard to keep her from danger.

"You and your other associates?" Her eyes remained wide, but this time with curiosity, her clever mind at work, no doubt.

"Yes. The theft of the Duchess of Grandon's diamonds is one such instance." He paused at the foot of the stairs that led up to his study. "Will you come upstairs? I have more to tell you."

Again she nodded, although he thought her eyes narrowed slightly before her velvety lashes obscured his view. He opened the door and they moved into his study. She walked to the hearth and he assumed restlessness kept her in motion.

"Why are you telling me this?" Her voice was absent of anger, so at least he'd accomplished that.

"I trust you." He moved to the sideboard and poured two glasses of brandy. Just a taste. "But I also want you to realize I'm prepared for perilous situations and heinous crimes. I've seen the darkness that lurks in the corners of London. I've lived in that darkness." He brought her the brandy and watched as she took a cautious sip. "I don't want you in the path of that darkness."

"That's very kind of you, but—"

"I care about you, Delilah." He hadn't planned on sharing *that*. He wasn't even sure why he was telling her all these things. Parts of his history he'd never confessed to anyone.

"I'm sorry about your past." Her eyes were clear and honest but there was an ache in her voice.

"It could be the reason I fear for your safety. I'm aware how fleeting happiness can be. How elusive." He finished his brandy and watched a series of emotions pass over her lovely face. She represented everything he'd lost that one morning when his father shoved him from the carriage. A safe and comfortable life. A promising future.

"I'm always careful." She swallowed and he wondered what she was thinking. "And resourceful."

"You did stab a mangy dog to help me." He breathed easier when a smile curled her lips.

"So that's how one earns your trust? By being fearless in all things?"

"Fearless, but not careless. I think you like to court danger."

"That's ridiculous." She set her glass down on the end table. "Are you going to share what you learned from Her Grace's driver?"

Hell, the lady was persistent. He almost laughed. In that way she reminded him of himself. "Didn't Oliver say he heard a mournful chime? He called it a sad bell, didn't he?"

"Yes. He likened it to the waterman's wherry. Since hundreds of rowboats and skiffs crowd the Thames, it hardly indicates a place to investigate, other than the knowledge he was kept near the water."

"True, and an excellent conclusion."

"Go on." Clearly, she wasn't leaving until she learned exactly what the driver had divulged.

"If I tell you the rest, I want your word you won't go hying off alone to see what you can discover."

She arched a brow but her gaze didn't waver. "I give you my word I won't go hying off alone to see what I can discover."

Her quick compliance brought him a moment of pause. But no, she wouldn't lie to him. Definitely not while she stood in his home and looked him in the eye. He breathed a satisfied sigh.

"The driver said the kidnappers were located near the base of the London Bridge across from St. Michael's on Mile's Lane."

"A man named Bert."

"You remembered."

"I remember everything."

"This doesn't mean Bert is sitting there waiting to be found, but many criminals keep to the places they regard as safe, especially if they've angered someone or are in wait of something."

"Like the diamonds."

"Exactly." He grinned down into her face. She was sharp, and true to her point, didn't miss a fact or intuitive conclusion. She'd make a good agent, although he'd never be able to concentrate on work if she was near, her fresh lemony scent and golden hair an enticement he struggled to resist.

"Is that it?"

Her question regained his attention.

"Almost." He drew her forward slowly, ready to let go at the slightest indication she wished to be released.

"Are you still angry with me?" He tucked a wayward wave of hair behind her ear as he murmured his question.

"Not nearly as much, although that may be the brandy." She didn't pull from his grasp and instead rested her hands lightly on his forearms.

"I'll have to be happy with that then." He touched his forehead to hers, not willing to ruin their newly formed truce. "Thank you for seeking me out and taking me to task. I deserved it."

"You did."

She gave him a slight smile then and he couldn't help but close the distance between their mouths. It was a tender kiss, a promise and apology all in one. When they pulled apart, they kept their faces close, sharing the moment a little longer.

"Thank you for trusting me."

"It was never about trust, love." She tensed at his use of the endearment and he wondered exactly what she was thinking. He angled his mouth and tasted her lips again, this time deepening their kiss and curling his arms around her to draw her lithe body closer.

When they broke apart, they were both breathless.

"I'll contact you if I learn anything at all."

She nibbled at her lower lip and he wondered if she fought to keep a renewed rebuttal inside. He didn't wish to tempt Fate, so he acted with alacrity.

"Let me walk with you back to the bookstore. I'm sure you want to get on with your day."

She nodded and moved toward the door. He was quick to follow.

CHAPTER 24

Delilah, Julia, and Phoebe rounded the first arch at the foot of the London Bridge, at one with the night, their black shirts and trousers blending seamlessly into the surround. They wore dark wool caps pulled low with all hair tucked out of sight and kidskin-soled boots that produced hardly any sound. With thick leather gloves keeping their fingers warm, they moved into the recessed culvert where unsettled fog lingered and the rancid stink of sea life hung heavy in the air.

"How shrewd of you to confront St. Allen and learn of this place," Phoebe whispered across the quiet.

Delilah had gone straight to the Wycombe and Company building after meeting with Sebastian, where she quickly relayed what she'd learned from the conversation. Her friends didn't comment on her relationship with Sebastian and she hadn't divulged anything personal or private, whether the retelling of his past or their bone-melting kisses afterward. Things with Sebastian were complicated and until she sorted out her own feelings, she saw no need to invite conjecture. From there, the Maidens had planned for this evening, and now execution was being put into action.

With Diana keeping watch on the town house, Julia, Phoebe, and Delilah arrived at Candlewick Ward and hurriedly crossed to St. Michael Crooked Lane beneath the London Bridge. They came together near the slimy stone soffit and spoke in hushed tones.

"Let's review our plan." Julia held up her gloved hand with fingers splayed as she spoke. "First we'll locate the hidey-hole. Hopefully Bert will be there alone, but there'll be no way to know until we peer through the window or interrupt his evening."

Delilah nodded, her pulse at a swift pace.

Phoebe grinned as she spoke, apparently at ease with their effort. "It would be beneficial if we can obtain our information with the threat of my pistol and not the use. The loud crack of a gunshot will rouse every rat out of its crevice and I'd rather not become the victim when we're here to apprehend the criminal."

"Well said. Let's take no unnecessary chances, especially since we're to split up," Julia continued as she raised her second finger. "Once we locate the shack, Delilah will go around back. I'll take either side and Phoebe, you'll have the entrance, whatever that might be. We'll use the element of surprise as our way in. I'm of a mind Bert is jittery and foolish. He's waiting for payment or hiding from an angry customer. Either way, he's sure to be on edge. I'm hoping by window surveillance we can determine his size, if he's alone, and most of all, if he has a weapon."

"That's asking a lot," Phoebe quipped. "But we'll make things work to our advantage."

"Agreed." Delilah looked out into the murky night. Was Sebastian here as well? Was he working in tandem with others? She shook her head, unwilling to lose focus.

"St. Allen described the location of Bert's hideout as being at the base of the bridge, but there's countless shakes and shanties lining the culverts. How will we know where he is?"

"Process of elimination." Again, Phoebe grinned, her teeth flashing white in the darkness. "It's a little game we play. Let's split up and locate Bert first. Then we can reassemble before we interrupt his evening."

"Good idea." Julia dropped her hands and looked toward the line of dilapidated tenements near the water's edge. She tugged at the chain around her neck and carefully pulled free a silver whistle. "I'll signal once we need to regroup."

"Then let's get on with it." Delilah began to move, disappearing into the blackness a few steps later.

Sebastian peered down the alleyway along St. Magnus-the-Martyr church before he continued toward the base of the London Bridge. He had a long knife in his boot, a dagger in his coat pocket, and a short cudgel in his hand. Tonight, he wouldn't be caught unaware. He wanted to believe Bert and Sullivan were incompetent, but one never knew what to expect.

Hearing movement near the first culvert, he moved silently until he had a distinct vantage point, but nothing was in view. Crooked Lane was home to an endless variety of thieves and no-gooders. The disturbance could have been anything. He moved toward the despairing line of shacks near the water. He knew the area well. Spending years on the street had afforded him the freedom to wander most anywhere. Fancy ballrooms excluded, of course. Although his work for the Crown now permitted him to assume entry there too, as long as he didn't get caught.

The first shanty was empty. The rank stench from the shallow water was unbearable, but as he moved down the line of dilapidated structures, the nearby water became deeper and the air more tolerable. He approached the second arch where a decent sized hovel leaned precariously against the stone wall. Candlelight lit the interior.

Slowing his steps, he braced his shoulders against the rough under-bridge and advanced closer, his attention drawn by a slim silhouette on the move to his right. He adjusted his hold on the cudgel, ready to strike the first blow just as Delilah slid into his path as gracefully as moonlight dancing on water.

"Fancy meeting you here."

Her hushed whisper caused a riot of reactions, some of them misplaced.

"Delilah."

"Sebastian." She offered him a brilliant smile.

"You're wearing trousers." He swallowed thoughtfully, the glow from the moon limning her profile in a golden aura.

"So are you."

"I'm supposed to wear trousers."

"Indeed, that's true." She moved closer with a few stealthy steps. "Clearly I don't do everything I'm supposed to do."

"How did you come to be here?" His eyes took her in from head to toe, noting with disappointment how her hair was tucked away under a wool cap. "How did you come to find this place?"

"Lord Hibbett took me on a lovely tour last week. He pointed out the most prominent historic sites along Upper Thames Street as we advanced to Temple Church. I paid close attention."

Sebastian beat back a wave of annoyance. This was neither the time nor place for irrational jealousy. "You gave me your word you wouldn't act on the information I shared."

"And I haven't broken it." She moved within a stride of him, her soft whispers reaching for him through the darkness. "You said *If I tell you the rest, I want your word you won't go hying off alone to see what you can discover.* And I said, *I give you my word I won't go hying off alone to see what I can discover.*"

"Exactly. That's how I remember it too, but you're here now." He kept his voice low but he couldn't stop exasperation from peppering his response.

"I am, but I didn't come *alone*." She stressed the last word as if she was quite proud of herself.

"That's just a twist of words."

"Clever, wasn't it?"

"You're a saucy minx at times, Delilah, and a powerful force at others." He had to hand it to her, she would make an excellent agent. He passed his eyes over her shapely backside perfectly outlined by her black wool trousers. Among other things.

"Have you discovered Bert's whereabouts?"

Her enticing whisper and wheedling question caused him to grin, no matter they courted a dangerous situation. "I wouldn't be standing here thinking about kissing you if I had."

"You're thinking about kissing me?" Her smile fell away and a wicked gleam lit her eyes. "I was thinking the same thing."

"Come here."

"No, you come here." Her chin rose a notch even though they negotiated inches.

He obliged immediately.

He wanted to tug off her cap and thread his fingers through her silky hair, but he knew better. He'd do nothing to place her in the path of danger, even if she insisted on placing herself there as frequently as possible.

He deepened their kiss, and when she slid her hands up his arms to the back of his neck and held him tight, his body ached with want. Why did she make him think things better left alone? She murmured his name as she withdrew, and for a moment all they did was breathe.

A whistle's melodic note sounded off to the left and she startled within his embrace, her hands coasting down his arms to settle in his grasp.

"I have to go." Her words came out in a rasp.

"Be careful, Delilah."

"I will. Always." She paused a heartbeat longer.

He flexed her hands in his before releasing her into the night.

"I think I've found the place we're looking for, and if Bert is inside and we can convince him to cooperate and reveal to the Duchess of Grandon why he took Oliver or how he was involved in the theft we'll leave him with a fat purse but no threat of arrest. We'll save that for whoever has the diamonds and threatened you and your aunt." Julia hurried with her explanation as the three-some followed her lead and moved below the bridge.

"That's a lot of ifs and maybes," Delilah said. "Why would Bert trust us more than the person who hired him in the first place?"

"The threat of exposure, and money." Julia patted her pocket. "Thieves are only loyal to whoever puts coins in their hand."

"Is this it?" Phoebe canted her head at a squat shanty house behind a stone support.

"Yes." Julia gestured for them to take their prearranged positions. "Delilah, make sure no one scurries out the back when I kick the door open. Phoebe, follow me as I rush in. The sooner we storm through, the more time we'll have to assess the situation and gain control. The only window is covered with a tarp, so I couldn't learn anything more than I've told you."

"Ready?" Phoebe asked, bouncing slightly on her toes.

"Ready." Delilah glanced over her shoulder once before she scurried to the back of the shanty. If they confronted Bert and located the diamonds or learned who waited on the collar, Aunt Helen would be safer. Delilah would speak to a runner in the morning. But without proof or further information, going to the authorities would prove useless and ultimately provide the scoundrels with a reason to disappear. She'd never be able to protect Aunt Helen or feel safe in her home again.

She waited in the dark, measuring each breath and listening for the sound of Julia's whistle, but all was quiet. Was Sebastian nearby? Had he also discovered Bert's hidey-hole?

Sebastian seemed different this evening. He'd accepted her sudden appearance and didn't attempt to censure her involvement. In fact, he'd encouraged her, sending her off warmed from his embrace.

A sharp stab of pain followed that lovely thought. He was an orphan. Raised on the streets without family or friends. How she wished she could rewind the clock and choose a different life for him. He deserved better. All street urchins and orphans did. Once this matter was resolved, she vowed to work toward improving the life of lost children and those without love and security.

She'd developed a deep fondness for him, one a wiser woman would avoid. Did it really matter that he wasn't a refined gentleman? Shouldn't a person be judged by their strength of character rather than a name or title?

He made her heart thunder with one glance, her pulse race with his smile, and his kiss . . .

The kiss they'd shared under the bridge was both tender and passionate, an expression of devotion more than a scandalous thrill.

The rough crack of splintering wood shook her from her musings. She tensed, ready to combat whoever might flee the property, but the sound of Julia's whistle met her ears almost immediately afterward and Delilah made her way inside.

"It's empty." Phoebe heaved a breath of frustration. "All that effort for little return."

"And now that I've kicked in the door, I doubt Bert will return. One glance at this mess and he'll know someone has found his hiding place." Julia's frown resembled their collective mood.

"So what do we do now?" Delilah asked, following the ladies as they walked up the river bank away from the culvert. No one answered at first, the quietude punctuated by a wherry's bell clanging offshore.

Sebastian tightened his hold on Bert's shirt and applied more pressure to his throat. "Talk faster. I'm short on patience this evening."

"Don't know what happened to the bloody diamonds," the man repeated, spittle gathering around his mouth. "The stones disappeared after we nabbed them."

"That story works if you mean to deceive the man who hired you and sell the diamonds yourself, but I'm familiar with Knox's business in Wapping. You'll not fence a pebble without me knowing it first."

"I don't have them." Bert extended his neck in an effort to loosen Sebastian's hold, his shoulders crushed against the stone wall, his feet barely skimming the ground. "If I did, I'd get rid of the cursed things. They're nothing but trouble."

It hadn't proved difficult to locate Bert at the closest pub. With a few well-placed coins and questions, Sebastian had hauled him out the back and into a nearby alley. And it served a dual purpose if Delilah was busy searching Bert's empty shack. At least she was out of the path of danger for the moment, although Sullivan was still somewhere.

"Where's your friend Sullivan these days?"

"I don't know." Bert gasped a stale breath. "He took off once things turned sour and we dumped the kid."

"And what of the threat to the ladies on Berwick Street?" Sebastian shifted his weight forward, anxious to gain the answers he needed.

"Don't know nothing about that." Bert squirmed against the wall.

"Are you sure? Maybe you should give it another think, Bert." Sebastian tapped his finger against Bert's forehead. "Rats enjoy a good chew on an unconscious body. Ears especially, and lips too."

Fear lit Bert's eyes and he stammered to answer, but then all hell broke loose.

The patter of dull footsteps entered the alley and elongated shadows arrowed along the stone wall. Delilah and two other women charged toward him. Recognition took hold. *The Maidens of Mayhem.* Their paths had crossed with his in the past. They were elusive, almost invisible, but it would appear tonight they assisted Delilah in her efforts.

Sebastian took in the scene over his shoulder but it offered Bert the opportunity he needed. A solid uppercut connected with Sebastian's temple and he staggered, his eyesight blurred. He flung an arm out in an attempt to catch Bert before he fled and his hands came away empty. Blinking to clear his head, he braced his palms flat against the wall, but to no avail. His legs gave way and he went down, darkness clouding his vision. He heard a female voice cry out even though his head began to throb and he could hardly keep his eyes open.

Two faces appeared in a shadow above his. Where was Delilah? What had happened to her?

CHAPTER 25

Delilah sprinted after the man who'd struck Sebastian, her heels spitting gravel as she gained ground. Familiar with the warren of backstreets and byways, the stranger held a distinct advantage but she was younger, faster, and she needed only to keep him in her sight. He darted left and disappeared behind a dilapidated clapboard structure that looked like it might have been a church at one time. Now it was nothing more than a skeleton of old memories.

She rounded the corner cautiously, unwilling to be deterred. He'd struck Sebastian. She'd acted immediately. Alone. Her heart thundered in her chest, but quitting when she was so close to apprehending the distasteful man was out of the question.

Moving silently, she advanced into the parish graveyard and mentally replayed the few words of conversation she'd heard as she'd entered the alleyway. Sebastian had located Bert. What had Sebastian learned? And was he conscious? Was he well?

She approached the far corner of the property where a length of fence had managed to survive over the years. If someone meant to hide and catch their breath, it would provide the ideal cover.

There was a shift of shadow and light. The air hummed with tension. She spun but it was too late. Bert appeared out of nowhere with a heavy rock in his hand.

"I hoped to outrun you, gel." He heaved another breath. "But you're too fast."

Delilah measured his size and noted the surroundings. No one knew where she was. The streets were desolate. The remains of the church blocked her sight line. The grave markers were a maze in wait to snap her ankle or cause a fall. She'd have only one chance to defeat him.

"You're a clever one, aren't you? I bet you're thinking about how you'll run away from me." Bert passed the rock from one hand to the other. "Pity for you, it looks like you've found your final resting place."

He lunged and she leapt over the nearest grave marker, losing her cap in the process. Her hair tumbled from its pins and she swept it from her face. She'd managed to keep another marker between them but she was still hemmed in on all sides. Her choices were limited until she could work her way to the street.

"What's the matter?" Bert scoffed. "Cat got your tongue? No matter. Worms will soon have the rest of you."

He lunged again and she evaded his grasp but her boot caught the edge of an uprooted marker and she stumbled, scrambling to regain her balance before he took advantage.

She almost succeeded.

"That'll do it." Bert wrapped his fist in her hair and tugged her across two grave plots to join him. He dropped the rock and pinched her wrists together in his meaty fist. "You weigh no more than a bag of feathers and yet you make so much trouble."

She kicked at his legs. If she could angle her body and use her knee on his bollocks, she could wrestle herself free. But it was no use. He had her reversed against his body, and when her boots connected with his shins it didn't make an impact, the soles too soft.

He dragged her backward to the clapboard wall and shifted his stance. He couldn't mean to kill her, could he? He'd returned Oliver. He wasn't a murderer. He was a petty thief and a poor one at that.

"You don't want to kill me."

"I'm not going back to Newgate. No snitch is sending me back." Bert wrapped one hand around her throat. "Just a little choke to keep you quiet and put you to sleep."

Delilah bucked against the clapboard wall, arching her back and resisting the pressure he applied to her neck. She blinked several times and saw a blur of movement several yards behind Bert. Another woman appeared. But it wasn't Julia or Phoebe. It was Eva. And she didn't move. She just stood there watching.

Delilah's struggle to breathe forced her face left and right, but no matter her thrashing, whenever her eyes looked to the grave-yard, Eva was there. Why didn't she intercede? Did she realize Delilah couldn't resist much longer?

Bert squeezed tighter and her body began to tingle. Her mind hummed with silence and blackness. She closed her eyes and summoned an image of Sebastian and how he'd looked in the moonlight tonight. How his lips felt against hers. The blissful sincerity in his kiss . . .

The thwap of a blade hitting the wall roused her. Bert's hand left her throat and she gasped for air, choking in an effort to fill her lungs as quickly as possible. Bert howled and went down. Delilah stumbled to the side, rubbing her neck and searching the dark-ness to understand what had happened. Eva approached and sat on Bert's back, although he didn't even try to rise, the knife pro-truding from his thigh enough to keep him immobile.

"Delilah!" Sebastian's voice rang across the graveyard and then she saw him, running toward her with a stricken expression. Julia and Phoebe followed a few steps behind. "What happened?" He'd reached her side and turned her gently to face him. Delilah swal-lowed, emotions of every sort clogging her throat. She didn't know where to begin.

"I got here just in time," Eva answered. "It would have been a much different outcome if I didn't intercede when I did."

Delilah met Eva's gaze, the double meaning of her answer not lost.

"I've summoned a runner through the Bridge Watch." Phoebe moved beside Delilah. "We should go."

"Yes," Julia added. "We've all had enough excitement for one evening."

"I'll wait for the runner. I'm in no hurry and neither is he." Eva applied pressure to Bert's shoulders and his whimpers grew louder.

"I'll walk with you then." Sebastian placed his hand on Delilah's arm, his grip firm. Was it relief that had him holding on tight or some other emotion?

"Are you all right?" Her voice sounded scratchy at first, but the more she swallowed the better it became.

"Yes." Sebastian brushed the hair from her shoulders, his eyes never leaving her face. "You've lost your cap."

Delilah tried for a smile and then initiated walking. The sooner she left the graveyard the sooner she could talk to Sebastian and explain what had happened.

He wanted to wring her neck. But in truth, that had almost happened. He couldn't stop staring at her, watching her, as if she might disappear or dissolve into moonlight right before his eyes. Her friends were on one side of her with him on the other, but the four of them kept silent. It was an odd trip back to the bridge.

"I'll see Delilah home." The finality in his tone brooked no argument.

The ladies eyed Delilah and when she nodded, they took their leave. Then he touched her elbow lightly and led her three blocks over to what appeared to the world as a poor man's tailor shop but at the turn of Sebastian's key led to the tunnel system below. He regretted the long walk and damp hallways, but he was determined to take Delilah to his home. Nowhere else would suffice.

"Does your neck hurt very much?" They'd shared few words and something fragile and not altogether comfortable seemed to travel with them.

"I'll be fine." She offered him half a smile and the tension eased. "Like your jaw."

If she could tease him, she must be feeling well enough. Although she wouldn't welcome a lecture on safety. He respected her choices even if they placed her in danger.

"The Maidens of Mayhem." He paused, gauging her reaction as they approached the stairs to his home. "They're helping you?"

"I left no opportunity untried when Oliver was taken."

"And now they're involved because your aunt was threatened?" She only nodded this time.

"I see." He didn't say more and climbed the stairs gingerly, anxious to see her inside where she could finally rest.

He poured her some brandy and watched as she settled on a couch near the hearth. He built a fire, too aware of the quiet in the room. He'd held her and kissed her this evening. She already owned a large part of his heart. And yet, he wasn't entirely sure what lay between them at the moment. Perhaps he should just ask.

"What is it?" He combed his fingers through his hair and sat beside her. "There are so many things I want to say, but you need to go first."

She hesitated and when she spoke her voice was nothing more than a wispy rasp. "She just stood there."

"Who?"

"Eva." Delilah turned to him, her slender brows lowered in confusion. "She watched Bert choke me."

"What?" Sebastian shot up and then just as quickly returned to the couch. "Tell me everything. What happened?"

"Bert already had the better of the situation. He had my arms pinned and one of his hands around my throat, but then Eva appeared across the graveyard and I knew I would be saved, that she would cause some kind of distraction. But she waited. She watched. She watched and she didn't do anything until the very last minute."

Rage lit his blood. He clenched his teeth so hard his jaw ached. How dare she. He'd have her removed from the agency. He'd write and speak directly to the prince regent if necessary. "I will take care of it. She had no right to allow you to be hurt."

It was the best reply he could muster, even though he wanted to find Eva immediately and vent his anger.

"Thank you." Delilah exhaled and her slender shoulders fell in a show of pure exhaustion. He brought her into his arms. Neither one of them spoke as the fire warmed the room.

"I can teach you techniques to protect yourself if you're ever attacked again." He could and he would. She needed to be better prepared if she insisted on running headlong into danger every fifteen minutes.

"You will?"

It was the first time this evening he'd heard her voice regain its usual buoyancy. Perhaps he'd surprised her.

"Of course I will." He gathered her closer. "I'll teach you every defensive move I know, although even I make mistakes. I turned away from Bert when I saw you running toward me. His punch and my carelessness caused what happened to you tonight, and I'm so very sorry, Delilah."

"I'm fine." She reached up and touched his jaw, running her fingers over the bruise. "I was worried about you."

"And I worried about you."

"We make a fine twosome." She may have tried for derisiveness, but he heard only accord.

"We do."

He lowered his mouth and brushed a kiss across her temple. He'd shown incredible restraint this evening, whether in confronting Bert, hearing of Eva's wrongdoings, or now when he wanted nothing more than to strip Delilah bare before the fire and offer her every comfort she deserved. But now was not the time for selfishness.

"I should be going." She sat up and adjusted her shirt, attempting to tuck the wrinkled fabric into the waistband of her trousers.

"I'll see you home in my carriage."

She nodded. "When will you teach me defensive maneuvers?"

She sounded so much more like herself, he had to smile. "Tomorrow evening. We can practice here. I'll send my carriage to the lamppost at eight."

"I'd like that." She huffed a breath as she stood and looked at the door.

"I—" And then he stopped, not wanting to give her anything else to think about tonight. But somehow, she knew.

Longing colored her eyes as she spoke. "Yes. I wish I could stay the night too."

All was quiet when Delilah reached home. The carriage ride to Berwick Street had been equally silent. She'd leaned into Sebastian's strength and heat, tired and at the same time invigorated by the evening's events. His kiss goodbye had spoken to her heart, but it was late and she was exhausted. Now in her bedchamber, she washed quickly with a wet cloth, yearning for a hot bath to ease her aches, even though she knew warm water and soap couldn't soothe away her complicated emotions.

It was Wednesday. On Friday she'd promised to take Oliver to the public gardens in Redman Square before his mother's birthday party, the celebration which had ignited the chaotic chain of events since their relocation to London. Had she never left Birmingham, she'd never have met Sebastian or the Maidens of Mayhem. Of course, she'd never have needed their help either.

Eva's actions were most disturbing. The woman had played a careless and dangerous game with Delilah's life. But to what end? Had Delilah perished, what did Eva stand to gain? Did she believe Sebastian would turn his affection to her favor once she'd caused Delilah harm? The logic in that conclusion was faulty on several points. Eva undoubtedly meant to scare Delilah and send a deliberate message. The woman could only believe the risk was worth the reward.

Despite these weighty matters causing unrest, Delilah fell into a deep sleep and woke the next morning refreshed. Downstairs everything was as it should be and she came to the breakfast table with a distinct plan for the day. She'd visit the Maidens first thing, though a delightful hum lived in her blood for later when she anticipated her meeting with Sebastian. Time would slow until she saw him again.

"Good morning, dear." Aunt Helen was busy with the jam pot and an uncooperative scone, but she paused and looked up from the task to smile broadly.

"It is a good morning." Delilah had chosen a high-necked day gown with dark lace around the collar. The last thing she wished to do was cause her aunt concern over the bruising on her neck.

"Tomorrow is Friday." Oliver quickly detoured her thoughts.

"Yes, it is." Delilah sat down beside him. "And we have very important plans, don't we?"

Oliver nodded vigorously, his eyes bright. "I can hardly wait!"

"Use a softer voice please, Oliver. It's early." Beth came into the kitchen carrying a fresh pot of tea. "Good morning."

"Things certainly have returned to normal." Aunt Helen looked across the table, completely at ease and unaware of the threat to her safety.

Just the way it needed to remain.

"Yes, and I couldn't be happier," Delilah agreed with a laugh.

"Nor I," Beth echoed.

"Mama, may I be excused?" Oliver eyed Delilah with an obvious widening of the eyes.

"Yes." Beth offered him a napkin. "Make sure to clean your face first."

Delilah joined Oliver on the lowest step of the staircase a minute later.

"You needed to speak to me?" She enjoyed Oliver's precocious nature and animated expressions. Someday she'd like to have a child. Perhaps more than one if she was blessed. The first step to that goal was a husband, but a pang of displeasure accompanied that thought.

"I've wrapped Mama's gift and I have it in my room." Oliver's cheeks rose in a grin. "Tomorrow we'll go to the flower gardens, won't we?"

"Just as we've planned." She patted his knee in reassurance.

"You won't forget?"

"No. Of course not. I'm looking forward to our outing." And it was true. The same trepidation that had accompanied her earlier feelings about venturing through London had vanished now. Offering Oliver another little pat, she rose from the step. She hoped to speak to the other Maidens of Mayhem before they went off on their own pursuits. They'd prearranged to meet at the Wycombe and Company building for half ten this morning.

Sebastian rubbed his palms together in an effort to control his temper. He'd asked Eva to join him and she was already ten minutes late. He paced in the hallway several strides before he heard the door close above.

He moved to the foot of the stairs to confirm it was she, and then on into the closest room.

"You wanted to see me?" This time it was definitely a question, not a statement. She had to know he wasn't pleased.

"What happened at the graveyard yesterday?" He needed to hear her version of the story and offer the benefit of doubt, but an ingrained sense of suspicion prevailed.

"It's a good thing I arrived when I did," Eva began, her expression unreadable. "It took the Bridge Watch another thirty minutes to arrive. It was a long time to listen to Bert's wailing."

"So you happened upon the scene and acted immediately." Sebastian noticed how Eva hesitated just the slightest. He'd known her long enough to understand the way her mind worked, but this went beyond anything he'd expected.

"At first I waited. Delilah had the situation under control."

Sebastian curled his fingers into a fist. Not by Delilah's account. She was being choked when she saw Eva. He blinked away the image of Delilah's bruised skin and the reddened marks left by the pressure of Bert's grip.

"Did you?" He drew a deep breath. "She isn't skilled in ways to overtake a man."

"Isn't she though?" Eva dared a smile and he lost any shred of control he had left.

He stood, the chair scraping back to the wall. "You let her suffer for no reason." He hadn't planned on raising his voice, but Eva's attitude was tinder to flame.

"I was lining up my shot."

"That's not what she says."

"How would she know? She was under duress."

"You allowed personal feelings to cloud your judgment."

"Isn't that rich?" Eva scoffed as she rose from her chair. "You're doing the same."

"Perhaps, but my actions aren't hurting anyone."

"Aren't they?"

A long minute of silence enveloped the room.

"I'd have thought better of you." He wouldn't check the contempt in his voice. Delilah might have died. *She almost did.* Had Eva not arrived in that moment, Delilah wouldn't—

It was the last thought that helped him reclaim clear thinking. Even though Eva reacted poorly, her actions saved Delilah's life.

"I'll need to include this in the report." Sebastian made to leave, unwilling to extend their conversation. "I'll relay the facts, untainted by personal issues, but there will be consequences."

Eva hadn't turned to face him as he'd moved to the door. He watched her straighten her back. When she didn't reply, he turned and left. She'd made her own decisions and she'd have to accept the outcome now.

CHAPTER 26

Delilah paused before the cheval glass in her bedchamber, the calm of the retired household a comfort. Aunt Helen was already in her rooms and the servants had closed the house. Knowing Sebastian's men watched the perimeter was invaluable reassurance.

She glanced at her reflection one last time and touched the bruises on her neck. She hadn't tried to hide them as she'd changed her clothes for her meeting with Sebastian. She'd survived and the evidence of her struggle emboldened her.

Slipping out of the house, she walked to the corner, where his carriage arrived with perfect timing. To her disappointment he wasn't inside and her mind returned to that night weeks ago when they'd ventured out to the Devil's Bedroom. How circumstances had changed.

She'd never gained access to Sebastian's home from the street, so when the carriage stopped before a neat three-story town house on the outskirts of Mayfair, she was taken by surprise. Not that he hadn't shown his discerning taste before. The interior of his study from carpet to draperies was evidence of impeccable taste.

He answered the door before she even touched the knocker.

"I let the servants have the night." He reached for her hand and ushered her into the foyer so quickly her skirts brushed over the tips of his boots. And then he pulled her into his arms and captured her mouth in a deep openmouthed kiss.

"I've been waiting all day to do that."

She took a minute to catch her breath. "Was it worth the wait?"

"You have no idea." But his expression fell as his eyes settled on her neck. "You're very brave, Delilah."

"I'm many things, I suppose," she said, hoping to restore the mood. "And I'm anxious to add master of defense to my list."

He laughed and the rich, rare sound bounced off the marble tiles. Desire licked through her. The man was terribly charming at times, but she'd come for a lesson in self-defense, not a romantic interlude. At least, not beforehand.

"I've cleared away the table in the drawing room so we'll have a carpeted area to practice." He started down the nearest hall, his fingers still linked to hers.

She took in every detail of his home, the fine cherrywood escritoire by the front door, engraved silver salver and framed beveled mirror above. They turned into the first room on the right where a lively fire danced in the hearth.

"You have a lovely home." She watched as he strode to the sideboard and lifted a crystal decanter.

"A little brandy before we begin."

"Won't liquor impair my reflexes?"

"Only a taste." He returned with two crystal glasses and clinked his to the rim of hers before he lifted it higher. "To your safety."

"And to yours." She took a hearty sip, the smooth burn of his expensive brandy adding another layer of heat to the room.

He finished his glass and set it on the mantel and she did the same.

"We should get started. We have a lot to do."

"I'm almost ready." She moved to the displaced table and promptly removed her gown.

"Your trousers." His face lit up like she'd just handed her the world.

"Now we're equally dressed. I thought it made more sense to practice in the appropriate clothing."

He angled his head right and left, one dark brow cocked in appreciative assessment. "I couldn't agree with you more."

Stifling a laugh, she rejoined him on the carpet. He looked into her face, all prior amusement gone, and gently ran his fingertips over her cheek before he touched her neck tenderly. "Women face threats men never need to consider."

"But now I'll be better prepared."

"Yes, you will," he said emphatically. "Let's begin."

"I already know one move. My father taught me when I was old enough to walk about Birmingham with the boy next door."

"I have a good idea, but you should tell me nonetheless. I'd rather we didn't practice that particular move this evening though," he jested. "And who was this lad walking about with you on his arm?"

She ignored his ridiculous question and tried to keep the laughter out of her voice. "A well-placed knee to the groin can be quite effective." She grew more serious. "Unfortunately, both times I was accosted, the attacks came from behind, rendering that particular move useless."

"Then come closer now and I'll show you more effective methods. Lean your back against my chest."

She did as she was told, her backside sliding against him in a way that elicited a low groan from his lips beside her ear.

"Keeping your hair pinned back is an excellent idea, although I prefer it out of its pins," he murmured.

"Let's stay focused, shall we?" Again, amusement betrayed her reprimand, but he immediately sobered.

"If I grab you from behind"—he banded a solid forearm around her waist—"what might you do to gain freedom?"

"I could scratch and punch at your arm or reach over your head and grab a handful of hair." She demonstrated the latter, sliding her bare fingers through the thick, silky lengths above his brow.

"Yes. Very good." His voice sounded strained. "That's one idea."

"Actually, that's two."

"Correct. I lost count there for a moment."

"Well, two *is* a rather large number." She bit her lip waiting for another quippy reply.

"There's no time for teasing when learning defense, Delilah." Humor laced his admonishment in kind.

"Indeed." She released his hair and wriggled against his chest to reorder their positions. That earned another groan.

"You'll be the death of me," he muttered near her ear. "If your elbows are free, you can jab backward into the assailant's ribs or stomp on his feet and legs. Aim for his ankle if he's wearing short boots. Now turn around and we'll practice a forward advance." He took her hand and opened it flat atop his. "The heel of your palm is a powerful weapon. With enough force and momentum, you can break someone's nose, even drive the bone up into the brain."

"Like this." She mimicked the motion twice, but on the third pass she stroked her fingers over his jaw instead. "What if I do this?" She went up on her toes and pressed a kiss to his lips. "What would happen then?"

His warm exhale swept over her cheek. The air between them became fraught with palpable desire.

"Then this might happen." He cradled her face, his fingers at play in the loose strands of hair at her nape before he released the pins and combed through the lengths.

Her heart thudded a heavy beat, her pulse skittered faster. She may have aimed to learn how to avoid capture, but at the moment she was ready to surrender.

Sebastian peered into Delilah's crystalline gaze and an ache swelled deep in his chest. When she'd nestled her backside against his trousers, he knew their lessons wouldn't last long. Now she tempted him in a way that resembled torture as much as pleasure.

"And what if I do this?" She traced a line along his shoulders, gliding over his biceps and down his forearms in a fleeting touch that counted his ribs and ended at the waistband of his trousers. She slipped her fingertips below the band and then just as quickly withdrew.

He sucked in a sharp breath. She was fearless and beautiful and unlike any woman he'd ever known. But two could play at her dangerous game.

"Then I would do this." He loosened the tie at her neck so the shirt gaped open and exposed the swells of her breasts beneath a dainty lace chemise. He took her hand in his, her slim fingers wrapping around in a tight hold. "Come upstairs. This room no longer accommodates us."

Delilah's heart beat a rapid tattoo. She loved this man. She loved him completely. It hadn't been planned or arranged, but it was true. The realization was both thrilling and distressing. No matter his fine town house and tasteful décor, he wasn't a proper gentleman.

Aunt Helen would be devastated.

But, maybe not. Her aunt wanted Delilah to be settled, and she'd found love, precious love. Sebastian was a respectable, hard-working, honest man with a caring heart and protective nature. He worked for the good of London and all its people. It could only be a work of Fate that caused their two lives to dovetail. But now was not a time for complicated considerations.

Now was a time for pleasure.

She followed him into his bedchambers without doubt of where they were headed or what they would do there.

Since last evening when she'd longed to stay in the security of his embrace, she'd counted the minutes until she could return. Glancing around his bedchamber, she noted the decadent furnishings, the large bed and multiple pillows, thick plush carpeting, and oversized chairs near the fireplace. Indeed, Sebastian enjoyed comfort.

He closed and locked the door before gathering her in his arms.

"You're amazing, Delilah." He exhaled, his chest rising and falling against her own. "You're so strong."

"As are you."

"In a different manner, perhaps." He looked into her eyes and she saw heartfelt honesty there. "You've fierce determination and unending courage, all woven together with beauty and grace."

She didn't know what to say to that and no reply was needed. He lowered his mouth and kissed her with such unabashed emotion her heart ached from it.

The kiss ended far too soon.

"What would you like to do now, Delilah?"

His voice was husky and the gruff tones of his throaty question rippled through her.

"I'd like us to go to bed."

She'd hardly finished her reply when he swept her up and carried her there, but they didn't lie down. Instead they stood side by side, each removing a garment in tandem. One for one, equal to equal. First their boots and stockings. Then their shirts.

Delilah paused, her eyes skimming over his bare chest, the brush of hair at the center and long lean line that led below his waistband. When he'd raised his arms to remove the shirt over his head, his hard-shadowed muscles shimmered in the firelight. His physique was beautiful, no matter countless scars marked his skin. She stood in only her lacy chemise and stays, her disrobing more complicated, but he didn't move, allowing her to have her fill before he assisted in unlacing her.

She turned her back so he would have access to the ties there and he nuzzled kisses along her shoulder, at first as soft as a feather against her skin. His attention soon turned to little bites and licks that caused her nerves to dance and nipples to tighten. A dull throb of desire made her wet between her legs. It seemed like forever until he worked the ties free, but at last her underthings were discarded. He caressed her from behind, his fingers warm, the rough texture of his skin another aphrodisiac. When he moved his palms over the tips of her breasts, she shuddered from the intensity of his touch. They both remained in their trousers. She turned, unwilling to suffer his sensual pursuit without recourse.

The look in his eyes was a gratifying reward. He reached for her and she stayed his hand with her own, bringing her fingertips to his chest, tracing the scars there, one by one, and coursing over his nipples, causing him to jerk with sensation now. She paused over one particular scar shaped like a bold X. It extended directly over his heart and she placed her palm flat, feeling the strong beat and cherishing the hard thrum.

"All we have left is trousers." His mouth hitched slightly as he eyed her in challenge.

"And whatever is left beneath." She worked the buttons on her waistband and shimmied the black wool down to her ankles. Then she stepped out and did the same with her pantalets. When she finally met his gaze, a wicked gleam lived there. "Your turn now."

He didn't hesitate and discarded his trousers and smalls to the carpet. They stood admiring each other's body, gloriously naked, but want quickly overtook curiosity.

Skin to skin they joined on the bed linens, the cool sheets against hot flesh adding another invigorating sensation. He plundered her mouth in a long, wonderful kiss, their tongues intertwined as their bodies longed to be. When he pulled back the slightest, he pressed gentle kisses to her neck and nipped her chin before he rolled her against him, her body fitted to his as if she were created for him alone.

She sensed his hesitation, perceived his indecision, and wanted to spare him. His body was all heat and strength, his erection pressed to her abdomen, yet he didn't move.

"I've never lain with a man before." She placed her hands on either side of his face and he raised his eyes to meet hers. "But I want this. I want you."

"Are you sure, Delilah?" He may have realized the futility in that question, considering their undress. "I would never hurt you."

"I know." She reached between them, shyly at first, and wrapped her fingers around his arousal. "You're so hard. Even here."

"Very much there."

And then words were no longer needed.

Sebastian placed his hand atop Delilah's gentle touch, guiding their interwoven fingers down his cock and up again. His restraint was all but decimated. He wanted her with a need he'd never known. But after another stroke he moved to the side, sliding his hands over her silky, smooth skin to explore her curves instead.

He'd learned at an early age that happiness was fleeting, memories often painful and nothing was guaranteed. But none of that mattered now. He only wanted to please the woman in his bed who'd somehow made her way into his heart. He couldn't offer for her as he wished he could. But he *could* give her pleasure upon pleasure.

He traced the seam of her thighs. She opened for him and he slid his fingers into her wet heat. She was drenched. His erection pulsed, his body anxious and ready, but he had other matters to attend. He lowered his mouth to her breast, the tip puckering on his tongue. She hummed a little sound he would always remember and stroked further into her folds, finding the ripe little bud, wanting to give her immeasurable satisfaction.

She wriggled her hips, her eyes closed and head against his pillow. He'd imagined her like this, her hair fanned across the linens, her fragrance of lemons now mixed with the musky scent of their love play. He stroked across her most sensitive spot one more time before he slid his finger inside her. She was tight and wet and before he could do more, she trembled, her climax coming hard and fast. Unwilling to relent, he caressed her, stroke upon stroke, until she clenched his hair in her hand and yanked him upward.

He listed kisses along her silhouette until they were nose to nose. Her cheeks were flushed, her eyes low lidded and glassy, and she'd never looked more beautiful.

Three words rose on his tongue. They were untried and new and still they begged to be spoken. But he smothered them because emotion was rarely the answer to anything, especially at a time like this. He wouldn't complicate matters for her. She deserved better.

CHAPTER 27

Delilah inhaled deeply and smiled, the intimacy of what transpired near overwhelming. She looked at Sebastian, his head on the pillow beside her. She was no accomplished mistress or knowledgeable paramour, but she realized he'd gone without while she'd found pleasure.

"What is this delicious debauchery you teach? And when does my second lesson begin?"

He too smiled before he marshaled his expression. "Always reaching for another goal, are you?"

She moved her hand down his abdomen and beyond until it rested on his erection. "Reaching. That much is true."

He growled something she couldn't decipher and moved above her, his weight supported by his lovely firm biceps, their bodies perfectly aligned. They stared at each other for the length of a few breaths. She wanted to believe it was the magnitude of their union, that their hearts were becoming synchronized and their joining, rare and precious. There were suddenly so many things she wanted to say, but she didn't dare speak and break the fragile moment.

He leaned down, angling his mouth over hers, kissing her until she couldn't hold a thought if her life depended on it. He deepened their kiss, his tongue both silky and rough. He rocked his hips against hers and she welcomed him, wrapping her arms around his neck to tighten their embrace.

His entire body seemed tense and coiled while beneath him she was pliant, nearly boneless with pleasure. The first nudge of his arousal at her core was clearly meant to prepare her, but she would have nothing of temperance now. She slid her soles against the linens and bent her legs slightly to allow him easier access. Instinct told her he needed momentum and force, just like the lesson he'd given her earlier.

He moved with her, his efforts determined and her body willing, while an electric hum of anticipation raced in her blood. At first her body strained to accept him, but she angled her hips, seeking him as he thrust until their goal was met. His sensual kisses and lingering caresses distracted from the sharp fleeting pain as he slid inside her.

They fit together completely, though she barely had a chance to relish the feeling before he withdrew. She objected, her complaint obliterated by his next thrust, and then their bodies caught rhythm. Every time he filled her, she experienced joy, only to be left bereft when he pulled away. The result was a pain-pleasure that stoked her desire and a wave of heat overtook her, lighting her blood and rolling through every muscle. She was certain he felt the same, his expression taut and muscles strained. He growled low and the vibration lingered in the tension between them. Then after one last thrust, he moved to the side and spilled himself on the bedsheets. Perspiration dotted his brow where he lay on the pillow beside her. She stared at him, memorizing the moment.

They must have fallen asleep. Sebastian squinted at the clock on the mantel, the firelight and candles barely enough for him to discern the time. Half two. He wondered if he should wake Delilah and return her home. They'd never discussed their plans further than the bedroom, and selfishly, he didn't want the evening to end.

"What is it?" She perched on one elbow and swept her hair to the side.

"It's so late. We fell asleep. I wouldn't want to cause your aunt worry. Would you like me to take you home?"

She huffed a little breath and he wondered if she was thinking about leaving.

"No." She lay down again, this time positioning herself closer. "As long as I return before dawn, I'll be able to slip upstairs undetected."

She didn't seem worried in the least.

He wanted to kiss her, to touch her again, but he waited. It was as if time held its breath, their night too short, reality all too ready to bring in the new day. What a fool he was to believe it would be so easy to make love with Delilah and then simply let her go. But he wouldn't think about it now and blemish their night together. It was better to talk about something else.

"Have you always lived here?"

Her question startled him even though it was an innocuous thing to ask. He had only to decide how much to share. He'd keep it brief. She already knew he was a child of the streets.

"For many years, my goal was simply survival. But as I became my own man, I needed validation of my worth. My father had tossed me out like a piece of garbage, out into the streets, but it was the streets that provided me with the knowledge to better myself. I used that knowledge to every advantage and came to secure the work I do now. It's dangerous at times, but it suits me." He exhaled fully. The words had come easier than he'd thought they would.

"What about your father?" she asked, her voice soft from the pillow beside him.

"He's out there somewhere, I suppose. Or deceased."

"But don't you wish to know what happened to him?"

"No. I wasn't good enough. I was his bastard son. He didn't want me then. I don't want him now."

"I'm so sorry." Her expression was soft with emotion. "What a fool he was. He must regret his decision."

"I doubt that, Delilah. Peers don't reveal their dirty secrets. Besides, I've made my life now. I've no reason to look back."

"I understand."

"Thank you for that."

"Is Sebastian your real name?" She sounded unsure if she wanted to ask the question.

"Yes."

"And St. Allen?"

"That's my name now. That's all that matters."

She didn't say anything more and he wondered if she'd connected the pieces he'd offered. He admired her clever mind. He was a bastard with blue blood. In some circumstances, he'd be tolerated. He might even be able to court her, marry her. But all that was assuming too much and fully out of reach.

No, he had no regrets. He remembered clearly what he'd lost that day, and because of it he'd become his own man, able to afford his comfortable lifestyle. A successful, skilled man who now worked for the prince regent.

Time to change the subject.

"With Bert injured and in the hands of the Watch, and Sullivan already on the run, I'd venture your aunt is no longer in danger, but my men will remain there as a measure of security."

Her eyes lit up. He'd distracted her effectively.

"Except the diamonds are still missing and the man who threatened me wasn't some Wapping miscreant for hire. He had refined speech and mannerisms."

Sebastian knew better than to doubt her attention to details. "I'll continue my investigation and assume the Maidens of Mayhem will work on your behalf. Pity, I'll no longer see you in trousers."

"There was something else I needed to mention." She moved even closer, their noses almost touching, and she threaded her fingers with his beneath the counterpane.

"Yes?"

"The Maidens haven't been working for me." Her voice dropped lower, as if the words were an intimate secret she'd decided to share. "They've been working *with* me."

"Of course." He smiled at the endearing emphasis she'd placed on the word. It was just like Delilah to want to be treated as an equal. "I understand."

"I'm not sure you do." She pressed a brief kiss to his lips. "I've joined their cause. I *am* a Maiden of Mayhem now."

He didn't answer at first. Did she expect his complete acceptance? He didn't like the idea of her putting herself in danger's path repeatedly, especially after they'd parted ways. That same intense ache formed in his chest. The selfish idea that their lives might cross in the future because of her involvement with the Maidens poked at his brain. But no, it wasn't worth the price of her safety. Still, he couldn't object. It would be the epitome of hypocrisy.

When he didn't immediately speak, she rushed on.

"I also plan on bettering the life of orphans and those who dwell in the streets. Ever since I searched for Oliver and visited the Lost Yard, I can't ignore the plight that plagues the place I now call home. I need to act."

Something inside him arrested when she said that.

Still she waited for his reply, and he forced an answer. "I see." It probably wasn't what she needed to hear, so he continued. "Then I should step up your self-defense training."

She was quiet for a long minute before she pulled her hand from his under the covers.

He'd said the wrong thing. Offended her. Hurt her feelings. It wasn't his intent.

"You mean, like this?"

Before he realized what she meant to do, she sat atop him, her legs on each side of his body as if she rode a horse. Her hair fell about her shoulders and her eyes glittered in the candlelight.

She looked exquisite.

He didn't need any more inducement to begin their next lesson after that.

It could have been the errand Delilah and Oliver pursued the next morning which brought about her effervescent mood, but she knew better. Last night seemed more a dream than reality and yet the subtle soreness between her legs testified it was all quite real. But along with that joy came the inevitable heartache. Eventually, she would want to marry. She couldn't bear the thought of spending her life with anyone other than Sebastian. This truth provoked such intense melancholy it threatened to overshadow the happiness in her heart. Her life was decided by circumstances much the same way his had been.

"Are we there yet, Delilah?" Oliver shifted on the carriage bench and pressed his face to the small square window.

It may have been the twelfth time he'd asked that question but Delilah didn't mind the distraction.

"One more block and we'll arrive at Redman Square. There are several public gardens where you may choose a bouquet for your mother." She put her gloves on and picked up her reticule. This morning she appeared as she usually did, a proper aristocratic lady.

"There. I see it!" Oliver exclaimed.

"Let's wait for the carriage to slow completely." She grabbed hold of his hand. Their past upset aside, she wasn't about to let Oliver scamper away today or any day going forward.

They entered the public gardens and Delilah was surprised so many people shared the space, given the early hour. Wrought-iron benches marked the walkway as the gravel path wound through plots of sweet peas, peonies, scabious, and delphiniums in a variety of bright colors. Oliver's eyes grew larger each time he looked in a different direction.

"This beats Mrs. Dunn's silly old garden behind the house."

Delilah bit back a smile. "I'm glad you're happy with the selection." She paused and removed a small scissors from her reticule. "Why don't you show me the flowers you'd like to include in your mother's arrangement and I'll cut the stems."

"I can do it," he immediately objected. "I know how to use scissors, Delilah."

"I'm sure you do, but I rather hoped you'd allow me to help in some way. Otherwise I'll have nothing to do but watch sparrows pick at worms, and I'm sure you know how boring that can be."

This notion caused Oliver considerable thought; his brows lowered as he sorted through his decision. "All right. That sounds reasonable."

This time Delilah couldn't help but laugh aloud, amused by her clever companion. They collected twelve flowers in a kaleidoscope of colors. When they finished, they sat on the nearest bench and Delilah removed a lacy handkerchief from her purse. Together they arranged the blooms in a pretty bouquet. They were nearly finished when a young girl approached, her tattered shoes and ill-fitting frock an immediate reminder of the children Delilah now noticed in every corner of London. In one tiny fist this child held a few lengths of ribbon.

"Buy 'o ribbon?"

The sweetness of her question spoke directly to Delilah's heart. The ribbons were frayed on both ends and most were as dirty as the little hand that held them, but she didn't hesitate.

"How perfect. Don't you think so, Oliver?" She smiled broadly at the child and ignored Oliver's confounded grouse. "I'd like them all, actually."

Delilah opened her reticule and removed four shillings. It was a fortune to pay for the ribbons and she couldn't be more pleased to do it. The girl gasped as Delilah pressed the coins into her hand and then before another word could be expressed, the child ran off.

"I thought we were buying a new ribbon," Oliver said, curiosity and confusion in his voice. "My mama doesn't like when things are dirty."

"We are going to purchase a new ribbon." Delilah looked down into Oliver's face, anxious to reassure him.

"What? Then why did you spend your money on these old things? None of them are any good. Mama says I'm never to waste money." He indicated the ribbons on the bench, his chubby finger hovering over the lengths without touching.

"It's true these ribbons are no longer useful, but the price I paid will help that girl buy food. Not just for today, but many days. Mayhap she may even share it with others. There's nothing that can replace a full belly, now is there?" Delilah scooped up the ribbons and tucked them into her reticule for later. They would serve as a reminder she had a lot to do in order to help London's street urchins.

Oliver patted his stomach as he agreed. "And my belly feels empty. Are we near the bakery? I think I smell currant buns."

"Perhaps we can stop at the bake shop after we visit the milliner for that ribbon." She gathered the flowers in the handkerchief, freeing one hand so she could grasp Oliver's when they returned to the carriage. His mention of a currant bun immediately reminded of her visit to the tea shop with Sebastian. Would that be how life proceeded? Where everything prompted a memory? She'd rather Sebastian and she made memories together going forward, not looking back.

He was a remarkable man, to have had such humble beginnings and succeeded so well in life.

"You know, Oliver, not everyone has dry clothing, a warm bed, and someone to kiss them good night in the evening."

"What?"

His incredulous expression almost provoked another smile, but Delilah was determined to teach Oliver about the world around him at a young age so he could understand from there on.

"Let's talk about it on the way to the milliner. We have a lot to do this morning." She reached out and Oliver took her hand.

"Yes, because tonight is Mama's party and I have the most wonderful present to give her." He beamed with pride.

"Indeed, you do," Delilah agreed. "Although I believe you are the present, Oliver."

CHAPTER 28

Sebastian sealed the letter and placed it to the side. Within the contents, he'd written a comprehensive update in the matter of the Duchess of Grandon's missing diamonds, but he'd also detailed Eva's actions. She'd allowed her personal feelings to overflow into her work. It was perhaps the most heinous of all mistakes for an agent.

And yet, he knew the same accusation could apply to himself. He was still digesting the news Delilah shared about her work with the Maidens of Mayhem. Naturally, he'd known of the group's existence and the good they perpetuated through London. He'd even learned one of the women recently left the team and married a duke.

Recalling that fact splintered his thoughts in several directions. Delilah had asked about his history, if that's what one would call the first fifteen years of his life. Could it be she was thinking about the future? Including him in that vision?

The sound of male voices jolted him from the muddle of these questions. Darlington and Vane entered the main office, their usual good-natured bickering alive in the air between them.

As expected, the two men went straight to the billiards table. Sebastian joined them, selecting his stick and chalking the tip while Tristan retrieved the iron from its place near the hearth.

He ironed the baize quickly before Malcolm unlocked the billiard box and placed the three ivory balls on the table. All this was done with swift execution, a habit learned from various nights when they played billiards into the wee hours while simultaneously working through unsolved problems in assigned cases.

"Any news on the Grandon situation?" Tristan leaned against the table's padded rail while he rolled up his shirtsleeves.

"Bert and Sullivan carried out the theft, returned with the boy, and lost the diamonds." He gave the succinct update as he aligned the red ball on the table.

"Any overlooked angles we should explore?" Malcolm took his shot, sinking the first ball and scoring three points.

"Not at the moment, although I'm of mind to pay Viscount Clayton a visit. He's the one uncooperative component of this matter."

"Good idea. He's in pretty low water with pockets to let. The situation is far beyond youthful recklessness," Tristan added.

"A man in need of funds is dangerous," Sebastian agreed. "Any other news being bandied about?"

"The duchess was seen in Hyde Park with Yardley on her arm yesterday." Malcolm set his cue against the wall. "Apparently, they're a public couple now, even though they've had a tumultuous love affair."

"Eva mentioned something to that effect," Sebastian commented begrudgingly. He didn't want to say her name and somehow evoke her company. It would be a long time before he could be civil in her presence.

"Speaking of Miss Fields . . ." Tristan hesitated. "Her departure is unexpected."

"Departure?" Sebastian made his shot and the ball bounced off the far corner.

"She sent each of us a message earlier," Malcolm added. "We assumed you'd received the same."

"I didn't." Sebastian's man of all things left the daily correspondence on the front hall salver. Sebastian had checked it this morning and also paused to relive Delilah's arrival and how the night had progressed so perfectly. To that point he was distracted, but he was also certain no message from Eva had arrived. "What did it say?"

"You honestly didn't get anything?"

"Get on with the telling." He regretted the note of annoyance in his voice, but he didn't have a good feeling about these messages, especially if he was specifically excluded. "I'm not playing a game here."

"You are, actually. And you're winning."

Ignoring Tristan's jibe, he gestured toward Malcolm to hurry him into speaking.

"Eva's done. Left. No longer working with us."

Sebastian took a minute to digest this news. Then he picked up his cue and made another shot. "Did she say why?" He sank one of the ivory balls in the far pocket.

"No," Malcolm continued. "But we thought you might know since you were both working on the Grandon problem."

How much should he share? His friends thought highly of Eva, partly enamored with the idea of a female who dedicated her life to covert operations. But Sebastian knew a different woman, a better one, who acted selflessly, faced danger without fear or complaint, all the while looking exquisite in black wool trousers. He smiled. Bloody fool that he was, he loved her. He loved Delilah.

"Everything is prepared for later." Delilah poured her aunt a cup of tea and then filled her own before settling on the chaise in the drawing room. "It seems as though this celebration has been a lifetime in coming."

"It has been." Aunt Helen added a little cream to her cup and stirred vigorously. "Have you heard from Lord Hibbett, dear? I suspect he's developing a fondness for you."

"No, I haven't," Delilah answered quickly, glad to have this quiet time with her aunt. She'd already decided to broach a particular subject, as it weighed heavily on her mind. She was not one to cower from difficult conversations and she hoped the information would be well received. "I don't feel the same way though."

"Oh." Aunt Helen appeared surprised. "Has he done something to put you off?"

"No. Nothing like that." Delilah rushed on. "He's kind and has always acted as a gentleman."

"I see."

Her aunt couldn't possibly.

"It's because I've developed affection for someone else."

"Oh, do tell." Aunt Helen's eyes glittered across the rosewood table. "Who is this lucky gentleman?"

"Well"—Delilah fiddled with the high lace collar below her chin—"when you meet him, you may recognize him as Lord Wintel from the Earl of Mumford's ball." There. That seemed a good place to start.

"Yes. I remember. A dashing gentleman with broad shoulders and piercing eyes. So tall, too. Impeccably dressed. Lord Wintel made quite an impression."

Delilah wanted to agree with Aunt Helen's accurate list of Sebastian's admirable qualities, but there was still so much to tell.

"That's the thing," Delilah continued. "Beth and Oliver know him as Mr. St. Allen."

Aunt Helen's smile fell away. "I don't understand. You said his name is Lord Wintel."

"Let me explain." Delilah clasped her hands in her lap. "St. Allen is his real name." *Although that wasn't completely true either. But it was the truth Sebastian accepted.*

Aunt Helen didn't reply and Delilah continued.

"He attended Lord Mumford's affair to complete a business matter and couldn't reveal his real name, so he posed as Lord Wintel."

"How odd." Her aunt busied herself with adjusting the spoons on the tea tray, and Delilah interpreted the gesture as distraction. Her aunt could only be uncomfortable with the explanation. The last thing Delilah desired was to portray Sebastian poorly.

"Mr. St. Allen assisted in Oliver's recovery."

"He left him on our doorstep?"

"No, no. He helped in the search. He's an honest man, Aunt Helen, and respectful and generous. I know how much you'd like me to make an esteemed match, and so you should know he's not of distinguished heritage."

"I see." Aunt Helen inhaled deeply.

Everything depended on this conversation, and Delilah had made a mess of explaining things. She wanted Aunt Helen's blessing if she could even dream of a life with Sebastian.

"You know, Delilah, before I married your uncle, I had a romance of the heart." Aunt Helen spoke softly, her eyes reminiscent. "His name was William and he was the handsomest man I'd ever met. He too was kind and of common birth. When my parents discovered my tendre, they forbade me from keeping William's company and arranged my marriage to your uncle within a week. But my heart was already given. How I loved William."

Delilah held her breath. She'd never heard this story before, had never considered her aunt's life before her marriage.

"But that doesn't matter now, does it?" Aunt Helen lost her dreamy expression and cleared her throat. "I married your uncle, God rest his soul, and he provided me with a pleasant life."

"What happened to William?" Delilah couldn't stop herself from asking.

"I don't know. I've always wondered, but I couldn't bring myself to ask. It was better that way. Not knowing. I don't think I could bear hearing he had married and grown a family. I moved to London with your uncle and I've been here ever since."

"I'm sorry." Delilah held her breath. Had her aunt shared that story to convince Delilah her relationship with Sebastian was of no significance? That life would continue despite her heart was given to someone else? Marriages among the aristocracy were rarely a love match.

"Cheer up." Aunt Helen's face regained its usual joyful mien.

"I'm not telling you all this to gain sympathy. I want you to know I understand. That I was once in the same place in life as you. Now tell me more, is your Mr. St. Allen a good man?"

"Yes." Delilah breathed a little easier.

"Do you love him?"

"Quite completely." Her chest grew tight as she said the words.

"Then I trust your judgment." Aunt Helen nodded emphatically. "Of course, I'll need to spend time in Mr. St. Allen's company, and you must always be properly chaperoned, but otherwise I have no objection to him courting you."

Delilah bit her bottom lip. If her aunt only knew. Still, she had to believe Sebastian felt the same connection, that he'd held back because of the differences in their stations, and that once he learned Aunt Helen had given her blessing, they might have a chance at a future. She couldn't wait to share the news.

Sebastian dropped the brass knocker and stepped to the side of the polished limestone stairs leading to the Duchess of Grandon's front door. Her Grace lived in a grand town mansion situated in the center of Mayfair, much like a queen among subjects. Her extravagant style and ostentatious personality were exemplified in every feature of the three-story structure, from the façade's smooth Portland stone to the elaborate pilasters which commanded one take notice.

The reserved butler who opened the door took Sebastian's card and placed *Lord Wintel* in the salon to await Her Grace's attention. He wondered if she would grant him an audience. He had nothing to provoke her to do so, other than the memory of his feigned love of Pomeranians. He scoured his memory now in an attempt to remember his fictitious dog's name in case she inquired. So much had happened between that conversation and this moment. Somehow time had sped by faster, and yet the investigation had almost slowed to a halt.

Either way, he'd fallen in love along the journey.

"Lord Wintel." Her Grace's voice snared his attention and he turned as she entered. She waved her glove in communication to the servant who trailed her that all was as it should be.

"Your Grace." Sebastian bowed low and accepted her proffered hand, where he placed a brief kiss. The duchess was fond of ceremony.

A series of sharp yips interrupted the greeting as two compact dogs with plumed tails ran into the room, their nails causing them to slide on the marble tiles as they collided with each other in their playful frenzy.

"You've acquired another dog?" Sebastian asked with purposeful curiosity. "Which one is Cygnet? They're both such fine-looking animals."

"That is true." Her Grace indicated a nearby overstuffed chair as she settled on an elongated chaise covered in bright pink brocade. "And they have quite a romance."

He might have been mistaken, but the dowager duchess's cheeks gained a rosy hue. Or it may have been due to the fuchsia fabric of the chaise. He couldn't be sure.

"There"—she pointed toward the larger of the two dogs—"that handsome dasher is Cygnet. And the other is Athena. Notice how she dotes on my boy. She's besotted."

Sebastian continued to probe, seeking more answers to a problem that became more absurd by the minute. "Cygnet was returned unharmed? I recall when we spoke at Mumford's event you were beside yourself with worry."

"Indeed, I was, though it was all for naught." She paused and adjusted one of the flounces on her gown. "I am sixty and eight, young man. I know you likely consider that ancient, but I've earned the right to be eccentric, fickle, or indulgent upon my whims. Time is fleeting and life is far too short, even by my standards, and I've already enjoyed more years than most. Cygnet's disappearance and subsequent return served to remind me of those facts. While Lord Yardley and I quibble over circumstance and detail, days and weeks fritter away in unhappiness. His elaborate ruse helped me gain clarity."

"Ruse?" Sebastian bit back his true opinion on that matter. Yardley's actions had endangered a child and caused countless people to put themselves at risk of harm. It was hardly a ruse.

"Yes." The dowager smiled and a glimmer of a younger woman shone through. "It is good to be adored."

As if the dogs were trained to agree, the dogs launched into a series of yips. But it was the movement in the hall that likely caused their reaction.

Lord Yardley entered the room wearing a loosely belted banyan in deep jade silk. His satin bed slippers whispered a shuffle as he moved forward. He portrayed the decadent nobleman, a man delighted with the fortuitous outcome of his extravagant masquerade.

"Your Grace."

"Good morning, my love."

Yardley took the dowager's hand and lingered over it, their interplay communicating more than their words.

"Lord Wintel called to inquire over Cygnet's safety," the dowager explained. "We'd previously discussed the matter at Mumford's."

"Is that so." Yardley angled his head and spared Sebastian an inquisitive perusal.

"With everything as it should be, I will take my leave." Sebastian stood and made his farewells. The dogs chased his heels as he advanced to the foyer, yet it wasn't so loud to override the lavish endearments which escaped the couple left behind.

He would never be able to explain the idiosyncrasies and peculiarities of the aristocracy and he dismissed his anger, refusing to allow it to ruin his mood. Problems were solving themselves, though others still existed. There was the matter of Viscount Clayton and the missing diamonds.

And more so, Delilah and her hold on his heart. He hadn't spoken to her and he needed to remedy that. She'd mentioned a trip into Redman Square and a gathering at her home this evening. If he were to call, he wondered if she'd be free to walk with him.

First though, he would pursue Viscount Clayton and learn more of the nobleman's unsatisfied greed. Sebastian hadn't gained knowledge of the missing diamonds from the duchess. Eva had shared that information. He'd have to approach the problem differently, because while he'd assured Delilah she was safe, with his men keeping watch, he wouldn't take any chance with her life or that of her family and friends.

CHAPTER 29

Delilah straightened the embroidered lace at her neck and confirmed it covered the bruises adequately. The marks left by the attack were tinged yellow now and fading, but she still worried someone in the household would notice. There really was no way she'd be able to explain her injury away without inviting a bevy of questions.

She'd come up to her bedchamber for a few moments' respite, but her nerves were having none of it and it wasn't simply the excitement of Beth's birthday celebration later. She missed Sebastian, and the desire to tell him about her conversation with Aunt Helen frayed her patience further. Where was he? Did he spend his days at the bookstore?

She touched her fingertips to her lips. What she wouldn't give for one of his kisses right now. He possessed the unique and wonderful ability to calm her even when she was at her worst.

She sat on the mattress and eyed the lantern on her bedside table. All she need do is put the lantern on the windowsill and he would be notified. But he could be in the middle of an important meeting or far from Berwick Street pursuing a righteous cause. Clearly it was wrong to summon the man just because she craved one of his kisses.

Falling backward on the bed, she closed her eyes and sighed.

Sebastian had her tied in too many knots to unravel. She recalled the intense look on his face when he was above her last evening. Nothing would ever replace the exhilaration of making love with Sebastian St. Allen. A light knock interrupted her musings and she rose to answer the door.

"This just arrived for you." Beth handed a note forward and Delilah quickly broke the seal.

> *Are you available for a walk at half three this afternoon? Put the lantern on the sill if you'd like me to call. —S.*

A rush of emotion swept through her and she gave an airy laugh. "How serendipitous!"

"So, it's good news." Beth looked relieved.

"Yes, and I'll need your chaperone at half three. Can Oliver help Mrs. Dunn with the preparations in the kitchen while we're gone?"

"Of course." Beth nodded.

"We'll return well before dinner and the party planned afterward." Delilah glanced to the bracket clock on the wall. There was still time for her to change her gown and tidy her hair. She'd need to put the lantern outside too.

With Beth's assistance, Delilah was perfumed and ready when Sebastian arrived. Aunt Helen was indisposed, resting from the flurry of preparations in the house, and therefore it rendered formal introductions unnecessary.

Delilah stepped out into the sunshine, with Beth following behind. She accepted Sebastian's elbow and then they crossed Berwick Street and walked around the corner where a modest square provided convenient privacy.

"This is a lovely surprise." He looked handsome in the afternoon light. She breathed deeply and savored his spicy cologne.

"I have news to share." He glanced over his shoulder to confirm Beth trailed several paces behind. "I visited the Duchess of Grandon this morning. Not only is Cygnet happily ensconced in a romantic relationship, but Her Grace and Lord Yardley have been mending fences." He waggled his brows. "Among other things."

"Oh my." She squeezed his forearm where her fingers rested, relishing the solid strength beneath.

"How is your neck? Does it still pain you?" His brows lowered with concern, though he couldn't see beyond the lacy frills of her collar.

"No," she reassured him quickly. "These high-necked gowns are more irritating than the bruises."

He offered her a mischievous smile and her heart turned over. "You always look lovely, but now that I've seen you in trousers, I'm ruined for everything else."

"You and my trousers!"

They laughed together as they followed a turn beside an ornamental fountain, though they soon fell into a companionable silence. Things were resolving swimmingly and she envisioned many more afternoons spent just like this one.

"That only leaves the missing diamonds and Viscount Clayton," Sebastian continued, unaware she mentally considered their future. "I paid a visit to the viscount, but he wasn't home. An associate of mine confirmed he's in a significant financial bind. Large debts and impatient collectors aren't an ideal mix. Desperation can drive a man to take drastic action."

"Like threatening my aunt's safety."

"Or worse."

This sudden somber turn in their conversation provoked her to lighten the mood.

"I also have news." She grinned up at his face, the late day sun causing her to squint. "I spoke to my aunt about our . . ." She hesitated using the word on the tip of her tongue. He'd never declared feelings for her or mentioned a day beyond tomorrow. Had she assumed too much?

"Relationship?"

She sighed, suddenly relieved. "Yes, that's the word. At first my aunt didn't understand your use of a fictitious name, but I explained it away as a business matter and she's given me permission to encourage Mr. St. Allen to call."

He didn't reply immediately and she rushed on, anxious to finish her thought. "To that point, we're having a small celebration for Beth's birthday tonight. I know Oliver would enjoy seeing you again. Considering it is the event which caused our paths to cross in the first place, I thought you might like to attend." Her voice climbed higher as she finished. What was he thinking? He hadn't said a word.

"I wouldn't miss it." He laid his hand atop hers. "But you didn't share your involvement with the Maidens when you spoke to your aunt, did you?"

"Heavens, no." He'd surprised her with his quick change of subject. His tone had changed too. "I would never cause her the unending worry of wondering where I was every night and whether or not I was safe."

"I see."

It was subtle, the shift in mood, but she sensed it nonetheless.

They'd come full circle on the path and crossed the road to walk back to Berwick Street, where he promptly returned her home.

"Until this evening."

Something didn't seem right. She wished she could go up on her toes and press her lips to his. She'd been after a kiss, after all. But that was not to be.

Sebastian followed Viscount Clayton to a seedy tavern not far from the King's Elbow. What a polished young dandy wanted with a ramshackle drinking establishment was left to speculation, but Sebastian knew the peer was in deep and floundering to remedy his situation.

Slipping into a booth unnoticed, Sebastian decided to watch Clayton and assess the situation before engaging him. He reasoned the viscount was here for either of two reasons: to meet someone and further his pursuit of the diamonds, or to drink cheap liquor and drown his sorrows far away from polite society where he'd be recognized.

What had happened to the diamonds? Bert claimed Sullivan left London in fear. Sebastian doubted either of the men were clever enough to hide their theft and fence the gems without Yardley or Clayton detecting the double cross. Furthermore, an intruder had threatened Delilah, and Clayton could fit the description she'd given. Could Clayton believe Oliver saw what happened to the diamonds and confided in Delilah? That she knew where to find the jewels?

A man entered the tavern, his black greatcoat drawing Sebastian's eye immediately. It was Yardley, and he took the empty chair at Clayton's table, where the two launched into a hushed conversation. Yardley left straight after, their exchange lasting no longer than a few minutes.

Gauging Clayton's level of inebriation, Sebastian summoned a serving girl and sent a tankard of ale to the viscount's table. When Clayton peered around the interior suspiciously, Sebastian turned away.

Again he waited, and after half the pitcher was consumed, Sebastian made his way to the table.

"Harper!" Sebastian greeted Clayton with a clap to the shoulder. "I didn't expect to see you here."

"I'm not Harper, you bloody imbecile." Clayton practically slurred the insult, his eyes reddened and weary. "Wait, I think I remember you from somewhere."

"People always say that when I'm solving their problems." The power of suggestion could go a long way when someone's judgment was compromised. "I'll order us another round."

He took the empty chair and signaled the server, who brought a second pitcher promptly. Clayton only grunted. He might have objected to the company but he didn't feel the same way about the ale.

"There's nothing like a drink to drown a man's sorrows," Sebastian commented, taking a conservative taste.

"Drink doesn't solve problems," Clayton grumbled. "It makes them worse."

Ignoring the viscount's contradictory logic, Sebastian pushed on. "What's troubling you?"

"Money matters."

Sebastian didn't respond and waited for Clayton to fill the silence.

"I've creditors demanding to be paid, and my only living relative has disowned me. She called me a squandering ne'er-do-well, among other things." Clayton washed away his complaints with another large swallow of alcohol.

"Couldn't you try to make amends?"

"There's nothing for it. My aunt won't see reason." Clayton heaved a breath, spittle speckling the scarred table between them. "She only cares about her pets. Yardley included."

"Most people despise disharmony within the family. You may have misjudged the situation."

"What do you know of it?" The viscount scrunched up his face and blinked rapidly, seemingly appalled Sebastian would question his reasoning.

"I could act as mediator. From the sound of it you have little to lose. Your aunt may reconsider. The decision you make in this moment could change your life. If we leave here and go straight to . . ." He paused on purpose.

"Mayfair." Clayton stroked his fingers over his mouth and straightened his shoulders, his drink-drenched brain busy at work. "That's where the duchess lives."

Sebastian remained quiet, allowing Clayton's desperation and contemplation to mingle and congeal. When Clayton stood, he staggered slightly and leaned on the back of his chair to regain his balance. Then he attempted to flatten the wrinkles in his waistcoat. Sebastian signaled the serving girl and paid their tab.

"Well," Clayton barked. "Come on then."

Sebastian followed the viscount outside, where he hailed a hack. Once on their way, he worked to convince Clayton his idea was brilliant, though he suspected the conflict to follow would be anything but redemptive. Would the Duchess of Grandon take pity on her nephew and forgive his transgressions? She didn't seem like someone who suffered fools or granted forgiveness easily. Things could very well implode. She didn't seem overly concerned with her heirloom diamonds either. But Sebastian wasn't of like mind. As long as their disappearance posed a threat to Delilah's safety, he couldn't rest.

There was no way to be certain what would happen, but as the hack pulled to the curb Sebastian knew they were about to find out.

The duchess wouldn't welcome the familial squabble being aired in an outsider's presence, and Clayton agreed it would inhibit their discussion, so that left Sebastian to eavesdropping in the hallway. Luckily, he was adept at the practice.

"What are *you* doing here?" Her Grace's acerbic tone rang across the salon. "I made it clear as crystal you were no longer welcome." The dogs punctuated her reprimand with a series of complaints. "I should have Yardley remove you. Are you in your cups, Clayton?"

There was no mistaking the disapproval in the dowager's voice.

"Your Grace."

Sebastian was impressed with the sincere note of humility Clayton managed, especially considering the amount of liquor bolstering his courage. The duchess did have a sobering effect.

"Stop sniveling and stand up. If you're going to bow you may as well continue to the floor and grovel at my feet with your apologies. You're a wastrel of a nephew. My only living blood relative and you're nothing more than a squanderer and spendthrift. What could you possibly have to say that would cause me to change my mind?"

"I'm sorry. Terribly sorry."

There was such a long silence after Clayton's apology Sebastian wondered if the two of them still remained in the room.

"You have Yardley to thank for my generosity."

So, the earl was also in the room. How convenient and conniving, the nobleman anxious to avoid the truth and smooth over deception. In the end, everyone received a modicum of what they were after.

"Recent developments have left me feeling charitable." Her Grace's voice expressed the opposite, each word said in a begrudging tone. "I have reconsidered, but I will not have you embarrass me in London with your negligence and tomfoolery."

"Yes, Your Grace."

Clayton actually sounded contrite.

"Your debt is forgiven. I'll see to the creditors who badger and blacken your name, but it's off to the countryside for you. Away from the temptations that plague you here in London. You'll do fine at Grandon House. Go home. Pack your things. You leave tomorrow."

"Thank you, Your Grace."

The dowager's harrumph was all Sebastian heard before he slipped out the door.

CHAPTER 30

Delilah rested her head on the rim of the tub and promised herself just another few minutes. She wanted to take extra care with her appearance tonight, but even the balm of her imported lemon soap couldn't soothe the niggling doubt something was wrong. She'd anticipated more than a cordial greeting and formal update when Sebastian invited her to walk earlier. Yet he'd never even mentioned their night together or the precious bond forged between them.

After she'd shared the news of her conversation with Aunt Helen, he'd seemed to pull away, and yet he'd accepted her invitation for this evening. It was all terribly confusing. If only emotion was as fundamental as crime, where determining right and wrong depended on concrete evidence and not feelings and moods.

She finished her bath and toweled dry, her mind replaying their conversation verbatim in an attempt to unriddle what might have changed between them. This evening she would dress and arrange her own hair so the guest of honor could also get ready for the party. She'd chosen a lovely gown in deep burgundy, and after she'd completed her layers of underthings and secured the buttons of her dress, she added ruby ear bobs and made her way downstairs. If only her emotions were as neatly put together.

For a household of five there was plenty of commotion. She

stood on the last step near the newel post when a knock sounded. Waving off Mrs. Dunn, Delilah walked to the door with Oliver catching her hems eagerly behind.

"Good evening."

Sebastian's deep voice worked better than her lemon soap to smooth her disquiet and she was tempted to believe everything was fine and she'd only imagined the earlier tension between them.

"Hello." Oliver stepped from behind her skirts.

Sebastian greeted the child with a firm handshake and offered a lovely bouquet of fresh blooms. "These are for your mother."

"We match!" Oliver exclaimed with excitement, the bouquet in his grasp held at a precarious angle. "These are just like the flowers we picked at Redman Square."

"Come in." Delilah widened the door and moved to the side. "It's almost time for dessert."

"I baked the cake with Mrs. Dunn today," Oliver continued. "She said no one will ever know part of the eggshell fell in." Full of energy, he ran toward the kitchen, leaving Delilah and Sebastian smiling after him.

"I'm glad you're here."

"You look beautiful."

"It's a special night," she added.

"Not as special as last night."

He'd leaned down to whisper this in her ear and her heart thudded triple time. They needed to talk. She had to know what he was thinking.

"There's a lovely view of the moon on the back terrace if you'd like to take a peek after gifts are given." It was another bold suggestion to add to her long list of improprieties, but she was fast discovering propriety wasn't always the best path to pursue.

"I'm very fond of the moon." A gleam of mischief sparkled in his pale blue eyes.

"As am I."

Enjoying their playful banter, Delilah was reluctant to move into the drawing room, but the only way to reach the end of the evening when they could talk privately was to make introductions. Time passed quickly in jovial conversation until at last the party was almost at an end.

One by one the presents were opened until it was Oliver's turn. He'd insisted on giving his gift last. Enjoying everyone's attention, he went to the hearthside basket where Aunt Helen kept a blanket for chilly drafts. He reached below it and removed a package wrapped in a bundle of lace and linen.

"Oliver, is that my fichu?" Aunt Helen's eyes widened in surprise.

"It was the perfect size," Oliver defended amid a round of laughter.

"I looked everywhere for that just yesterday." Aunt Helen's smile softened as she shook her head, bemused.

Beth sat in the walnut armchair, visibly uncomfortable to have all eyes focused on her. Oliver rushed to her side and placed his present in her lap. Then he kissed his mother on her cheek. The room fell quiet in appreciation and anticipation, but Oliver soon jolted everyone from their sentimental reverie.

"Open it, Mama! I've waited so long to give it to you."

Obeying her son, she gently pulled the satin ribbon loose and the fichu fell open to reveal a thick leather band with a double row of round diamonds. The stones caught the light from the fireplace, glittering and winking their brilliance across the room.

Everyone gasped, albeit for very different reasons.

"Cygnet's collar!" Delilah couldn't believe her eyes. Oliver had hinted at a special gift for weeks now and she'd never considered the mention beyond a child's belief his gift was most special.

"But it can be a necklace or a bracelet for you, Mama." Oliver looked around the room, proud and pleased with himself. "Or we can get a dog!"

His last suggestion evoked another round of laughter.

"Fine work, young man. The Duchess of Grandon will be much relieved to know her heirloom diamonds have been found."

Sebastian stepped forward and Beth gently placed the diamond collar in his outstretched hand.

"You mean we can't keep it?" Oliver asked with a mixture of shock and anger. "I took it when that nasty man didn't know it. He didn't deserve such a pretty necklace, but you do, Mama."

"Let's talk about it tomorrow, Oliver." Beth took her son's hand and steered him out of the room. "I wonder if there's any cake left. Would you help me check?"

"And just like that the last piece falls into place," Sebastian murmured beside Delilah.

"The last piece?" She hated how uncertain she sounded, but her heart gave a little twist when he'd said those cryptic words. Surely, he spoke of recovering the diamonds, but what of their relationship?

"Let's go out on the terrace now."

Delilah glanced at her aunt, who nodded with a smile. Taking Sebastian's elbow, they moved through the rooms and out into the brisk night air. As promised, the full moon shone overhead.

"I'm confused." She turned to face him with her hip pressed to the balustrade. "I thought when we were together the other night you felt the same way I did." She swallowed, suddenly unsure of everything or mayhap nothing at all.

"I do." Sebastian exhaled a long breath, his expression intense. "I do, Delilah. But then you told me you've joined the Maidens of Mayhem. That you'll continue to seek out danger, break down doors, confront criminals and risk your life. You said you would never worry your aunt over your alliance to the league, but I'd worry. It would worry me. I'd worry every time you were out of my sight."

He ran his fingers through his hair and waited, as if beseeching her to interrupt and tell him she wouldn't do it anymore. That she'd break ties with the Maidens. But she had no plans to leave the group. She'd only just begun to work toward resolving injustice.

"I could say the same of you," she objected with disappointment. "You take all the same risks."

"It's not the same."

"Why not?"

He didn't say anything for several minutes. He stood, staring at the moon, and each passing second forced further uneasiness to cause her doubt.

"It's not the same because I've never loved someone before. I've never given my heart into someone else's care. I've never had someone care about me." He drew her into his arms and placed a kiss to her forehead. "But I do now, Delilah. I've opened my heart to you and you've filled it completely. I couldn't bear to lose you. That's a chance I'm unwilling to take. Not when I've just discovered how love is supposed to feel."

"I do love you, Sebastian, and it isn't fair or right your life has been without genuine affection. I'm so sorry. And I do understand your hesitation. But you also run toward danger. You also risk your life. You willingly fight for just causes and yet you won't fight for the most important joy life has to offer. Don't push me away because you fear losing me. Pull me closer so we can have the most wonderful future together."

He breathed deeply and his hold on her tightened.

"I vow to you I will always be sensible, careful, and honest." She went on: "I won't take unnecessary risks because I carry your heart right beside mine. Will you do the same?"

"Of course, because I love you," he answered immediately. "And now I know you love me. And when someday you're expecting our little one?"

His words sounded so tentative and fraught with caution, her heart expanded to near overflowing.

"Then I will happily leave restoring justice in London to the other Maidens of Mayhem." She pulled back far enough to look him in the eye, his chiseled profile outlined in moonlight, his pale eyes aglitter. "Besides, I'll be too busy preparing for our babe."

"I suggest we start practicing immediately after the wedding then," he said with a grin.

"Very clever." She went up on her toes, seeking the kiss she'd wanted for what seemed like forever. "Very clever indeed."

*   *   *

Delilah entered the Duchess of Grandon's drawing room, anxious with her errand in the new light of morning. She had good news to share with Her Grace, but that paled in comparison to the knowledge she would soon be Sebastian's wife. Her life had changed in every way imaginable since she'd come to London, but nothing compared to the love and security she experienced in his embrace, his kisses, and their delicious late-night assignations.

"Why have you come, Lady Ashbrook?"

She would soon be Lady St. Allen, able to retain her title and *also* able to keep her secret identity with the Maidens of Mayhem. It filled her with thrilling anticipation.

"I have something to return to you, Your Grace."

Delilah sank into a low curtsy and then approached the fuchsia chaise where the duchess sat with Cygnet nestled in her skirts.

"I believe this belongs to you." Removing the diamond collar from her reticule, Delilah placed the valuable gemstones in the duchess's hand.

"How do you come to have this?" The duchess assessed her with a discerning stare. "Were you involved in Cygnet's disappearance and the theft of his collar?"

"No, of course not, Your Grace." Delilah needed to choose her words carefully. "The child who petted Cygnet that morning was in my company on Jermyn Street. He too suffered an ordeal, but information he shared led me to pursue the miscreants who caused the incident. Eventually, the collar was recovered." Hopefully she'd relayed enough to satisfy the dowager and also protect the many secrets she'd collected along the way.

"You're an ambitious gel. I'll give you that." The duchess glanced at the collar draped across her palm. "Why didn't you keep the diamonds? They're worth a good fortune. My feckless nephew, who has not a speck of conscience, would have sold the stones without hesitation."

"That would be dishonest, Your Grace." Delilah smiled. "I couldn't live with myself thereafter. I believe in good works."

"As do I." The duchess nodded as if in deep thought.

"I've great plans to improve the life of orphans and those left to the streets. I'd like to petition for funding to be given to the Foundling Hospital and with hope, support additional homes where the boys and girls can live comfortably. Educators and governesses will give lessons. Everyone will benefit. The children most of all, as they become more attractive to families who wish to adopt, parents who mayhap haven't been able to have children of their own." She hadn't prepared her words beforehand and she realized belatedly she'd gone on too long, in too passionate a tone. The duchess would label her an idealist, or worse, an intellectual for her progressive ideas. Not that she would mind either label.

"Indeed."

Without warning, the duchess rose from the chaise. Cygnet was caught by surprise and barked in objection as the fabric beneath him slipped away. Her Grace walked toward Delilah with a keen look in her eyes.

"Use this to fund your cause, my dear." The Duchess of Grandon extended her hand and offered the diamond collar. "It's provoked so much trouble and tribulation, I'd like to believe it was meant for something more meaningful. When I pass, I shudder to think what my nephew would do with it, but you will serve London well with the price it brings. I've never been blessed with children. No one should suffer the hardships of life on the streets."

"I couldn't agree more." Delilah hesitated. "Are you certain, Your Grace?"

"Without a doubt. Now take yourself away with it. Lord Yardley awaits me in the gardens."

"Thank you." Delilah gave herself a little shake, surprised and excited by the unexpected outcome. "Thank you very much."

EPILOGUE

It was a glorious afternoon for the wedding celebration. The London sky took on a rare shade of blue, a mixture of wondrous aquamarine and sparkling sapphire, while the sun beamed proudly like a diamond set high to share warmth and light with everyone who'd gathered in the garden. Guests ranged from dowager to commoner, child to canine, donned in their finest attire for the joyous occasion. Floral displays were plentiful. Bouquets and decorative arrangements rich with bold peonies and delicate calla lilies, blushing ranunculus, and maidenhair ferns, lined the aisle and marked areas where cushioned chairs were arranged for conversation and respite.

Delilah viewed the scene before her and sighed, the exuberant rush of contentment, gratitude, and overwhelming emotion almost too much to contain. Across the lawn she spied Oliver as he chased after Cygnet, the child's laughter as loud as the dog's energetic bark. Scarlett and her husband, the Duke of Aylesford, were touching their champagne glasses in their own intimate moment while to the left, Julia, Phoebe, and Diana stood engrossed in discussion. But they paused now, as if somehow they'd sensed her attention. The Maidens looked up to meet her eyes, and Delilah returned their smiles.

"Shall we begin to say our goodbyes?" Sebastian leaned down to whisper into her ear and a delicious shiver raced through her.

"I couldn't have asked for a more perfect day." She turned her gaze up to meet his, and the spark of desire she saw in his eyes told her the evening promised far more pleasure. "But I suppose we should begin thanking the guests and saying our farewells. All good things come to an end sooner or later."

"I couldn't disagree more."

His words were meant for her only, and she paused, caught by surprise. Hadn't he just suggested they take their leave? "What did you say?"

"I couldn't disagree with you more," he repeated and gently pulled her closer, shielding her from the crowd as he turned them behind a large ornate vase overflowing with greenery. Then he tugged her closer still, until the delicate white lace of her wedding gown was pressed against the smooth black wool of his tailcoat. "Good things, like our love, shall never come to an end. The years ahead offer us an unspoken promise of laughter, passion, and joy."

"Why, Sebastian St. Allen." She wriggled closer still, each of his exhales now a tickling whisper against her forehead. "Under all that strength and brawn, you have the heart of a poet."

"Since you're the keeper of my heart, my love, you should know."

His answer was nothing more than a murmur against her lips as he leaned down and took her mouth in a kiss that expressed everything his words had declared not two heartbeats beforehand, and promised all the happiness the future could hold.

ACKNOWLEDGMENTS

Writing a book is a huge endeavor, one I could never achieve without the encouragement and support of the fabulous people I'm grateful to have in my life.

First, my heartfelt thanks to Esi Sogah, my amazing editor, who graciously shares her expertise and knowledge, along with the Kensington publishing team, most especially Jane Nutter, who patiently answers my many questions and emails.

To my readers and the historical romance community, thank you for reading and recommending my book. I appreciate all of you!

To my family and friends, I'd truly be lost without your support, especially my parents, Theresa and Sam, and Aunt Mary Ann, who tolerate the many phases of my writing process without complaint—or are kind enough not to complain when I'm listening.

Don't miss how it all began
in
DUCHESS IF YOU DARE,
the first in the Maidens of Mayhem series.

And be sure to read the
the Midnight Secrets series
LONDON'S WICKED AFFAIR
LONDON'S BEST KEPT SECRET
LONDON'S LATE NIGHT SCANDAL
LONDON'S MOST ELUSIVE EARL
available now from
Anabelle Bryant
and
Zebra Books.

Visit us online at
KensingtonBooks.com
to read more from your favorite authors,
see books by series, view reading
group guides, and more!

BOOK CLUB

BETWEEN THE CHAPTERS

Visit us online for sneak peeks, exclusive
giveaways, special discounts, author content,
and engaging discussions with your fellow readers.

Betweenthechapters.net

Sign up for our newsletters and be the first
to get exciting news and announcements about
your favorite authors!
Kensingtonbooks.com/newsletter